FALSE HORIZON

ALSO BY JOSEPH REID

Takeoff

FALSE HORIZON

JOSEPH REID

Text copyright © 2019 by Joseph P. Reid
All rights reserved.

Published by Thomas & Mercer, Seattle

www.apub.com

Amazon, the Amazon logo, and Thomas & Mercer are trademarks of Amazon.com, Inc., or its affiliates.

ISBN-13: 9781503959361
ISBN-10: 1503959368

Cover design by Kirk DouPonce, DogEared Design

Printed in the United States of America

FALSE HORIZON

PROLOGUE

Yeager Airport, Charleston, West Virginia, October 11

Unlike the other passengers, Joseph Boswell Simpson didn't press forward to the waist-high gate separating them from the tarmac. The fenced-in patch of damp concrete outside the terminal door reminded him of a livestock pen, and he knew from his childhood what happened to animals that got taken out the chute.

Instead, the twenty-six-year-old leaned a shoulder against the exterior wall of the building. There, shrouded in the predawn darkness, he hung his head and wondered exactly how big a mistake he was about to make.

Judging by the acid scalding his throat, Boz—everyone around St. Albans called him "Boz"—figured it was pretty huge.

Bigger than the things he'd been keeping quiet about for the last three years.

Bigger, even, than the lies he'd been telling his wife that whole time.

The latest one of those had come at bedtime the previous night, when Delilah had noticed him shaking. But it wasn't the fifty-minute airplane flight that had him spooked, not really. While he preferred the outdoors to confined spaces, he'd flown successfully four times in his life. Twice as a kid, on those rare occasions when his father had enjoyed a good-enough year that the family could afford a few days at

Disney World. Once more, two years back, for their honeymoon in the Bahamas. And then, of course, three weeks ago.

This very same route to Pittsburgh.

That was the trip that had made a mess of things. Left him wondering now whether he'd make it onto his late-morning return flight.

Or, if he did, whether anything would ever be the same.

Why, Boz wondered, hadn't he insisted on making the four-hour drive? Sure, the internet company had offered to pay for the flight, but he could have turned them down. He could have told them he was scared of heights. Or that little puddle-jumper planes were the worst for the environment; he'd read that somewhere. Hell, anything to avoid taking that flight.

But he had taken it. And now, here he was.

Boz squeezed his eyes shut. He thought of his wife, the way she'd lain sleeping when he'd left. Peaceful. Hair swept back like she'd brushed it that way. On her side, an extra pillow clutched between her knees to relieve the stress on her back, now that the little peanut was starting to show.

From the day he'd met her, Delilah Marie Richards had always been way too good for him. He knew that. Everyone in the whole damn county knew it.

Which was exactly why you took that flight, to earn her—

Boz stopped the voice in his head before the lie spun out too far. He'd lied enough already.

Truth was, he hadn't traveled to Pittsburgh for Delilah. Not when it came to taking the flight, anyway. The job? The extra money? Sure. The chance to maybe move somewhere nice? Absolutely.

The chance to get free from Chas Miller?

Most of all.

But not that flight.

The flight had been all about him.

As he'd parked the truck that morning and cleared security, as he'd stopped to buy a cup of coffee near the gate, he'd been playacting: pretending he was someone important. Someone who had "a plane to catch."

God, it had felt *glorious*.

So good that Boz had forgotten Kaitlyn Stallings worked the register at the Kanawha Café inside the terminal. A tiny young woman with loud freckles painted across her arms and forehead, Kaitlyn was Chas's second cousin on his mother's side.

That was one thing about Chas: he had so many cousins spread across the county, you never knew where you might run into one. And whenever you did, Chas would know exactly where you'd been and what you'd been doing.

This morning, Boz had bypassed the café. He didn't need to see Kaitlyn again, and he didn't want any coffee. He'd briefly considered slamming down something stronger on the drive to the airport but decided against it. His stomach was already wrecked, and it'd be just his luck to get pulled over or, worse, to run into some other Chas cousin who'd snitch on him, too.

The airline agent emerged from the building, wove through the crowd, and unhitched the latch on the metal gate. Passengers flooded from the pen, dragging their rolling suitcases down the crosshatched path to the plane. Boz pushed himself up off the wall and ambled after them.

Off to the right, daylight was breaking. From the damp ground and the way the horizon softened at the first hint of sunrise, he guessed the low-lying clouds would hang around all day.

That was the kind of "local knowledge" the internet people in Pittsburgh had said they wanted as a boost for their fishing app. Getting paid for stuff he already knew sounded like easy money to Boz, who'd never had very much. Of course, that's how he'd been consoling himself since he'd gotten involved with Chas in the first place. And the money had come in handy—at first, all he'd needed was a couple thousand bucks to pay off Delilah's engagement ring and make sure they had enough for the wedding. Now, with a little one on the way . . .

Boz ignored the luggage cart parked at the base of the stairs up to the plane. The whole idea behind the backpack was that he could keep it with him. After clambering up and ducking through the door, he shuffled down the narrow aisle to his seat, the window on row 4. He tucked the bag at his feet, clipped the two ends of his seat belt together, and yanked the loose end until it was snug.

Once more, Boz found his hand shaking. Lying again, he blamed the cold and his shitty canvas coat.

Crossing his arms tightly against his chest, he forced his eyes shut and summoned the warmest thought he could: the sun in the Bahamas. He'd never felt anything that blazing hot. So intense, it seemed to generate its own physical pressure: pushing on you, squeezing you. Making it difficult to breathe.

God, breathing felt hard now, too.

Boz inhaled sharply through his nose, then swallowed over the lump in his throat. When he glanced up front, the flight attendant was pulling the stairs up into the cabin. Once they were stowed, she closed and sealed the front door with a heavy clunk.

He instinctively turned to the window. Outside the small circle of Plexiglas, the engine roared to life. Louder than a chainsaw but lower pitched, it nearly drowned out the prerecorded safety announcements that played over the PA system. Beyond the now-spinning propeller, the sky had lightened to a dull gray that matched the underside of the wing. After a few moments, the scenery shifted as the plane began to taxi.

Their roll down the runway took less than forty-five seconds. As they cleared the edge of the airfield, Boz watched the terrain drop several hundred feet down to the brown water of the river, the incline making their climb seem even steeper and more dramatic. After leveling off, the small plane banked gently, turning northeast and gaining altitude. In the dim light, the wooded hills below appeared charcoal black. Narrow plumes of silver mist rose from the ground, adding to the impression that some sort of massive fire had thoroughly scorched the earth and then been doused.

Contrary to the apocalyptic look of things, though, Boz knew the landscape below was thriving: a dense patch of rural wilderness, virtually identical to the one west of here where he'd first met Chas Miller three years ago.

It had been spring then, the woods teeming with does and their new, spindly-legged fawns, when Chas had arrived at the store with another guy, looking for a turkey-hunting guide. Although they carried rifles, the pair hadn't been dressed like any kind of hunters Boz had ever seen—no camo, no gear. Just T-shirts and jeans, like they were headed to the movies instead of into the forest.

Boz had immediately recognized Chas's face. Everyone in the county knew him, whether they bought from him or not. Given Chas's reputation, Boz decided he should keep quiet and be polite.

It hadn't helped.

They hadn't been hunting for ten minutes when Chas started asking questions. Which direction the river flowed. Which way the interstate was. Whenever they came across a game trail, Chas or his buddy would ask its length and where it led.

Boz did his best to answer in the fewest possible words, hoping Chas might think he was slow and end the trip early. It didn't happen; the pair kept him out until the hunting day officially ended after lunchtime. And the two never did shoot anything except a couple of old stumps, whooping and hollering as they splintered the rotten wood. When he dropped Chas and his partner back at their car, Boz had sighed with relief.

Until they'd returned to the shop two weeks later. Upon being told they could choose their guide, Chas strode over, wrapped an arm around Boz's shoulders, and proclaimed, "This here's my guy."

Once again, Boz had kept his mouth shut on their drive out to the woods. After they'd stalked several hundred yards into the forest, though, Chas started talking. About how he was willing to pay for loyal help. And all the good things he'd heard about Boz.

Chas had produced a stack of bills as thick as a deck of playing cards. After stripping off three hundred-dollar bills, he'd shoved them into the breast pocket of Boz's flannel. Even as he'd stood motionless, Boz couldn't help but notice that Chas's partner had his rifle up and ready.

And that was how Boz had come to work for the most powerful drug dealer in Kanawha County.

Mostly, he'd done simple stuff. Showing them trails, guiding them through the forest. The few times he'd actually seen any drugs, it was just shrink-wrapped packages of weed. From what Boz had heard on TV, states were legalizing pot, so where, really, was the harm in that?

Thinking back to it now, Boz ground his teeth. He squeezed the tip of the armrest between his fingers and palm, as if he might peel the plastic strip back off the metal. He'd hoped the interview in Pittsburgh would be his ticket out—would save him and Delilah and the baby from all the dumb decisions he'd made. He'd never thought it would lead to more trouble, more lies.

Or to this flight.

Because while Boz didn't know exactly what was waiting in the bag he was supposed to retrieve for Chas in Pittsburgh, he knew it wouldn't be pot.

Pushing back against the headrest, Boz reclined the seat the few inches it would go and forced his eyes shut. He told himself all this would be over before noon. He could pick up Delilah and take her out for lunch. She was craving meat these days—maybe a burger at Dwight's. They both deserved that.

Or at least *she* did.

As the engine droned on, Boz took several deep breaths through his nose. The heater had finally kicked in, overdoing it so now the cabin felt warm and stuffy. His muscles finally relaxed, and when they did, the blackness seemed to spread from his eyelids to the rest of him.

A sudden jolt and loud noise got Boz's attention.

As he was thrown forward, his eyes flicked open. He didn't know if he'd dozed off—if so, he wasn't asleep anymore.

His first thought was turbulence—he'd experienced that once before. But this hadn't been any little bounce; the impact made it seem more like a car crash. Thankfully, he had his belt on tight.

Whatever happened had changed the plane's momentum. Rather than continuing straight, it was angled up and to the side, as if banking into a steep turn. But the turn didn't end. Instead, the airplane continued listing, eventually tipping all the way over onto its side.

Boz glanced quickly to his right—now the equivalent of down—and then to his left.

He blinked twice.

Outside, the sky had turned a brilliant blue—they must've risen above the cloud cover, up where the sun was shining. But as his eyes struggled to adjust to the light, he sensed that the view out the window was too bright. Almost blinding.

That seemed wrong somehow.

For the first time, Boz also noticed the sound—or lack of it. The cabin was much quieter than before.

Eerily so.

When his eyes finally focused on the world beyond the window, he understood why.

The engine was missing.

And, along with it, most of the wing.

The front of the plane began tilting downward now, as if starting a dive. Boz felt almost weightless for a moment, until the seat pressed into his back and pushed him along. In addition, the window seemed to drop away from him, while the other side of the plane began to rise.

Boz wondered what exactly was happening until he realized they were starting to spin.

Slowly, at first. Then faster.

The airplane ended up taking three full minutes to drop all the way to earth.

During those 180 seconds, the plane spun until the second wing gave way and ripped off. Completely deprived of power, the cabin lights went out. Without the rotation bleeding off speed, the fuselage accelerated until it reached terminal velocity. Luggage and other items flew through the cabin. In the dark, people cried, and screamed, and prayed.

Boz didn't notice any of it.

He thought about Delilah the whole way down.

CHAPTER 1

Los Angeles, October 25

Because it was a Tuesday, I turned my target papers around after the first shot.

Don't get me wrong—I like bull's-eyes. But so few bad guys go around wearing them.

Flipping the papers over, aiming for the tiny hole you made in the back side of the plain white sheet—if you can even see it—felt more realistic. Plus, I was hunting for new challenges these days.

Regulations require federal air marshals to take target practice every day unless they're flying. Given that marshals typically spend two to four days each week on airplanes, that translates to one, maybe two range sessions per week.

Except I wasn't an air marshal anymore, not like before. A few months back, a crazy woman named Berkeley had emptied a full mag at me in a thunderstorm. While she hadn't succeeded in killing me, she did compromise my covert status. After the incident, the Service decided my face was too recognizable; suddenly, I couldn't fly anonymously anymore. Instead, they'd offered me a new, tongue-twisting role as Tactical Law Enforcement Liaison and Principal Investigator, which meant they'd send me wherever Service-related cases popped up.

So far, though, there'd been only one. The only other airplanes I'd been riding were to see my godkids in Texas—a flight drought that had planted my ass firmly in the basement firing range five times per week.

I'd taken up all kinds of new drills to fill the time. Dry firing—shooting with no bullets in the gun—to focus on my trigger pull and eliminate any twitches. "The Dots," firing six shots in five seconds from a holstered start. The "Walk-In, Walk-Out" drill, in which you hit targets from various yardage markers.

All the extra practice helped. I'd been a pretty good shot before—best marks in the office—but if real work didn't pick up soon, I figured I'd enter one of those interagency shooting competitions to see where I really stood against the best of the best.

Once I'd slung my hundred rounds, I made my daily pilgrimage upstairs. Exiting the elevator, I looked across the maze of cubes that filled the center of the floor toward my boss's office in the opposite corner. Although his lights were on, I was in no particular rush to hear Vince Lavorgna tell me that "no news is good news" for the eighty-fourth straight day. Plus, I had a gift to deliver to Loretta, so I headed to her cube first.

I began tracing the outer wall toward the nearest entrance to the maze. Halfway, I passed the small exterior office they'd assigned me as part of my new job. With its window shades drawn and all the lights off, the darkened doorway stood out from the others along the row.

I didn't break stride as I walked past it. If anything, my pace increased.

Offices make me . . . uneasy.

I'd had one before—a nice corner like Lavorgna's, only bigger—back in my former life as an electrical engineer. And that was the thing: I'd left all that behind with absolutely no plans to return. So, unless Lavorgna ordered me to move in, I'd just leave my things in the same cube I'd occupied for the past two and a half years.

On my way to Loretta's, I listened for the telltale click-clack her long nails made against her keyboard as she booked travel for all the marshals in the office. It was quiet, noticeably so, and a moment later I learned why.

As I drew up to her wall, she peeked up over it, looking at me like she'd caught me on my way to the cookie jar. "So-ooooo," she said, drawing out the word in her raspy warble, "is today the day?"

Even in heels, Loretta Alcott barely reached my shoulder, which left me staring down through her gold-rimmed spectacles. "The day for what?"

Her eyebrows rose. "Can I see it?"

"See what?"

She crossed her arms and glared over her glasses. "You know very well what I'm talking about, mister."

Given that we'd had this conversation every day for the past two weeks, I certainly did. But that only made teasing her more fun.

"Let's see it."

I glanced off to the side. "I don't know if I'm ready."

"You talked nonstop about getting that thing after Austin. Then, once you supposedly built up the nerve—"

"The nerve?" The ink lining both my arms is a pretty good testament to the fact that I'm not afraid of needles. But from her grin, I could tell Loretta was enjoying the game, too.

"You won't show it to anyone. Did you even get a new tattoo, or did you chicken out?"

"The scabs take time to heal."

"Oh." She gave a single, pronounced nod. "Well, are they healed enough today?"

Sighing, I undid the first two buttons on my shirt and pulled the left collar aside. The new ink sat just beneath my collarbone: the name *Emma*, with two pairs of linked music notes for the *m*'s.

Loretta's grin grew wide enough to take up all the slack in her aged face. She nodded approvingly. "Bet she likes it. Must make her feel loved."

Before I could respond, a voice thick with a Philadelphia accent called out from over my shoulder. "I thought I heard you two talking."

Turning, I spotted Lavorgna coming down the row. I barely managed to brace myself before he slapped a heavy hand on my shoulder. Built like an NFL linebacker after decades of lifting weights, he didn't know his own strength.

"Loretta, our young friend here needs to get to DC on the first available flight."

"Reagan or Dulles, Mr. Lavorgna?"

"Reagan. He's been granted an audience with our number-one benefactor before heading out into the field. C'mon, Seth, I'll fill you in." Lavorgna took two steps back toward his office.

"Just a sec." I produced an envelope from my pocket and pushed it into Loretta's gnarled fingers. "Happy birthday!"

She blinked several times. "It's not my birthday."

I tried to look surprised. "Are you sure?"

She took a heavy breath, her nostrils flaring. "My birthday's in *February*."

"Jeez—I must've gotten the dates mixed up. You and Bob should still enjoy the gift, though." Before she could speak, I spun and hurried after Lavorgna.

When I caught up with him mid-hallway, he asked under his breath, "Food?"

"Uh-huh. One of those services that mails you ingredients and a new recipe every few days."

Ever since I'd found Loretta making a ketchup sandwich in the coffee room from a stolen slice of bread two years ago, I'd been buying extra food and passing it to her. Her husband, Bob, was on his second stint fighting cancer, and the bills had long since consumed whatever savings they'd accumulated over the years. She was too proud to accept handouts, though, which forced me to get a little creative sometimes, like pretending I had leftovers I couldn't finish before I dashed out of town. I'd always wondered whether Lavorgna knew, but I should have guessed. Although he'd settled into life behind a desk, little escaped the former undercover agent.

Once we reached his office, he ushered me in, then shut the door.

"What's this new case?" I asked, slipping into a guest chair.

"A weird one."

I winced. Although he'd predicted that bodyguarding Emma would be a cakewalk, the heavily armed gang targeting the teenage singer had chased us halfway across the country, nearly killing us several times.

"It's that plane crash a couple of weeks ago. They want you on that."

"The one back east? News said it was a bird strike."

Birds hit commercial aircraft all the time, but most strikes were harmless. A single bird, particularly a small one, couldn't do much damage to a giant metal-skinned jetliner. A whole flock could be a different story—Canada geese had knocked out both engines on the so-called Miracle on the Hudson plane that famously made an emergency landing on the Hudson River.

"Who's my contact?" I asked.

"That's the weird part." Lavorgna stroked his black beard. "You're meeting up with Special Agent Mitchell Devers in Pittsburgh."

I gave him a quizzical look. Normally, the National Transportation Safety Board handled crash investigations. "FBI?"

"We haven't seen an innocent crash in a long, long time."

People often comment on how safe flying is compared to riding in a car, and it's true: despite billions of flight hours logged annually, only one person had died in a US-certified airline incident in eight years. If the FBI was involved with this one, it signified a whole range of possibilities.

"What's the look for?" Lavorgna asked.

I realized I'd been making a sour face. "After Austin . . ."

"You don't trust them?"

"Kind of hard to." The lead FBI agent assigned to Emma's case had secretly used us as bait, making a bad situation even worse.

"You should call Melissa Cooke," Lavorgna said. "I'm guessing she can give you an idea of what to expect."

A psychologist by training, Cooke worked in a special division of the Bureau's Critical Incident Response Group, or CIRG. She'd helped me deal with the crazy woman who'd almost killed me—Cooke had even taken two of the bullets meant for me in that thunderstorm. "I will. And I'll help however I can."

Lavorgna leaned back in his chair and smiled. "Something tells me you'll find a way. You're a fast learner."

When he tapped his own ear, then pointed at mine, I knew he was referring to the earpiece I wear. I use it to pump a steady stream of content—books, articles, podcasts, whatever text I've converted—from a player in my pocket into my left ear. My brain has this condition where, unless my adrenaline's pumping, it needs to be constantly distracted; otherwise it'll spin off in a thousand different directions. Lavorgna hadn't believed me about that until he'd forced me to demonstrate. After I'd collapsed into a drooling, twitching mess on his floor, he'd been pretty understanding. Particularly since listening to all that in the background helps me study up on things.

"Who's this 'benefactor' I'm supposed to meet?"

"Representative MaryAnne Rapp. She's the ranking member on the appropriations committee, and her district is in West Virginia, so this case is doubly important to her."

I'd never heard of her, and my face must have said as much.

"You don't follow politics?" Lavorgna asked.

"Not if I can help it. You?"

"No more than necessary." His face contorted into a strained expression. "The good news is, Rapp likes us—likes you. She's one of the people who approved the idea of you becoming an investigator." He paused. "Be on your best behavior, Seth."

I cracked a grin. "Always, sir."

"I'm serious." He shot me a look I knew better than to question. "Rapp's our best ally on the Hill—we lose her, the whole Service could be in a world of hurt."

The midmorning departure Loretta found me left just enough time for a couple of quick preparations.

First, I dashed back to my Manhattan Beach house. As I steered down 18th Place, the beach became visible at the bottom of the hill. With the morning sun shining and a breeze whipping up three-foot faces, it looked like perfect surfing conditions. Thankfully, I'd caught sets every day this month, so the idea of missing a few didn't pain me as much as it might have.

Pulling into my garage, I was greeted by the buzz of automatic saws and the banging of hammers. The arrival of Guillermo, the contractor fixing the damage Emma's attackers had done to my place, meant my trip was well timed. With new drywall almost up and the windows getting mounted, his crew would need to paint next. The fumes could dissipate while I was gone.

After raiding my closet for cold-weather gear that I jammed into an oversize duffel, I drove back to LAX. On the way, I left Cooke a quick voice mail. By the time I reached the terminal, first class was already lined up to board.

I used the remaining moments to text the older of my two godkids in Texas. Now nine, Michael had been begging their mother, Shirley, for a phone. While she'd refused his request, as a compromise, she let him message me whenever he wanted. We'd recently started trading "Emojis of the Day," and this might be my best chance to send today's.

Thinking of Representative Rapp, I settled on the American flag and pressed "Send" before starting down the jetbridge.

A few minutes later, I shoehorned myself into a middle seat in the dead center of coach. That was one air-marshal perk I missed: guaranteed aisles. I'm not the biggest guy, but I'm not the smallest, either; that little bit of extra room made all the difference. Plus, I could work in an aisle seat. While I'd left the electronics industry behind, I still tinkered in my spare time, patenting inventions on the side. Flights were one of my prime opportunities to doodle and work out the ideas bouncing around in my head. With my elbows pinched into my ribs and my knees braced against the seat in front, though, there was no way to reach the pad and pencil trapped in my laptop bag, let alone do any sketching. The people on either side of me leaned away—either because they were polite or scared of the guy with the shaved head and tattoos—but even so, I knew I was in for a long four and a half hours.

At least I had the earpiece. Despite the airplane's Wi-Fi cutting in and out, I managed to download a series of articles about Appalachian 303. Running the articles through special text-to-audio software, I set myself up with several hours' worth of content about the doomed flight.

The jet stream must have given us an extra boost—we landed in DC ten minutes early, pulling up to Gate 22 as the sun was dipping behind the building's wave-shaped roof. While I'd been learning about the low-speed efficiency of turboprop engines during my flight, Michael had sent me a robot emoji, and Cooke had texted that she would come up from Quantico to meet me for dinner. I fired off a quick response to her with a proposed location as I walked up the jetbridge.

When I stepped into the terminal, I was surprised to find a young man in a crisp blue suit standing at the edge of the seating area with a sign bearing my last name.

I nodded as I drew up to him. "That's me."

He kept his eyes locked on the doorway over my shoulder. "I don't think so." From his baby face, I halfway expected his voice to crack as he said it.

"No, really. I'm—"

"Listen, pal," he said, finally facing me. Although I had him by a good six inches, his expression left no doubt how important he thought he was. "This is government business. If you don't back off, I'll call security."

I pulled out my badge holder and let it flip open in front of him.

His eyes widened as he scanned it, then looked me up and down again. His Adam's apple bobbed above the fancy knot in his tie. "Congresswoman Rapp sent me to collect you. She's arranged a conference room here in the airport."

"Then lead the way."

When we reached the main concourse, I couldn't help glancing up—to me, Reagan is one of the prettiest airports. Particularly in profile, its wavy roof and several-story wall of glass facing out to the tarmac remind me of the Asian terminals I used to travel through as an engineer. While those could feel antiseptic inside, little touches make Reagan seem distinct and historic. Instead of industrial epoxy over concrete, Reagan's floor is shiny black terrazzo, accented by patterned inlays of art deco–style lines and rectangles in gold and white. Standing on it, you realize the ceiling several stories overhead isn't some single, monolithic structure, but rather an interconnected series of domes that gives the vaulted atrium a cathedral-like feeling. Circular skylights at the peaks of the domes combine with the wall of windows to flood the concourse with natural light. And while most airports go for boring white walls, Reagan's exposed metal girding is done in a bright yellow—against the dark stone, it really pops, creating a lush, vibrant environment.

The greeter—whose name I learned was Nick—led me to the far end of the concourse, then down a long corridor of doors, the last of which turned out to belong to a small meeting room. A woman was seated alone inside, poring over papers. She glanced up, smiled, and stood, pulling a pair of bifocals from her face. Her purple pantsuit was stylish but understated; the only jewelry she wore was a simple gold cross on a chain around her neck. "You must be Seth Walker," she said in a refined-sounding twang. "It's a pleasure to finally meet you."

"Thank you," I said, shaking her hand. "Do you prefer *ma'am* or *Congresswoman?*"

Rapp tossed her hand in the air. "I've been called much worse than either one. Have a seat."

With Nick gone, sitting alone with Rapp staring at me intently felt a bit like being called to the principal's office. Lavorgna's instructions rang in my ears.

"I have to say, ma'am, it's quite an honor to meet a member of Congress."

Rapp's smile broadened. "You're sweet to say that. If I'd known you were so dashing and polite, I'd have called you to DC sooner—you could've helped me win over a couple of votes last term."

I shifted in my seat. "I doubt it, ma'am—that really isn't my element."

"Well," she said, folding her hands on the table in front of her, "let me start by taking this opportunity to thank you. For your service, and for helping make my job easier."

"How's that, ma'am?"

She looked at me sideways, her smile frozen in place. "I'm sure you know my committee doles out the lifeblood of this place—money—and there's always more open hands than dollars to fill them. I'm facing a lot of pressure from my colleagues, Mr. Walker. One—from a state with no major airports, mind you—thinks your Service ought to be dismantled completely. I can fight off something that drastic, but I've got deficit hawks on my committee who'd like to cut your funding by thirty-five percent. I don't have to tell you, that kind of reduction would mean some very significant changes in the Service's day-to-day operations. And *personnel*."

The emphasis Rapp put on that final word hit me like I'd grabbed a live wire back in our electronics laboratory: an initial jolt, followed by all my nerves seeming to fire at once.

At first, I assumed she meant my job was in jeopardy. Because I couldn't fly undercover anymore, it made sense I'd be considered expendable. At that thought, my brain switched almost immediately into damage-control mode: calculating the cost of fixing the house, tallying how many patents I had in the pipeline. All kinds of things.

But then another, darker thought struck me: Did Rapp know about Loretta?

The more I considered that, the further my stomach sank. Loretta booked all of our travel—in theory, rendering her indispensable. But if they decided to automate or handle bookings through some central service . . .

Loretta was more than some office staffer to me. Although she was probably only a year or two older than my parents, she reminded me most of my grandmother—my dad's mom—who'd died back when I was in college. They had similar blue-black hair, styled just so: dyed, straightened, and sprayed stiff. Both had warm eyes that twinkled with the slightest hint of mischief. And, much as my grandmother had welcomed me into her South Carolina home every summer, giving me a refuge from being the "new kid" as we moved between each of my dad's military-duty stations, Loretta had been the first to make me feel welcome in LA.

These days, Loretta's income was all she and Bob had. With it, they were barely scraping by. Without it . . .

Rapp interrupted my thinking, shaking a finger at me. "You have the power to provide me with a great counterargument to my colleagues, Mr. Walker. Whether we're talking about terrorism, smuggling, or human trafficking, you're at the tip of the spear. Travel and technology are making the world a much smaller place—I think we need people like you to help us navigate it safely."

The way she'd transitioned to campaign-speak and turned on the compliments, I almost believed them. I could see why people had voted for her.

"Take this crash you'll be investigating. Twenty-nine people died—mostly my constituents—and their families deserve to know why. But if that plane had struck an urban area, the death toll could have been much, much higher. That's why, inside this tragedy, I see a perfect opportunity to demonstrate what your Service can do. If you discover something improper downed that plane, for example."—she paused and cocked her head—"that would give me a very powerful anecdote to share."

I caught myself blinking at her blankly—was I really supposed to hope someone had taken down Appalachian 303? The room, already small, seemed to have shrunk around us.

Rapp leaned across the table, ensuring our eyes were locked. "Do you understand what I'm saying, Mr. Walker? How critical this case is?"

The skin on my arms tingled; my heart fluttered in my chest. "Uh—yes, ma'am. I understand."

"Good." She nodded once before leaning back in her chair. The smile returned. "Then it sounds like I can count on you to give this your highest level of dedication."

"I'll do my best."

"I certainly hope so. An awful lot of people are counting on you."

CHAPTER 2

My head still swimming from the meeting with Rapp, I had a half hour to drop my things at the airport hotel, don warmer clothes, and get to the restaurant. Maybe less, since Melissa Cooke tended to be early to everything. Thankfully, the place I'd suggested sat just a couple of blocks from the L'Enfant Plaza Metro stop.

I spotted Cooke from two blocks away, already pacing the sidewalk in a long woolen coat, the collar turned up against the cool night air. Her auburn hair was pulled back into a tight French braid, exactly as I remembered. She noticed me when I hit the corner and met me halfway.

"Long time, no see," she said, giving me a polite hug.

"How're you feeling?" I went extra gentle, unsure how well her injuries had healed.

"They say I'm good as new." She nodded back at the restaurant's crimson awning. "What is this place?"

"You've never heard of Li's Golden Noodle House?"

She shook her head and gave me a suspicious look. "All the Chinese restaurants I've been to in DC are in Chinatown."

"C'mon, then. You're in for a treat."

Inside, the narrow restaurant was dim, illuminated only by flickering candles on the dozen or so white-clothed tables. But what the place lacked in visuals, it more than made up for in aroma: the air was thick with the smells of sesame, garlic, and soy. We'd been at the hostess stand only a moment when a Chinese woman in a red ankle-length gown appeared from the back of the house. Seeing me, she smiled broadly and bowed her head several times.

I returned the courtesy. "*Nǐ hǎo*, Zoey."

After greeting us in English, she led us to a table, where I exchanged a few more pleasantries with her in Mandarin. Once Zoey had gone, Cooke said, "I take it you've been here before."

I grinned. "Zoey and her sister, Alana, are twins, from Zhejiang province. I worked with their dad overseas. When they came for college, I offered to pop in and check on them now and then. He wanted them to learn science and return home, but they liked it here and went into the restaurant business instead. They've got one on each coast—Alana's place is in Long Beach, just south of me."

Cooke's eyes narrowed. "There's always another surprise with you, isn't there? Another layer to the onion."

I shrugged. "It usually helps to keep people guessing. You being the obvious exception." She and I hadn't exactly hit it off as friends on our first case together. More like the exact opposite, since she'd mistakenly concluded I was a double murderer.

"You know, figuring out people's secrets is literally my job description." She cracked a smile for the first time. "Speaking of which, there were a couple of questions I never got to ask you."

"Oh no." I gave an exaggerated eye roll, hoping it might dissuade her. Deep down, though, I knew better—I'd seen firsthand what a bulldog she could be. Interrogation was one of her specialties, so I guessed that even if I refused, she'd break out her bag of tricks and have her way with me.

"Come on," she said. "Just simple stuff."

"Like what?"

"Like, why does a guy on the fast track toward the job he's always wanted suddenly drop out, move cross-country, and become an air marshal?"

I chuffed. "That's your idea of *simple?*"

Cooke smiled but kept staring at me.

I might not be a world-class interrogator, but I'd paid close enough attention during the hour of air-marshal school on questioning suspects to know what she was doing: waiting for the silence to turn awkward enough that I'd break it. I also knew she'd probably read enough about me that lying wouldn't get me anywhere—I was going to have to figure out a way to dodge what was coming. "Who says a job in electronics is what I always wanted?"

She crossed her arms, gave her head a little shake. "I saw *Silence of the Lambs* at a sleepover when I was twelve, and the very next day I checked out a book on forensics from the library. This job was *my* dream."

Reveal a little about yourself, bond with the subject. God, she was smooth.

"You—I've seen the way your mind works. I'm surrounded by technical people, but you're . . . off the charts. I'm guessing as a kid you ripped things apart just to put them back together."

I waited a long moment before answering. "Maybe."

"So, why leave? You'd just been put in charge of a whole division—"

I tried to select my next words as carefully as possible. This answer would be my best chance to get away without talking about Clarence, about things Cooke didn't need to know. "That job . . . wasn't what I expected. I figured I could do more good someplace else."

I studied Cooke's face as I spoke and sensed her measuring every word. There was just enough truth in what I said that I hoped she'd believe it.

Zoey rescued me. Returning with a pot of tea, she poured out two small cups while explaining that she'd asked the chef to whip up a few special items for us. Finally, with a small giggle, she said, *"Tā hěn piào-liang. Bàba huì gàosù nǐ hé tā jiéhūn."*

Sensing an opening, I hung my head dramatically as she departed.

"What was that about?" Cooke asked. "What did she say?"

"That you're very beautiful. And that her father would tell me to marry you." Which was probably true—Zoey's father had teased me about settling down and starting a family for years.

I couldn't be completely certain in the dim candlelight, but Melissa Cooke might have blushed. Even if not, the comment caught her sufficiently off guard that she reached for her teacup with both hands and asked quickly, "Are you healed up?"

"Yeah. My shoulder took the worst of it—doctors say it could pop out again, but it's about as good as it's going to get." With my elbow bent, I rotated my left arm to demonstrate. It still felt normal despite the cold air outside, giving me hope that the combination of rehab and paddling out into the Pacific every morning had done the trick.

"I heard how you protected the girl. But I meant Dallas."

"I got off easy in Dallas." I reached for my own cup, keeping my eyes focused on the dark bits swirling around at the bottom. "You and Grayson took all the—"

"I'm not talking about bullet wounds, Seth."

The silence caused me to glance up reflexively. Our eyes locked.

"You gonna psychoanalyze me now?" I asked. "The shrinks in LA all pronounced me fit for duty, you know."

"I'm just asking as a friend. Losing someone like Sarah is traumatic. You don't just forget—"

"Forget?" I yanked back the sleeve of my sweater to reveal my right forearm. There, between my other tattoos, was a heart with the letters *S* and *A* inside.

Cooke focused on the ink. "Her initials?"

"Yeah."

I looked down at them, too. Probably stared longer than I should have. I used to take Sarah Allen to places like this, although we'd never been to Alana's restaurant in Long Beach together. And now, after what that Berkeley woman had done, I never would. There wouldn't be any more candlelit dinners for us. Any more anything.

When I finally looked up from my arm, I found Cooke's eyes still on me. "You did everything you could have."

"Truer words were never spoken." I smiled grimly.

"I'm serious. What happened to Sarah wasn't your fault."

My smile broadened. "We both know that isn't true."

"In psychology, there's a concept called 'subjective guilt.' It means—"

"Feeling bad even though you didn't do anything wrong. Yeah, I've heard all about it. And 'survivor syndrome.' I told you, I've seen the shrinks." What Cooke didn't understand—what she couldn't possibly comprehend—was how much I'd *actually* done wrong. To Sarah. And to Clarence before her. I more than deserved the guilty conscience I was hauling around, but right now, the only person I needed to worry about was Loretta. "Is there anything you can tell me about Appalachian 303? Like, what the hell is the FBI doing investigating a bird strike? And why am I getting pulled into it?"

Cooke's face straightened. "You've seen the news stories, then?"

"Yeah, I've seen them."

"Well, they're complete bullshit. We fed that bird-strike stuff to the reporters to buy time, but the truth is, NTSB's engineers still have no idea what happened to that plane."

Cooke's words hung on the air, mixing with the heavy scents from the kitchen as Zoey returned with a tray. One by one, she set down between us several serving dishes containing fried oysters, a seafood soup, steamed dumplings, and *dan dan* noodles.

"*Xièxiè,*" I said, thanking Zoey and bowing again.

Pointing with my chopsticks, I explained each of the dishes, and we started taking portions for ourselves. After Cooke fumbled several times with a slippery dumpling, I asked, "Do you need a fork?"

She shot me a fiery look, then stabbed one chopstick into the center of the dumpling to lift it. After biting in, her expression softened. "Wow."

I had to agree—the dumpling shells had a perfect consistency, the filling a tangy-but-earthy mix of pork and vegetables. I let us get a bite or two of everything onto our plates before continuing to press her. "There's got to be some clue, somewhere . . ."

Jaw firmly set, Cooke shook her head. "We know they'd reached cruising altitude. They lost the left engine and wing first—"

"Wait, they lost the whole wing?" That certainly hadn't made the news. Contrary to what most people think, airplane wings aren't attached to the sides of the fuselage, but to the bottom or the top. The connections of the wing spars—the rigid "bones" inside the wings—are so solid that the two wings actually function as a single piece.

"It was in the pilot's Mayday call," Cooke said. "But we have no idea what caused the damage. They didn't have visual contact with anything."

"What about radar? Or the black box?"

"Our techs scoured both. No sign of anything unusual."

"Explosives?" I asked.

Cooke shook her head again. "That was the first thing they looked at, but wrong kind of debris. An explosion would have shattered or melted pieces of the fuselage. Gunfire would have left holes or tattered the wing. This was like something sliced clean through."

"Those planes have metal skin," I said. "That means—"

"Something hit the plane. Hard. And we have no idea what."

I blinked several times. "Was there extra debris? Anything to show what made contact?"

"As you can imagine, there's a zillion tiny pieces to sort through. But, as of now, we haven't found anything."

The back of my brain kept spinning on the math, the forces involved in a collision that devastating. "Anything big enough or strong enough—"

"Should have been visible to everyone, I know. The technical side of this has everyone stumped." Cooke took another long sip of tea. "That's why the Bureau's involved, and that's why the agent in charge decided to call you in. To figure out who did this. And how."

I grimaced.

"What?"

"I'm just thinking about everything the Congresswoman said is riding on this case."

Cooke's eyes grew steely. "The big worry, obviously, is there's some kind of new mystery weapon out there. Something we're completely defenseless against."

"So why go after a puddle jumper with it? Why not something bigger?"

She shrugged. "A test, maybe? We've checked the manifests—it wasn't like anyone important was aboard. No one's claimed credit. That's worrisome, too."

"But you're convinced it was something unnatural? Not some mechanical thing, bad maintenance?"

Her eyes locked on mine. "You know as well as anyone, wings don't just fall off airplanes, Seth. They just don't."

As we helped ourselves to another round of food from the family-style plates, I switched gears. "What about this guy Devers—what's his story?"

"He's solid," she said. "Smart. Did a tour in the army, saw some pretty heavy action. Then double-majored in history and criminal justice at Kentucky on the GI Bill. He's got some pet theories about what's going on, and he can be a little hardheaded. But you of all people should understand that."

"Ouch." I slapped a hand over my heart. "You know, your buddy Franklin almost got the girl and me killed."

"Franklin's not my buddy." Her eyes flashed in a way that suggested a story behind the comment. "But Devers is different. He'll have your back."

We continued picking at the food until finally Cooke stretched her arms over her head. "I should get going—I've got a long drive."

"Thanks again," I said, "for coming up here, and for the intel. It was nice seeing you."

"You, too. But you're not getting rid of me just yet."

"Huh?"

"This case is important enough, CIRG has been tasked with overseeing it. Which means—"

"You're the agent in charge? You're my boss again?"

Although Cooke didn't answer, her grin told me all I needed to know.

The tiny airport hotel Loretta had booked me wasn't particularly comfortable, but I didn't get enough sleep for it to matter. By four thirty, I was trudging back to Reagan with the duffel slung over my shoulder, listening to more press clippings about the crash. I considered getting an early jump on "Emoji of the Day," but I didn't want to wake Shirley accidentally.

After a long wait beneath the concourse's bright lights to clear security, I ended up boarding at the gate next to the one through which I'd arrived. The early flight to Pittsburgh was only half-full, everyone looking bleary eyed and quietly sucking on their cardboard cups of coffee.

One downside to my brain condition is that I need my sleep. If I don't get at least seven hours, I'm not at my best; less than six, and I really get scattered. Making matters worse, I have to avoid caffeine, which can send my brain into overdrive. With no chemical help to stay awake, I began dozing after takeoff and didn't stir again until touchdown.

Where Reagan's terminal is shaped like an E, Pittsburgh's is an X; we pulled in toward the far end of one of the spokes. Inside, the gate area was mostly empty, but I had no idea what Devers looked like. I started walking and had gotten out past the final rows of chairs when a voice called out behind me.

Turning, I found a man about my age clad in dark jeans, a stylishly cut powder-blue shirt that set off his dark complexion, and black Ranger boots buffed to a high shine. While the boots and his throwback high-top fade combined to give him an inch on me in height, he was built thinner, leaner than I am.

"Walker?"

"Devers?"

We shook hands, and almost immediately he was steering me toward the hallway.

"We've got a National Guard chopper waiting," he said. His voice was deep, with a hint of a drawl. "It'll take us down to New Martinsville, the town closest to the crash."

After grabbing the duffel, we set off down a series of back hallways and utility staircases that dumped out onto the tarmac. When we emerged outside, Devers donned an electric-blue insulated vest; the temperature was at least five degrees colder than DC, and our breaths formed small white clouds as we walked. A cart ferried us across the field, where we boarded a Black Hawk, and in five minutes, we were wheels-up over the treetops, headed south.

It's funny—while heights give me knee-liquefying vertigo, I can fly in just about any kind of aircraft, no problem. I think it's something to do with being enclosed. The flight down to West Virginia was no different: I had my cheek planted against the glass, watching the lush hills speed by a few hundred feet below us.

We'd been flying about ten minutes when Devers began talking over the intercom.

"Where you from?"

Although that question always causes a pinch in my gut, I tried not to show it. "Navy brat. Moved all over the place."

"I'm guessing that didn't include West Virginia?"

"Nope. You?"

"Little coal-mining town in eastern Kentucky."

"What's it called?" I asked.

"Lynch."

My eyes darted over to him.

Devers flashed a broad, sarcastic smile that seemed to bare all his gleaming white teeth.

"You're kidding, right?"

Shaking his head, he said in a thicker accent than normal, "I'm the son of a black coal miner, raised in Lynch, and now I carry a gun for the United States government. Can't get more American than that." He let out a deep laugh, then pointed out the window. "We're almost to the site."

I turned back to the glass but didn't see anything except more rolling hills, thick with trees showing off their fall colors. After another minute, though, the helicopter banked, and that's when I noticed it: a narrow seam cut into the foliage, exposing the dark ground. If you looked carefully, you could see the opening had been made by force—branches cut, tree trunks split open.

"Must've been hell hauling the wreckage out," I said.

"Got lucky. There's an old mining road a quarter mile from here. That let the NTSB boys get in and pull it out piece by piece."

After circling the area three times, the chopper leveled off and resumed its original course.

"Cooke told me the engineers don't know what downed the plane."

"Maybe that's what the pocket-protector brigade says. But if you know what's going on around here, it's pretty obvious."

I ignored the engineering insult. "What's that?"

"This part of the country hasn't exactly been a national priority, okay? Ever since I got posted up here, I've been trying to warn folks that something bad was gonna happen."

"Why?"

"The Green Way."

"The Green what?"

"The Green *Way*," Devers said. "Richard Chu's little band of ecoterrorists."

I knew a little about Chu. He'd made a billion in Silicon Valley before dropping out to focus on what were supposedly philanthropic causes. But I'd never heard of this Green Way. "You mean folks who run around the forest, tying themselves to trees?"

"Oh, the Green Way does a lot more than that. Chu's guys call themselves 'disruptors'—they aren't shy about breaking stuff. Ever since fracking started up here, the Green Way's been causing trouble. Once they brought in drones—"

"Wait, drones?" I hadn't studied drone tech very much, but I'd been thinking about getting my godkids a small one for Christmas. Michael wasn't particularly interested in electronics beyond a phone, but Rachael, the five-year-old, was already saying she wanted to be an engineer like her dad, Clarence, had been.

Devers nodded. "They send 'em up with cameras, film themselves attacking the fracking pads, then post the videos online. But it's not just that—they drop stuff, too. Couple weeks ago, they dropped fireworks."

"What happened?"

"Got lucky—the pad wasn't active. But they do that again in the wrong place at the wrong time . . ." He flared his fingers like an explosion.

"What kind of drones are they using?" Commercial radar is set to ignore small objects like birds. If a small-enough drone had attacked Appalachian 303, it might explain why it hadn't been detected. And, unlike birds, drones had enough metallic parts that if one got sucked into an engine, it could cause a lot of damage.

"Little quadcopters—the kind you see people flying on TV."

"So you're thinking . . ."

"Mm-hm," said Devers.

"But Appalachian 303 got hit at twenty thousand feet," I said. "I'm pretty sure commercial drones can't get that high."

Devers shook his head. "I'm telling you, Walker, these Green Way guys are well connected. Hollywood, Silicon Valley—bunch of richie-rich liberals funneling them money out the wazoo. With those kinds of resources . . ." He shrugged. "You'll get to judge for yourself."

"How's that?"

"The county sheriff radioed while I was waiting for you. A new pad's going horizontal today—that's gonna be our first stop."

CHAPTER 3

I'd never seen chaos quite like the fracking-pad protest.

I could tell something serious was about to go down even before we landed. After showing us the crash site, the pilot flew the Black Hawk leisurely until we hit the Ohio River, then dipped the nose and picked up speed. Zigging and zagging a few hundred feet up, we rose to dodge the occasional I-beam bridge, but otherwise stayed low enough that the downwash roiled the river's surface, sending fingers of froth toward the banks.

At each major bend, the helicopter banked, giving us a view of the contrasting landscape on either side of the river. To our right, the Ohio shoreline featured little hamlets, their houses scattered across grassy fields tucked neatly against the hillsides. On the left, craggy rock outcroppings and dense forest came right to the water's edge, except where they'd been pared back to make room for smokestacks and concrete cooling towers. Other than a few splashes of color, the trees here had mostly dropped their leaves; together with the underlying rock, they painted the landscape in a deathly gray palette.

As we rounded a final turn, the chopper banked hard left, streaking over the first neighborhood we'd seen on the West Virginia side. At the end of an inland cul-de-sac of small houses with smaller lawns, we reached a clearing bookended by short, squat buildings. At first, I thought we might put down between them, but then I spotted the county sheriff's black SUV—gold star on the door, flashers spinning—parked in a large lot just beyond them.

The Black Hawk eased down toward a square concrete landing pad near the vehicle. Devers was out the side door before the chopper's wheels even touched, like this was some kind of tactical assault. As he beelined for the SUV, I followed clumsily with the duffel slung over my shoulder. I was still clambering into the back seat of the truck when the sheriff gunned the engine.

"Sorry," she called back while keeping her eyes fixed on the road ahead. From behind, all I could see was her coal-black hair, cropped simply at her shirt collar, and the thick, powerful hands she used to grip the wheel. "I'm sure we'll get to introductions later, but we've only got a couple of minutes until they start."

The dashboard clock said 7:48 a.m.

"I thought fracking was kind of constant?"

Devers turned in the passenger seat. "This site's a little unique. There's already a vertical well installed, so all the company needs to do is push a little deeper and go horizontal. They're doing that this morning. Everybody knows, so we figure the Green Way does, too."

At the cul-de-sac's intersection with what appeared to be the town's main street—ironically named Energy Road—we turned north. After two minutes following the river and leaving civilization behind, we veered onto an unmarked road that cut steeply up into the woods. Oddly, compared to the gray, crumbling asphalt we'd just traversed, this unnamed track appeared new and freshly paved, and while trees closed in from both sides, the SUV hummed along, relentlessly climbing as the sheriff kept it floored. By 7:56 a.m., we emerged onto a flat clearing the size of a football stadium.

Overall, the fracking pad itself looked much less impressive than I'd expected: just one giant tower in the center, surrounded by clusters of tanks, trailers, and generators painted industrial yellow. The entire area was ringed by a chain-link fence topped with razor wire. While numerous pickups were parked together inside the compound, two SUVs matching our own were aligned outside in a V beside the fence's main gate, which was chained and padlocked shut. Deputies in black jackets stood on either side of the trucks, hands on the grips of their pistols, eyeing the tree line.

The sheriff pulled our SUV alongside the others. When she climbed down from the driver's seat, she turned out to be nearly as tall as Devers and me. Even discounting the bulky vest pressing out from inside her black uniform shirt, I could see she was powerfully built, with broad shoulders and muscular legs.

After being shielded by the tinted glass and forest canopy, my eyes squinted to adjust to the bright sunlight in the clearing. The dirt at our feet was sandy in color but more like baby powder in consistency—every step seemed to stir up a small cloud, and a fine coating of the stuff stuck to my boots. Its odor was in the air, too—dust mixed with the sweet smell of rotting leaves.

While I'd prepared myself for an onslaught of industrial noise, compared to the howl of the SUV's engine, the compound seemed eerily quiet. Birds chirped to the morning sun, and leaves rustled in the wind, but otherwise the sheriff's greetings to the deputies were the only sound.

"Any sign yet?" the sheriff asked in a voice twangier than Devers's.

"Nothing," a deputy said.

"Watch the road," she said. "They love to block the way in and out."

Devers checked his watch.

As he did, a new noise appeared in the air. Faint at first, seemingly carried on the breeze. Like bees buzzing.

Tiny shapes appeared in the sky at the back edge of the compound. As they approached, you could gradually make out spinning rotors—quadcopter drones. Five of them.

"That's the Green Way," Devers said.

Like a fighter jet in one of those Super Bowl flyovers, one drone peeled off from the formation, rising vertically until it was barely recognizable. The other four continued forward, flaring into a wide square. Once they'd cleared the fence line, they descended together until they were hovering a couple of stories above the ground.

Workers emerged from the trailers inside the compound—one or two dozen men in matching hard hats and coveralls. Several carried large wrenches or hammers. One had a shotgun.

The men clustered together, looking up at the quadcopters warily. For a moment, it seemed as if the uneasy standoff might persist.

Until the first bombs dropped.

One of the quadcopters swooped in from the side. As it did, two small football-shaped objects detached from it, hurtling downward at the workers like heavy water balloons. One missed completely, creating a dark splotch on impact with the soil. But the other landed close enough to soak the two or three nearest men.

They immediately recoiled.

"Butyric acid," Devers said, inching closer to the fence. He raised an arm to his face, covering his nose and mouth.

"Acid?" one of the deputies asked.

"Stink bomb."

A moment later, the smell wafted to us: the vile, acrid odor of vomit and rot.

Two of the drones made three strafing runs, dropping pairs of stink bombs each time. As the workers recognized the pattern, they dispersed, making it harder for the drones to hit any of them.

Focused on the smell and avoiding the ordnance dropping from the sky, no one was paying attention to the other two drones as they drifted toward the rear edge of the fence. Without warning, crackling noises erupted from the back, and plumes of smoke rose from the ground. Almost immediately, the chain-link fence was engulfed in a massive white cloud.

A loud buzzing sound—much louder than the drones—ripped through the air. If the workers knew what that noise was, you couldn't tell; they remained frozen, unsure where to direct their attention.

Finally, after a long moment, about two dozen figures charged through the cloud.

They were clad completely in black, faces obscured by a hood, scarf, and goggles. Most carried backpacks strapped high on their shoulders. And each seemed to play his or her role with military precision. One group of six made immediately for the central tower, scaling the metal ribs with ease. Another squad, armed with what looked like old-fashioned scissor-type bolt cutters, headed for the tanks. A final few dispersed around the compound, their motives unclear.

Upon seeing the intruders, the workers' initial surprise evaporated, and they started toward the figures. But before they could take even a couple of steps, the smoke drones swept forward, dropping additional fireworks that exploded loudly and filled the compound with thick smoke. From our vantage point, these new clouds completely obscured what was happening inside the fence.

"C'mon," Devers said.

He took off, sprinting along the fence line to our right. Together with the deputies, I followed.

The ground was slippery with fallen leaves, and I had to focus to keep my footing. But every few strides, I stole a glance inside the compound. The tower climbers had now risen above the cloud: two were already nearing the apex, which looked to be at least the equivalent of a ten-story building, while the others had paused at intervals along the side.

As we rounded the first corner of the fence, a breeze began working in our favor. At the back of the compound, the original smoke started to drift away, revealing a large hole cut in the fencing. The secondary clouds in the middle of the compound softened into a dull haze.

From what little I could see, black-clad figures were making mischief everywhere: at the trucks, affixing boots to their wheels; at the trailer doors, messing with the knobs; chopping away at hoses and lines leading to the tanks and generators. The ones on the tower appeared to have done the most damage, as the climbers at the midsection had woven a silver cable or chain back and forth through the ribbed supports until it looked like some kind of giant spider had spun a tangle of webbing around it. Meanwhile, those at the top had attached and unfurled a long, thin banner—although the wind caught the emerald-green fabric and blew it backward, the vertically arranged letters plainly proclaimed, "Respect the Earth!"

With the smoke dissipating, we weren't the only ones who could see the Green Way disruptors. The workers did, too. Although far less coordinated than the Green Way operatives, they began charging toward the insurgents' positions. Before they could intercept any of the black-clad figures, however, a shrill whistle sounded.

In unison, all of the Green Way people immediately stopped what they were doing and began retreating toward the hole in the back fence. Most were far enough away from the workers that they had no problem outracing any pursuit. The unexpected noise also froze some of the workers momentarily, adding to the disruptors' head start.

The climbers on the tower weren't so fortunate, however. Although they attached ropes at their respective positions and rappelled down, by the time they reached the ground, several workers had encircled the base of the tower. And as other workers abandoned their pursuit of the runners, they joined their comrades until the climbers were completely surrounded and outnumbered.

We'd drawn nearly even with the tower, almost at the midpoint of the side of the fence. The circle of workers had begun to close in, raising their tools and leaving little doubt what would happen next.

Except for the drones.

They swooped down together, targeting the workers who stood between the black figures and the hole in the fence. Although the machines had apparently spent all their ammunition, they had surprise on their side: hearing the hornet buzz rapidly approaching from behind, the men flinched, ducked, or spun around, creating a narrow break in the circle.

All six figures bolted for it.

Four got through, clearing the fence hole as Devers, the deputies, and I were reaching the second corner. As we slowed to round the turn, the disruptors sprinted for the tree line only yards away.

Devers jerked a finger from the deputies to the runners, sending the police off on a diagonal course to try to intercept them, while he and I continued toward the hole in the fence. From my position at Devers's heels, I could see the two remaining disruptors on the ground inside the compound where they'd been tackled from behind.

"Stop! FBI!"

Although Devers yelled at full volume, the workers either didn't hear or didn't listen. The crowd had engulfed the downed climbers, dragging them to their feet and restraining them by the arms. One particularly burly worker approached the captives, holding a wrench the length of a baseball bat. Looking like a major-league slugger, he hefted the tool onto his shoulder.

"Don't do it! FBI!"

Devers ran quickly ahead of me, but not fast enough.

The muscular worker stepped forward and began rotating his shoulders. Then he swung the head of the wrench into the side of the first captive's knee.

I wasn't sure if I heard or imagined the sickening crack the leg made when it folded inward. But the disruptor's scream was real—it sliced through the morning air, raising the hair on my arms.

We weren't the only ones who noticed: the drones had circled around, lining up single file for another pass.

This time, though, the workers were ready. The one with the shotgun moved between the wrench swinger and the oncoming quadcopters. He raised the butt of the gun to his shoulder and waited, letting the lead drone close the distance.

When he finally pulled the trigger, the sound of the gunshot reverberated around the site.

Somehow the lead drone dodged the fire, banking away at the last minute, leaving the second drone to catch the buckshot. It teetered in midair momentarily, looking almost drunk before clattering to the ground.

The second Green Way climber was struggling mightily against the crowd. Not wanting to suffer the same fate, the intruder dropped to their knees. That led the workers to draw the person's arm out straight. This time, the wrench swinger heaved the heavy tool behind him to deliver a two-handed overhead blow.

Given what the wrench had done to the other's leg, I expected it to chop the arm clean off.

But he never got the chance.

Devers collided with the wrench swinger at full speed, driving his shoulder into the man's ribs. The worker crumpled; Devers tumbled over and past him, skidding to a stop a couple of yards away. The wrench fell between them.

Startled by the commotion, the shotgunner turned, swinging his barrel around so that it pointed directly at Devers.

Although I'd been charging ahead, I pulled up and drew my Sig. Before I could tell him to stop, a woman's voice boomed through the compound: "Everyone freeze! You drop that shotgun this instant, or so help me, I'll shoot it right out of your hands!"

All eyes turned to the front of the compound. The sheriff held a car-mounted microphone in one hand while aiming her own pistol at the shotgunner with the other.

He hesitated, lowering the weapon a few inches.

"You heard her," I said. "Put it on the ground and step back!"

After glancing between the sheriff and me several times, he complied. By the time I felt safe enough to look up, the three remaining drones had already climbed high into the sky and were curving back toward the wilderness from which they'd come.

Devers rose, brushing the powdery dust off his pants and vest the best he could. Still breathing heavily, he flashed me the same sarcastic smile he'd worn in the Black Hawk.

"Welcome to Wetzel County, Walker," he said. "It's wild and wonderful."

CHAPTER 4

When the sheriff and I finally got around to introducing ourselves, she told me her name was Heather Simon.

By then, we'd returned to her office, a narrow room on the first floor of the courthouse. Set on a corner at the southern end of New Martinsville's business district—a stretch of several blocks that bent like an L off Energy Road—the building stood out from the brick storefronts and Victorian-style houses that lined the street. Only yards from the river, it was cut from rough earthen-colored stone and featured tall spires at its corners and a large central clock tower that gave it a historic look. Inside, though, it felt more like an outdated DMV: industrial metal furniture, analog clocks whose hands ticked loudly as they moved, and little metal plates above each doorframe to identify the office holders.

Unlike the deputies who shared the office next door, Sheriff Simon had a private office with her name stenciled on the pebbled glass inset in the door. Otherwise, the perks seemed few. The walls stood bare; a small set of shelves contained nothing but some unmarked black binders. While her desk held a flat-screen monitor, underneath it I saw the bulky metal shell of an outdated PC.

Simon sat semireclined in a rolling, high-backed chair whose grainy honey-colored wood matched both the door and the chair-rail moldings encircling the room. "You see the look on that fracker's face when he found out I was the one with a bead on him?" Her hair swept at the top of her collar when she talked. "Bet he's not used to taking orders from a *girl*." Her pale-blue eyes gleamed.

Devers had chosen to lean against the windowsill instead of folding his long frame into one of the guest chairs. "I was surprised you arrested him at all, tell you the truth. No jury around here's going to convict him for pulling a gun to fend off the Green Way."

"Jeez," she said, "you're in a mighty forgiving mood. You're the one he almost shot." When Devers didn't react, she tapped a finger on the desktop. "Nobody points a shotgun at a member of law enforcement in my county without getting arrested—at a minimum. If folks don't understand that, it's going to be pure chaos around here. And that's not even mentioning that poor girl—"

"Poor girl?" The FBI agent pushed away from the wall, his voice rising an octave. "You mean the terrorist who—"

"Who's probably never going to walk right again, if she walks at all," Simon cut in. "She's facing ten years, but she's the one people are gonna feel sorry for, losing her career and all."

Everyone in the compound—law enforcement and workers alike—had been surprised to discover that, beneath the black hood and scarf, the injured climber was a young woman, her brown hair braided into tight cornrows. Once we'd gotten back to headquarters, one of the deputies had printed a news profile featuring a wholly different picture of her: smiling broadly, wearing lots of makeup and a USA leotard. A gymnast who'd barely missed going to the last Olympics, she'd apparently passed on a college scholarship to join Richard Chu's fight against fossil fuels.

"Besides," Simon said, "she had spunk. People around here respect that."

Unlike her disruptor colleague, who'd sat near catatonic after dodging the threat to his arm, the woman had cursed a blue streak while the paramedics worked on her. Then she'd spat at—and hit—the shotgunner as she'd been carried off to the ambulance on a gurney.

Devers's head dropped for a moment. "At least you see now, right?" he asked me. "What I was telling you in the chopper?"

"I mean . . ."

"Oh, c'mon, Walker—Chu has those Green Way guys trained up like an army. The drones are his little air force."

"The disruptors were supercoordinated, I'll grant you that. Well equipped. But that thing"—I pointed to the cardboard box on Simon's desk containing the remains of the drone that had been shot down in the compound—"there's no way one of those crashed Appalachian 303. You talked about keeping our eyes on the ball—*that's* the case we've got to solve."

"Just because we saw that drone today doesn't mean it's the only one they've got. The Green Way doesn't care how many people get hurt—"

"The only people who got violent today were the frackers," I said. "The Green Way trashed some property, but they didn't have guns or kneecap anybody. If Sheriff Simon—"

"Heather," Simon cut in. The corners of her mouth had turned up in a noticeable grin.

"—if Heather hadn't called ahead to the paramedics, who knows what would have happened to that woman."

Devers looked at me as if I were crazy. "She was *trespassing*! She cut through their fence, jacked up their drill, then tried to run away."

I could feel my face starting to flush. "And that gives them the right to cripple her?"

"No! Hell, I'm the one who tackled the guy with the wrench, remember?"

"Textbook technique, by the way," Simon said.

Devers glanced over at her, nodded, then turned back to me. "But if she's not in that compound causing havoc in the first place . . ." He paused for a breath. "Look, it makes sense that some kind of drone took out that plane, and the only ones around here using drones are the Green Way. We ought to haul Chu in right now—"

"Hold on a sec," Simon said, then turned to me. "You said Chu's drones couldn't have brought down that plane. How come?"

I stood and stepped to the box containing the fallen drone. "I used to be an engineer, but I didn't work on drones, and I haven't had a ton of time to research them. One of the few things I do know, though—and I even double-checked it during the drive back here—is that the highest these things can fly is about eleven thousand feet. Appalachian 303's altitude was almost twice that when it . . . had its problem. So if we're searching for a drone collision, it couldn't have been with one of these."

"I'm not saying it was one of *those*," Devers shot back.

Simon stared at a spot on the far wall between Devers and me and chewed her lower lip. When she finally did speak again, she was looking at Devers. "I don't like Chu or those Green Way characters any more'n you do. But we've got to keep in mind, they're not the only folks causing trouble around here."

"What kind of trouble?" I asked.

Simon's eyebrows rose, as if she wondered how much time I had. "You can start with those fracking boys we tangled with today. The way these pads work, they draw folks from Texas, Oklahoma, Wyoming, all over. Workers drift in from out of state for a few weeks, help set up, then move on. Don't ask me why, but the gas companies never seem to hire local.

"That means we've got a whole bunch of strangers flashing cash and getting drunk on the weekends. They hassle women, get in fights—and we're the ones who've got to break it all up. At the same time, every miner in the county, employed or not, sees coal prices dropping as these frackers move in."

"Hard to see how that would affect Appalachian 303, though," I said.

"You never know," Simon said. "An awful lot of miners are veterans. They're well armed, plus the mining companies keep plenty of explosives around. You tell me something blew up, that's one thing I'd consider, even if it isn't necessarily top of my list."

"What *is* at the top of your list?" I asked.

She cocked her head and sighed. "You seen the news lately? We've got some drug problems around here."

"You think drug dealers brought down an airliner?"

"If you'd told me a couple years ago that we'd have a thousand overdoses in a year, I'd have said you were crazy, but that's where we are now. Used to just be the meth cookers we had to worry about hiding up in the woods—now it's heroin. That gets brought in all sorts of ways: trucks, boats, you name it. Few months ago, we caught a guy flying a load in on one of those ultralights—you know, one of those glider things, with the fan on the back?" Simon pantomimed a propeller spinning with her finger. "I'm guessing drones aren't too much of a stretch."

"Huh," I said. "How big is the county?"

"Three hundred fifty square miles."

"That's a lot of forest to search."

Devers, who'd slumped back against the windowsill, shook his head. "We don't have time for all that. Another pad goes online tomorrow—we need to stop Chu *now*."

"Before we go charging off, we ought to do a little homework," I said. "If Chu does have some bigger, badder drone we haven't seen, we're going to want a way to bring it down. It might take me a few hours, but if I do some research—"

"I may have a shortcut for you on that." Simon's eyes twinkled again as she rose, pulled on her jacket, and wrapped a scarf around her neck. "Let's take a drive."

When we emerged from the courthouse, half of the sky had been overtaken by a dark front of flat-bottomed clouds. Simon turned the SUV toward the sun and drove us out of downtown, following a creek whose water looked as still as it was muddy brown. Eventually, we settled onto Route 7, a two-lane highway that wove back and forth, tracing the creek as it stretched eastward.

We'd navigated through several bends when Devers asked, "Where are you taking us, exactly?"

"We're headed to Hundred," she said.

I wasn't sure I'd heard her correctly from the back seat. "Where?"

"Hundred. Little town on the other side of the county. They named it for Henry Lee Church—a British soldier in the Revolution, lived to a hundred and nine. At least, that's what most folks say."

"Are they wrong?" I asked.

Simon smirked at me in the rearview mirror. "Some think they named it after Church's wife. She made it to a hundred and six."

"Please tell me this is where Chu is hunkered down," Devers said.

"It might be, but that's not why we're going," Simon said. "At least not at first. I want us to talk to Wesley Hughes."

"Who's that?" I asked.

"He's a local boy, enlisted in the air force after high school."

"Does he know about drones?" I asked.

"Hell yeah—probably knows more about drones than anybody in the state. He flew Predators in Iraq and Afghanistan before retiring last year."

"You gotta be an officer to fly, Heather," Devers said.

"I know that." Simon rolled her eyes. "Wes got commissioned after he was in. Local paper wrote a bunch of articles about him."

"Any chance this guy's gone in with the Green Way?" Devers asked. "That was some slick formation flying this morning."

She grunted. "Not a chance."

"You know him?" I asked.

"Wes and I . . . went to high school together. Not the same class— he was a couple years ahead."

"I detected a little pause there," Devers said, his voice dropping to a sly tone. "Older man, huh?"

"Don't get all jealous on me now, Mitchell," Simon joked. "Besides, he's turned into a bit of a hermit."

"How's that?"

The sheriff paused, her mouth pressing into a straight line. "Wes's dad died when we were kids—diabetes—so his mom was the only kin he had. Right after he got back, she got real sick and passed. That took a toll."

"And?" Devers asked.

Simon sighed heavily. "Folks have been talking—it all could be just idle gossip, mind you—but they're saying that somehow he's . . . not the same, you know? Like, maybe he's got PTSD or something. He tried a couple of jobs, but nothing's quite worked out."

Devers shifted in his seat. "If he needs money, Chu could have thrown cash at him."

"I highly doubt it," Simon said. "From what I hear, Wes has been scraping by on the little bit he gets from the VA every month."

As Route 7 continued winding through the countryside, tracing the valley formed by the narrow creek, we appeared to be the only vehicle headed east. Although the area was heavily wooded, tiny houses dotted either side of the road, rarely within shouting distance of each other. Some had hay laid out in their yards; others seemed to serve as both dwellings and storefronts. Virtually all were painted white and had some kind of satellite dish pointed into the sky.

Simon knew the road and kept the SUV well above the speed limit. Still, the cloud cover seemed to be outpacing us—it wasn't long before the sun disappeared and the sky came to match the bleached gray of the pavement speeding below us.

In the back seat, I used the time to get my own research started. Pulling up as many drone articles and white papers as I could on the laptop, I ran them through my software and loaded them onto my audio player. By what I guessed was the midpoint of the drive, I had a narrator chattering in my ear about lift-to-drag ratios and how designers were altering propeller shape to reduce interactions between multiple rotors.

When a sign indicated Hundred was two miles away, Simon turned onto a single-lane switchback. A handful of small houses with neatly manicured lawns stood at the base of the road, but wilderness seemed to take over completely as we started to climb. Every so often, we'd pass an unmarked driveway cutting up into the woods, but otherwise, the road itself was the only constant reminder of civilization, and even that was mostly buried beneath a layer of fallen leaves.

With no room to spare on either side of the SUV, Simon's speed decreased significantly. A fine drizzle—barely more than mist, but which people back home in LA would have called rain—caused her to switch on the wipers.

After several minutes creeping along that way, we reached a section where the land on the right-hand side of the road was fenced off. Three wires had been strung between periodic wooden posts, like the livestock fencing I used to see in Texas. But here, the thick foliage became an integral part of the barricade: the wires wrapped around or through tree trunks wherever they rendered the posts unnecessary, while bushes and lower-growing foliage swallowed the wires in many places.

After a couple of miles of fencing, Simon eased the SUV as far off the road as she could and coasted to a halt. Just ahead, a large metal gate blocked a gravel driveway. Although the metal panel bore a superficial coating of rust, it still looked sturdy enough to discourage intruders. "Keep Out" and "No Trespassing" signs had been posted on either side, and in case the point wasn't clear enough, "Private" had been spray-painted across it in tall black letters.

Simon slid out the driver's door, and Devers and I followed. In addition to the precipitation, the cloud cover had lowered the temperature significantly—my breath now formed pale puffs of smoke, while the cool air and moisture tickled my bare scalp and ears. I tugged the zipper on my leather jacket up a couple of inches.

Even more than the weather, though, the most noticeable difference between here and New Martinsville was the odor in the air. Acrid and ugly. Like rotten eggs, but even stronger than the Green Way's stink bombs. The air seemed thick with it.

"What's that smell?" I asked.

"Fracking fumes," Simon said. "There's an active pad about a mile away—as the wind changes, the exhaust from the compression stations moves around."

She stepped to the gate and tested it with her hand. Secured by two heavy chains fastened with large padlocks, it wasn't going anywhere. Although a plastic mailbox had been mounted at the top of one frame post, no call box or other way to contact the residents of the property was visible.

"I don't think your boyfriend wants visitors," Devers said.

She shot him a look.

"Do you know his phone number?"

Simon chuffed. "If I had that, I would have spared us the drive. His mother's landline got turned off years ago, and I doubt he has a cell." Cupping her hands to her mouth, she yelled, "Wesley! Wesley Hughes!"

As she cocked an ear, listening for a response, Devers and I exchanged looks.

"Listen, Heather," he said. "Maybe we should—"

"We'll just have to climb it," she said. And before he could get another word out, she'd hoisted herself halfway over.

Devers muttered something under his breath as he and I approached the gate.

The gravel inside the barrier, overgrown with weeds a half-foot high, crunched softly as we landed. Tree branches knitted together overhead, making it seem more like dusk than lunchtime. Even in the dim light, the narrow trail snaked noticeably up the hill until it disappeared around a rocky outcropping a hundred yards ahead.

"Be careful," Simon said, "both of you. Folks around here tend not to like unannounced visitors. And Wes may be more suspicious than most." Crouching by the fence, she dug around in the leaves until she located a long fallen branch. She used it to begin poking the ground ahead of her as she walked.

She'd gone maybe three yards before her hand flew up. "Whoa!"

Devers and I drew alongside her and watched as she shoved the branch forward into a significant depression hidden by the weeds.

Devers grabbed another stick and began sweeping the ground. Gradually, he cleared away enough leaf litter to reveal a ditch two feet wide and at least a foot deep.

Lining the bottom were sharpened metal spikes.

"Those'll take out a tire," he said. "Or your foot."

If Hughes had rigged the ditch to stop someone from approaching, he'd probably done more than that. Glancing up and around at the trees, it took a moment, but I eventually spotted what I was looking for.

"There," I said, pointing at a spot maybe ten feet over our heads. A small green box was tethered to a nearby trunk. "Looks like a trap camera. So he can watch if someone gets stuck down here."

"You thinking it's motion sensitive?" Devers asked.

"Maybe," I said. "Or he installed some kind of pressure sensor down in the ditch. Either way, he could be watching us now."

Simon turned to the tree, removed her hat, and waved at the small box.

"He's gonna recognize you, right?" Devers asked.

"He should."

"That's not super encouraging when we're talking about crazy booby-trap hermit man."

"Let's keep going," she said.

"How far is the house?" I asked.

"Not far. After that bend"—she pointed to the outcropping where the driveway disappeared—"you go over a little ridge, and then it's all downhill. Maybe a quarter mile total."

We each hurdled the ditch, then started forward again. A few feet farther, Simon's stick struck something hard on the ground. Once again, Devers bent over and swept at the spot. Two metal tire guides—movable ramps mechanics use to work under cars—lay in the weeds.

"Guess we know how Hughes gets himself in and out," Devers said. He straightened to his full height and turned to take another step.

I glanced ahead of him for some reason, and something unnatural caught my eye.

"Wait!" I shot my arm out and grabbed his shoulder. "Heather, use your stick. Up high this time."

Simon raised the branch in front of her, at arm's length and perpendicular to the ground like a drum major's baton. Slowly, she inched past Devers. Less than six inches from his chin, the wood snagged on something that dug into the bark and bent the stick back toward her face.

Holding the branch steady, she crouched and swung herself underneath the invisible obstacle.

"Metal wire," she said once she stood back up. Simon removed her scarf and draped it over the top.

Once you knew what to look for, the taut wire was vaguely discernible against the mottled coloring of the forest behind it, but barely. It stretched to a tree trunk on either side of the driveway.

Devers, who'd frozen when I grabbed him, now set his foot down and took a deep breath. "This is insane. We're never gonna make it to the damn house."

"Wesley!" Simon yelled twice more, but still no response.

"He might not even be here," Devers said. "Could've gone out for a gallon of milk and left his booby traps guarding the place."

"Just a little farther," Simon said. "You can see the house from the ridgeline. If his truck's missing, we can go."

"No way," Devers said. "This is a total distraction from what we ought to be doing, and we're up against God knows what here in the woods. What's next, land mines?"

As they argued, I tried to think what might convince Simon to leave and return later. When I opened my mouth to speak, Devers turned toward me.

His eyes widened. But they weren't trained on my mouth or my face.

I followed his gaze down to my jacket.

A glowing red dot was hovering over the zipper.

CHAPTER 5

Figuring whoever was on the other end of the laser sight would be eyeing me carefully, I tried hard not to move. Or even breathe.

That last bit actually proved to be the easy part. Controlling my pulse was a different story—my heart wanted to explode out of my chest.

But I kept my chin tucked against my collarbone, my eyes focused on the red dot hovering over my sternum. So much so that, when it disappeared suddenly, I wondered if that meant a bullet was headed my way.

After a moment passed, and I wasn't dead, I glanced up to find that Simon had stepped directly in front of me.

"Wesley Allan Hughes!" Her voice had turned angry now as she directed her words toward the rocky outcropping. "I know it's you up there in them trees. Don't you pretend you can't see me through that damn sniper scope—get your ass down here!"

Simon's tirade seemed to have absolutely no effect. Unable to see the front of her uniform, I checked Devers's face—his eyes remained locked on Simon's heart.

"Wesley, I have known you since you were nine years old. I really don't think you want to shoot the county sheriff, but if I'm wrong, let's go on and get it over with. Otherwise, come on down here, and let's talk like civilized human beings."

When another long silence followed her words, I wondered if it might be someone other than Hughes behind the scope. Simon's shoulders rocked rhythmically from all the yelling, but I had to imagine that she, too, was growing concerned by the lack of any response.

"Wes?" she called one last time. Her voice, quieter now, seemed to have lost some of its strength.

"What do you want here, Heather?"

The question came suddenly from our left, and we all spun to face it.

Although we hadn't heard anyone approach, a man stood just a few yards away, off the driveway in the woods.

My hand instinctively flew back to the grip of the Sig, but I didn't draw it. The man carried a shotgun, albeit lazily, the barrel pointed at the ground. No rifle, no scope—had the laser dot been a trick? Dressed in dirt-smeared overalls and a green flannel shirt, he had a messy mop of brown hair and several days' growth on his face.

I swear I heard Simon exhale. After a moment, she tromped forward into the brush. "First thing I want from you is a hug, you big goon. I don't think I've seen you since your mom's service."

Hughes didn't move as Simon wrapped her arms around him, squeezed, and then released him. When she took a half step back, she rapped the back of her hand lightly against his chest. "Scared me half to death with that laser thingy. Is that for real?"

He blinked at her twice, but his expression didn't change. "Who are these men? What do you all want?"

"They're from Washington, DC—we need to ask you a few drone questions. Can we head back to the house and sit for a bit?"

Hughes glanced from Devers to me and then back again. Without a word, his eyes dropped to the ground, and he started walking, first onto the grown-over gravel, then following the path back toward the outcropping.

Simon hurried after him, waving at us to follow.

It was a good thing we had Hughes leading the way. Mirroring his movements and following his footsteps, we were able to avoid three more wires, another ditch, and likely countless other booby traps we couldn't see. I noted at least four more places where trap cameras had been installed to watch portions of the driveway—any or all of them could have been rigged to explosives, automatically fired weapons, or who knew what else.

As Simon had described, the farmhouse sat in a clearing just over the ridge. The driveway ended in a broad circle of gravel that was home to a beaten-up pickup and a one-horse trailer. The house bordered the drive, while a larger structure—a barn?—loomed in the distance beyond it. Thick woods like those we'd prowled through encircled the clearing, while the front of the house overlooked what might at one time have been a yard, but had now transformed into an expanse of tall grasses. I didn't see any animals or crops other than a small wooden box that I guessed served as a chicken coop. Next to that, several wooden lean-tos had been erected and used to drape various skins and pelts—the largest looked to be a deer, but there were quite a few smaller ones that could have belonged to rabbits or squirrels.

Hughes led us around front, giving us a good view of the house— overall, the place seemed to be a confusing jumble of mismatched parts. The entire structure sat atop stacks of concrete blocks that raised it several feet off the ground and created a dark, open crawl space underneath. For some reason, the ground floor had two front doors flanked by windows of different sizes, all of which faced onto a covered porch. The second floor appeared more symmetrical, but an additional section that included hayloft doors instead of windows protruded out over the porch roof.

All of the house's siding seemed to be real wood, although its white paint had long since grayed and chipped, the wooden boards underneath bent and splintered. Shingles were missing from sections of both roofs; uneven cement stairs with copper-pipe railings led up to the porch.

Without pausing, Hughes climbed the steps and entered through the left front door, which he'd left unlocked—apparently a fringe benefit of having the property booby-trapped. Simon followed without a word. Devers and I shot each other uneasy glances before mounting the stairs and stepping inside.

After the odd exterior, the interior layout was reassuringly straightforward. The ground floor had been divided into a series of small, square rooms. With few windows and none of the old-fashioned light fixtures lit, each of the tiny boxes was extremely dim. The wooden floorboards—untreated oak, from the look of them—creaked as you crossed them; the plaster on the low ceiling was chipped in places.

More than anything, though, what added to the cramped feeling was the sheer amount of stuff that had been packed into each room. Piles of books and newspapers littered the floors, to the point where footpaths cut between them. The walls were similarly crowded with maps, pictures, and military memorabilia—virtually every inch of space had been claimed. Unlike the skewed piles lining the floors, though, everything on the walls would have bubbled a level. No dirt. No grime. Swords had been freshly dusted. The glass in every frame looked freshly polished.

As we progressed from room to room, it became apparent each one was themed around a particular armed conflict. The first room we'd entered contained images from the Revolution. Another, pictures and relics from Vietnam.

Devers must have noticed, too—the pained expression he'd worn since leaving New Martinsville had evaporated, replaced by wide-eyed, open-mouthed awe. At several points, he stopped and squinted for a better look at particular pictures or medal sets we were passing.

The largest room, which might have been the dining room in any other house, contained Civil War memorabilia. Devers spoke up before

Hughes could reach the next doorway. "Sir, I just gotta say, all this"—he gestured around at the walls—"is something else. I could spend hours in here—I even saw a patch from my old unit, the Dagger Brigade, back in one of the other rooms."

If Hughes appreciated the compliment, you couldn't tell.

"It must have taken years to find all this stuff. How long have you been collecting?"

"Not collecting. This is my family."

Once it became apparent Hughes wasn't going to say more, Simon added, "Wes's family has served, I'm pretty sure, in every war the United States has ever fought. That's what his mom always said, at least. Right, Wes?"

He nodded.

Devers's eyes grew even wider. "Anyone famous? Anybody fight in the big battles?"

Hughes gave a one-shouldered shrug.

"Wasn't there someone in the Civil War your mom always talked about?" Simon asked. "The Battle of Antietam, maybe?"

"The first Bull Run," Hughes said.

"Big defeat for the Union," Devers said.

Hughes nodded. "But there were some small victories along the way." His voice swelled to the loudest volume we'd heard so far. "My great-great-grandfather was part of Sherman's force that ambushed the Confederates and sent 'em retreating in the morning."

"I'm from Kentucky," Devers said, stepping over piles to stand next to a large frame. "This looks like a big ol' map of Louisville."

"Yep." Whether from Devers's excitement or his own, Hughes's eyes lit up for the first time. "My great-great-grandfather's brother served under Bull Nelson there. He was one of the ones racing around the city, fortifying it against a Confederate attack."

Devers shook his head in admiration. "That's *some* family history right there."

Hughes eventually led us to a kitchen in a rear corner of the house, where he waved us into simple, unmatched chairs surrounding a wooden table. Two sets of windows met here, making it the brightest room we'd visited. As I worked my way around to one of the chairs in back, I couldn't help but notice the window frames had been nailed shut.

Simon sat across from me, and I watched her face for any signs of nerves or stress while keeping my right hand perched by the Sig. She seemed perfectly relaxed.

Hughes himself dropped into the final chair, rolling up the sleeves of his shirt before draping his arms on the tabletop. While the front rooms had been no warmer than outside, here the temperature seemed a few degrees higher, perhaps from the wood-burning stove.

Simon patted his hand. "You been taking care of yourself, Wes?"

"What?" He glanced down at his arms, which caused me to do the same. The skin on one of his forearms had reddened, and once he noticed it, he rolled the sleeves back down again and rebuttoned them. "That's nothing—I just got into some poison ivy last week."

"Actually," Simon said, "I was thinking you look like you could use a double helping of your mom's cobbler."

Talk about understatement. Although Hughes was reasonably tall—an inch or two over six feet—his head sat atop a slender neck that matched his narrow arms. His cheeks were sunken, while his shoulders poked out sharply from beneath the fabric of his flannel.

"I'm getting by," he said.

On closer inspection, Hughes's dark hair didn't look merely unkempt—it was a greasy, tangled mess. His skin, naturally pale, was coated in a visible layer of grime.

"You sure are serious about home security, Mr. Hughes," Devers said. "You had problems with trespassers or something like that?"

"I just want to be left alone."

"You mind if I help myself to a glass of water?" Simon asked, rising from her seat. "I know where the glasses are."

"Sit," he said. "I'll get it." Hughes rose and retrieved a mug from one of the cabinets. "Do you two—"

Devers and I both shook our heads.

Hughes filled the mug from a plastic jug in the corner.

"You switched to bottled, huh?" Simon asked.

"Well pump's out," he said. He returned to the table and took his seat. "You mentioned drones—what's this about, exactly?"

"Did you hear about an airplane that crashed near here a couple weeks ago, Mr. Hughes?" Devers asked.

He shook his head.

I hadn't noticed a television, a computer, or any other way he might get news.

"We're wondering whether a drone might have been involved in the crash," I said. "Heather mentioned you were the local expert."

Hughes gave Simon an annoyed look. She simply smiled in response and patted his hand again. "Go on, Wes, tell them about the things you did. You should be proud—"

His head whipped back toward me. "I flew Predators and Reapers. But I don't really see how that helps you."

"Do you think a drone collision could bring down an airplane?" Devers asked.

"Depends. What kind of plane? What kind of drone?"

I explained what little we knew about the problems the plane had suffered.

Hughes scratched at the sleeve covering his rash. "Little turboprops like that don't have too much thrust—if there was a collision on takeoff, the pilot might not have been able to recover. But the FAA restricts airport airspace, so that shouldn't happen."

"You mean geofencing?" One of the manuals I'd listened to explained how drones' GPS systems were preprogrammed so that they couldn't fly into certain "fenced" areas, including airport airspace.

He nodded.

"This incident happened at cruise altitude," I said, "not takeoff. So . . ."

He blinked at me several times. "How high?"

"Twenty thousand feet," I said.

He grunted. "Nothing civilian flies that high."

I glanced over at Devers. "I've read the maximum ceiling for a commercial drone is about eleven thousand."

Hughes leaned back and crossed his arms. "Theoretically, maybe. But that's not a real number."

"Why not?"

"FAA caps 'em. Same as geography—they're programmed not to fly over fifteen hundred feet. So you'd have to monkey with their code to get them above that."

"Okay," I said. "Let's assume that's not hard to do."

"It's probably not," Hughes said. "But then you've got other issues."

"Like?" Devers asked.

"Like control," Hughes said. "Our platforms had two-way satellite communication—that's how come we could sit at Creech in Nevada and fly drones in Iraq. There's a lag 'cause the signals have to travel so far, but you've got a dedicated link. Commercial drones use radio control, but that's got all kinds of issues. Interference. Range. You go too far and you're BVLOS."

"Bee-what?" Devers asked.

"Beyond visual line of sight," Hughes said. "You can't see the drone with your own eyes, and you can't tell what's around it."

Devers's eyebrows arched. "Plenty of drones have cameras."

Hughes sighed. "Video's on a whole different frequency, and that's got a much shorter range. You go up more than a few hundred feet, good chance you're flying blind. And that's if you can even get there."

"What do you mean, 'get there'?" Devers asked.

"Power is altitude," Hughes said. "Commercial drones run off an electric battery—there's only so much charge, so you can only go so high. And the harder you push the platform, the less performance you get. That's the whole reason military drones were built around a traditional power plant. We would have loved the quiet of electric, but there's just not enough power.

"Best battery life I ever heard about in an electric drone was ten minutes. That was a couple years ago. They're probably better now, but that means you get what, twenty minutes? Thirty? It probably takes you ten minutes to climb, another ten to descend. So you got almost no flight time."

Batteries.

The word wedged in my brain. Chu had made his fortune in tech—he'd led three successful startups in a row. One of those, a company named Amplify, designed batteries for hybrid cars. I made a mental note to follow up on that. In the meantime, though, I had a more pressing question for Hughes. "Any thoughts on the best way to knock a drone out of the sky?"

"You mean besides just shooting it down?"

I nodded.

Hughes stared off into space a moment. "Surest way would be to take over its comms. If you controlled the platform, you could do whatever you wanted."

"If its communications are encrypted, though—"

He nodded. "I was just gonna say, it may be difficult to hack. Our drone comms were as secure as anything the government had."

"Any other way?" I asked.

Hughes paused a minute, then shook his head. "Not that I can think of."

Although I hadn't listened to all my articles yet, some described the idea of overwhelming a drone with radio waves. While you might not be able to *control* the drone, if you could drown out its operator's signals, it'd be forced to revert to a set of backup commands. I realized I'd need to look at that more.

The back of my brain was calculating how strong the signal would need to be when Devers spoke again. "We appreciate all your time and help, Mr. Hughes. Heather, don't we need to get moving to make it to our next stop?"

The look he gave her said Devers wasn't going to wait, no matter what Simon said. But she glanced at her watch and rose from her chair. "Yeah, we should go. Thank you, Wes. When this whole thing is over, I'm gonna be back here with a plate of cookies for you."

For the first time, Hughes managed a slight smile.

"One last thing," I said, standing up myself. "Is there any chance someone could've gotten their hands on a Predator or a Reaper, like the ones you flew?"

Hughes shot me a look like I was crazy. "Only a couple ever crashed, and we worked pretty hard to destroy those. A new Predator costs four million bucks, and it's not like you can just go down to the store and order one up. They're government contract only."

That raised an important question, something I'd need to follow up with Cooke about.

"It's a good thing, too," Hughes added. His eyes drifted down to the table once again. "Drones kill. That's all they do, just watch and kill."

CHAPTER 6

Once we'd carefully made our way back to the SUV, I switched my phone to speaker and dialed Melissa Cooke.

"Progress?" she asked.

"Process of elimination, maybe." I recapped the events at the fracking pad and what little we'd learned from Hughes. "So, assuming there was a collision, it had to be with something bigger than what we've seen so far."

"You really think someone got their hands on military tech?" she asked.

"Maybe," I said. "But are we completely sure the military wasn't involved, that they weren't testing something secret that might have caused this by accident?"

"DOD confirmed it had no assets in the area at the time of the crash," Cooke said. "We went through that with them when we were chasing down air-traffic reports."

"Do you believe them?"

"Why wouldn't I?"

"Because if we're looking for something military grade, the military's the first place to look," I said. "And it wouldn't be the first time a government agency lied to protect something."

Cooke's silence on the other end said my point had registered. "I'll ask again," she said, "and confirm it one hundred percent. But I'll also put a feeler out to intelligence to see if we have a sense someone's gotten ahold of our drones."

I could see Devers's lips had pressed into an uneven line. "What are you thinking?" I asked.

"For me," he said, "this all comes back to money. Whether you're talking about some black-market refurbished drone of ours or something new built from scratch, that takes big bucks. Richard Chu is the only one around here with that kind of bankroll."

"We're going to question Chu next, Melissa," I said, deciding not to mention the Chu/battery connection for now.

"Keep me posted," she said.

After we hung up, I checked the scenery flashing by. Although we were on another two-lane road bracketed by hills on either side, this one felt narrower than Route 7. Fewer houses, denser foliage, and the tree branches seemed to encroach into the roadway even more than before. The dashboard clock said it was nearly 3:00 p.m.

"Where are we headed?" Devers asked the sheriff.

"Pine Grove. A little town about halfway back to New Martinsville, but a touch farther south."

"And that's where the Green Way is set up?" I asked.

Her eyes flashed up in the rearview mirror. "Not exactly."

Devers sighed heavily. "I don't understand—"

"Chu isn't staying in a motel, guys," Simon said. "He and his people are camped out, they move around. You saw my whole force back at the station—I don't have the manpower to put someone on them full-time. But I know someone who'll know where they are."

A small sign and a blocky, white government building announced our arrival at the Pine Grove city limit. From there, another meandering creek led the way to downtown proper. The first landmark we reached—an old cinder-block warehouse painted sky blue—turned out to be an American Legion post. A marquee and blinking-arrow sign announced that bingo was held every Monday night at six.

We turned right, crossing a narrow concrete bridge to a small intersection where the streets weren't marked, but a hand-painted speed-limit sign had been posted on the sidewalk. While the road we'd been following continued up and over a ridge, another crumbling asphalt street spilled down to our left, crossing the creek again toward a redbrick schoolhouse.

Simon pulled the SUV into an empty gravel lot and silenced the engine.

When we climbed down from the truck, the rancid odor had disappeared from the air, replaced by a crisp cold that stung my nostrils in a good way. Uphill from the empty lot, houses were perched atop grassy mounds that strained against cracked concrete retaining walls holding them in place. Downhill, past a marquee for a Chapel of Victory church that was nowhere in sight, a small hexagonal building sat alone overlooking the creek; the oversize black satellite dish mounted on its roof seemed to contradict the stacks of books visible inside and the "Public Library" sign hammered into the ground next to it.

Simon started across the street, where several abandoned brick storefronts stood side by side. The first was the most impressive: a two-story structure with an intricate facade, its arched doorway—boarded over with plywood—faced out to the corner and had "Bank of Pine Grove" chiseled in stone above it. The next one had a rusted metal awning protruding out over the sidewalk, further shading its darkened plate-glass windows.

The final storefront was by far the humblest—barely more than a narrow doorframe and a glass-block window. Unlike the others, though, this tiny little building showed signs of life, as four people sat in lawn chairs blocking the entrance. Poster-board signs leaned against the blankets covering their laps, bearing handwritten slogans like "Coal is King" and "We Need Gas to Pass."

Sheriff Simon approached the man seated closest to us in the quartet. With dark age spots on his balding scalp and stark white hair, he looked to be in his mid- to late sixties.

"How's it going, Harv?" she asked.

"Chilly now. Was better while the sun was out."

"I hear you," she said, flipping the end of her scarf over her shoulder.

He raised a silver thermos from the sidewalk. "You need a cup?"

Simon chuckled. "Shit, Harvey, I got no way of knowing what all you spiked that with. Getting a DUI two weeks before the election ain't gonna help me."

That drew laughs from the old man's companions and made him grin. "It'd make me vote for you," he said. "Twice."

"Brittany Anne inside?" Simon asked.

"Sure is," Harvey said. "She in trouble?"

"No, nothing like that."

"You should arrest her," the woman seated next to Harvey said.

"On what charge, Cathy?" Simon asked.

"Riling everybody up."

"I'll check my statute books back at the station, but I don't know that 'riling up' is a punishable offense."

"That lawsuit she filed last month," Cathy said. "If they close the mine, everyone here'll be out of work. Including my husband. That's an awful lot of lives to throw away for some damn lizards."

Simon shrugged. "I'll see what I can do. For now, why don't y'all let us through." She squeezed between their chairs and pushed her way into the building. Devers followed her directly; I smiled at Harvey, which earned me a curt nod.

Behind the heavy wooden door stood a single room not much larger than Lavorgna's office back in LA. The walls stood bare except for a navy-blue banner draped across the back wall, whose gold lettering read, "Appalachian Center for the Environment and Society." In the center of the room, two desks had been turned to face each other. Only one was occupied—by a young woman whose chestnut hair was tied into long, tight pigtail braids.

As I let the door go, it slammed shut loudly behind me.

"Hello, Sheriff," the young woman said in a voice that was even higher pitched than I'd expected.

"Fighting the good fight, Brittany Anne?"

"Yes, ma'am," she said. "ACES fights every day." Dimples formed in her ruddy cheeks.

"Let me introduce my friends, here," Simon said, identifying us in turn. "Guys, this is Brittany Anne Donohue, founder of this little organization."

Donohue bounced to her feet and shook our hands. Barely over five feet tall, she wore a gray WVU Mountaineers sweatshirt over black leggings and Chuck Taylors. The shoes, in particular, reminded me of Emma, the young pop singer I'd bodyguarded in Austin. She hadn't had a Glock 19 strapped to her right thigh, though.

"Cathy's still mad at you about the lizards," Simon said.

"Amphibians. Yeah, I know." A tiny crystal stud on one side of Donohue's nose glinted in the light as she talked.

"What exactly does your Center do?" I asked.

"We educate folks about the toll the energy industries are taking. We try to get people to see that there are other paths to the future."

"With lizards?" Devers asked. "Or, amphibians?"

Donohue kept smiling. "The Cheat Mountain salamander. It's a federally threatened species that only lives on mountains in five West Virginia counties, and nowhere else. One of the coal companies, Mountain Energy, just applied to do mountaintop-removal mining on a series of those. If their permit gets expanded, there's a real good chance they'll ruin a huge chunk of the salamanders' remaining habitat."

"So salamanders over people," Devers said.

"Have you ever seen what mountaintop-removal mining does?" she asked, circling back to the computer on her desk. "Instead of digging a tunnel down and pulling deposits out, they essentially slice the top off the mountain to grab all of it at once."

"My daddy risked his life down in tunnels like those," Devers said. "We never knew if he was coming home at night or not. What you're describing sounds a heckuva lot safer and more efficient."

"Oh, it's efficient, all right," she said. "Problem is, they've got to put the mountaintop somewhere once they carve it off. Most times, they just push it off to the side, but that fills a natural valley and can cut off water supplies, redirect rivers—all kinds of things."

We peered over Donohue's shoulder as she clicked through a series of pictures on her computer showing wooded hills like the ones we'd been driving through all day. But the tops of some of them had been flattened into what looked like dirt fields.

"Still," Devers said, "salamanders?"

"It's not either/or," she said. "Several years ago, they found a chemical in lizard saliva that helps treat diabetes. People need to realize we've got more raw natural resources than just what's underground."

"Brittany studied to be a lizard expert in college," Simon said.

"Herpetology major, yes, ma'am," she said. "If we throw away these things that could potentially help us in the future, we're shooting ourselves in the foot."

"Speaking of shooting . . ." I nodded at the khaki holster on her leg.

Donohue blushed. "My parents."

"Are you a good shot?"

"I don't know that I'd win any trophies or anything," she said sweetly. "But on my eighth birthday my grandpop took me out in the yard and set up coffee cans for me to knock down with a Henry Mini Bolt .22. Ever since then, I've gone hunting with my brothers and shooting with my dad. When I told my parents I was opening the

Center, they gave me this." She shrugged. "My job isn't exactly the most popular one in the county."

"I'm hoping you can help us," said Simon. "We need to talk to some of the Green Way folks, ask them some questions about what happened out at the New Martinsville pad this morning."

Donohue's face grew solemn. "Sheriff, you know ACES isn't—"

Simon put a hand on her shoulder. "I know you're not in with those crazies, hon." Then she cocked her head. "But I'm guessing you know where they're camped out."

The young woman closed her eyes and nodded.

"Great. If you draw me a little map—"

Donohue pulled a parka-style jacket off the back of her chair and began wriggling into it. "I'll just show you—it'll be easier. Besides, I've been cooped up all day. Give me just a sec."

From a canvas shopping bag next to the desk, she extracted a large tinfoil-wrapped baking dish. After peeling off the foil to reveal several pieces of fried chicken, she carried the platter back to a microwave sitting on the floor in a corner. Once she'd heated it, she took it out and said, "Let's go."

Outside, Devers, Simon, and I navigated through the protesters' chairs to reach the street again. After locking the door to the Center, Donohue turned and handed the baking dish to Harvey. "I thought you all might be hungry, Mr. Nelson," she said. "It's getting awfully cold out here."

"Thank you, Brittany Anne," he said. With a smile, he took a drumstick, now steaming in the chilly air, and gave the dish to Cathy. She passed the dish on without taking any food, but the other two protesters each began eating a piece.

"Y'all have a good night," Donohue said. "I'll grab the dish back from you tomorrow." Then she stepped between the lawn chairs and strode past us wearing her sweet smile.

◆ ◆ ◆

Donohue took the front passenger seat of the SUV, leaving Devers to pile in the back with me.

"I've never seen that before," he said.

"What's that?" Simon asked from behind the wheel.

"Environmentalists feeding protesters."

"If you don't mind, Mr. Devers, I prefer the term *conservationist*," Donohue said. "That goes over a little better around here. But, yeah, we feed everyone we can. Like it says in the Bible, 'Give some of your own food to those who are hungry, your light will rise in the dark, and your darkness will become as bright as the noonday sun.'"

"You said *we*—how many people work at the Center?" I asked.

"Oh, it's just me for now," she said. "But there's other groups around doing similar work. The Center for Coalfield Justice up in Pennsylvania, the Ohio Valley Environmental Coalition down in Huntington."

"The Green Way," Devers said.

She turned back over her shoulder. "We're not like them, Agent Devers."

"Seems like you want the same things," he said.

"If you mean we're both against fracking, then absolutely. But when chemicals leaked into the water supply last year and no one in Pine Grove could drink from their taps for a week, the Green Way wasn't around to help."

"You don't partner up with them? Maybe take some of their money?"

Donohue let out a high-pitched giggle. "If the Green Way was paying me, the Center'd be a whole lot nicer than it is. My budget for the year is twenty-four hundred dollars. Half of that'll go to printer paper and ink, and the other half I'll spend at the grocery store buying food for events. I'm not getting rich at this."

"Why do it, then?" he asked.

"Because these are my people—my relatives, my neighbors. I want to save this town—"

"Save it? From the mine?" Devers grunted. "These towns only exist 'cause of what's underneath them. U.S. Steel built my town—it *owned* my town. Back then, Lynch had ten thousand people. Black folks, white folks—hell, we had people from thirty-eight different countries. Eventually, U.S. Steel sold the town; then they sold the mine. Now, Lynch is six hundred people on a good day. The mine is the town, and the town is the mine."

"You sound just like the people who live around here," Donohue said.

"That's 'cause they're right."

"I understand folks need jobs, believe me. My father was a miner, and one of my brothers is, too—"

"Wait, you got miners in your family, and you're doing this?"

"I do this *for* them. And for everyone like them who lives around here."

He shook his head and leaned forward, elbow on his knee. "The only reason I'm sitting here at all is 'cause of a coal mine. They hired my granddaddy when no one else would give work to guys that looked like him. The only reason my brothers and I had food on our table or clothes on our backs was because of my daddy's paycheck from the mine."

"Nothing says mining jobs are the only ones people around here can do."

Devers grunted again and leaned back in his seat. "It's not like they're gonna be writing apps for your iPhone."

"Don't be so sure," she said. "There's a group training ex-miners to code. They're already comfortable working with machines, so it turns out they make great programmers. Plus, there're plenty of other options. People already come here to fish and hunt and white water raft—why couldn't we make more money off tourism?" Donohue turned back to the window, her reflected expression troubled. "I don't worry about fracking as much as some other folks do. It's not that fracking's not bad—it is, and it's doing horrible things we don't even understand yet. But most people around here have caught on. The fumes, the noise, the traffic—people are against it. Now, whether the gas companies can buy their way around that by donating to the politicians, we'll see. But people don't trust the gas companies anymore, if they ever did. Mining's different. People here are willing to give the coal companies pass after pass. Just last year, the plant up in Natrium leaked chlorine gas—"

"Part of New Martinsville got evacuated over that one," Simon said.

"—while the coal-fired power plant leaked mercury into the river. That's Mountain Energy; they're the big company around here. But CarbonPro's down south, and they're no better."

"Those coal mines are paying people—"

"Fewer and fewer people," Donohue said. "It's more machines than miners nowadays. And, what, we're just supposed to give them every last drop of blood we have, wait till they don't need us at all anymore? Or till all the coal is gone? What happens then?" A smile spread across her face. "That's been the funny part, seeing the coal companies panicking because fracking's cutting into their margins. They were all for the free market when it gave them an advantage over workers. But now that the price of natural gas is undercutting them, they want subsidies, they want protection."

Simon had steered the SUV out of town, and again we were following the creek and the railroad tracks that paralleled it. After a minute, we reached a point where the only structures visible were spherical white tanks on the opposite side of the tracks. Then, following a narrow stand of trees, we passed some kind of pumping station before a hairpin turn diverted us in a different direction.

"That back there was an extraction and fractionation plant," Donohue said. "On one side, it collects all the gas shunted down here from the various rigs and pressurizes it for transmission. On the other side, they're making propane and isobutane."

"Sounds good to me," Devers said.

"I don't know how you can say that."

"I can say it because I humped a rifle around Iraq for four years. Gas here means we don't need oil from over there. Keeps us all safer—better for everybody."

"Maybe," Donohue said, "if it wasn't leaking, like the EPA figured out a couple years ago. And that's not even counting the emissions from the compressor stations farther up the lines. They push the gas here, but they end up dumping a ton of pollution into the air."

"Was that what we smelled back at the Hughes farm?" I asked.

"Yep," Simon said. "Some folks think the odors make them sick—people complain about headaches and nosebleeds and stuff. But the gas companies always say there's no science to back that up. And they have all this data they say shows they're complying with the regulations."

"What do you think, Sheriff?" I asked.

"No idea," she said. "I just know on certain days, when the wind's blowing right, my dog won't go outside when I open the door."

After the extraction station, signs of civilization dwindled until we were left with nothing but telephone poles and high-tension wires, and even those were often swallowed by the surrounding vegetation. The rural scenery continued for perhaps ten minutes until we once again rounded a bend to discover a small cluster of buildings.

This time, the prominent landmark at the entrance to town was a three-story cinder-block firehouse with a "Jacksonburg VFD" sign above its garage doors. Simon turned there, but as in Pine Grove, the hamlet offered little else: two short residential streets, and we entered the wilderness again.

"This is one of the state's wildlife-management areas," Simon said. "About fourteen thousand acres where folks can hunt and fish."

Donohue gave Simon directions, and she pushed us deeper into the forest. The terrain grew steeper here, too, the surrounding peaks butting up against the road instead of being set back from it.

After several more miles, Simon turned into a small dirt lot. A few pickups were parked at one end, but the rest was filled by high-end SUVs—Audis, BMWs—bearing license plates from all over the East Coast. Several also had bumper stickers supporting various environmental causes.

"This it?" Devers asked.

"Yes, sir." Donohue pointed to the trees. "The Green Way's camp is right up in there."

CHAPTER 7

The hike up into the woods wasn't easy. Although a trail had been cut through the trees, the terrain was steep, and a thick layer of leaves hid holes, stumps, roots, and other obstacles. Mist continued to fall, adding to the damp chill in the air and rendering the leaf litter even slipperier. Still, with Simon and Donohue leading the way, we eventually made it up and over the first ridge, where the ground gradually plateaued.

A quick check of my phone showed it was approaching five o'clock; I shot a quick text to Michael with today's Emoji of the Day, a snowflake, since it felt like we might be seeing them any minute. Daylight was noticeably waning, but after a few hundred more yards of walking, we began to see the dark silhouettes of tents backlit by the crisp, yellow glow of small campfires.

When we reached the first of these, I could see the encampment was much larger than I'd anticipated. Two or three dozen pup tents had been assembled in concentric circles over an area the size of a football field. In the middle, several four-wheel ATVs were parked around a much larger tent. Unlike the others, this central tent was illuminated both by a large fire and a set of portable lights, like the kind construction crews use at night on the freeway. But instead of a generator, it was plugged into a stand-alone box roughly the size of a shopping cart. As we drew closer, I could see thick wires snaking outward from it to the outlying tents.

In all, I saw maybe a hundred faces, mostly illuminated by the blue light of computer screens or phones. The youngest looked to be in their twenties, like the gymnast who'd gotten hurt at the pad, but there was a wide age range, including several with white hair and thick beards. Most looked well heeled, though, wearing expensive gear from the North Face and Patagonia.

Simon made straight for the central tent. When she reached it, a man and a woman stood from their field chairs to block her path. "Can we help you?"

"I need to see Richard Chu," Simon said.

"I'm not sure if he's here," the woman said.

"This is important." Simon's voice sounded serious, but completely in control, not wavering a bit. "It's about keeping you all safe."

The flap to the large central tent opened, and two men climbed out. As they did, I tried to peek inside—I thought I saw at least one quadcopter, but the canvas slipped back down before I could be sure.

I immediately recognized Chu: his face had been plastered on more magazine covers than some supermodels'. Like many of the others around camp, he had a fleece jacket on with the collar turned up, but he also wore baggy cargo shorts and sandals, despite the temperature. His dark hair was pulled back into a tight ponytail.

"Nice to see you again, Mr. Chu," Simon said. Then she turned to his companion. "I don't believe we've met."

"Darwin Hartley," he said in a thick cockney accent. Hartley stood nearly a foot taller than Chu—he was easily six foot eight—but with narrower shoulders and thin, sinewy limbs. He crossed his arms, trying to look menacing.

"Darwin just joined us recently," Chu said. "He's my number two around here. What'd I hear about a threat to our safety, Sheriff?"

"Quite a performance your folks put on this morning. I'm here to ask you not to repeat it tomorrow."

Chu grinned and shrugged. "I have no idea what you're talking about."

"Your folks were at the pad that went horizontal in New Martinsville this morning. We both know that."

"If you're saying a fracking operation got shut down, that's obviously great news," Chu said. "But what you're suggesting sounds like trespassing. I wouldn't know anything about that." He called to outer rings of tents, "Any of you trespass at some fracking pad today?" When no response came, he turned back to Simon and shrugged again. "We're just enjoying all the wild splendor that West Virginia has to offer."

"I'm not interested in games," she said. "I'm not here to entrap you, or whatever you're thinking. I just know that young woman got hurt today, and I don't want anything like that happening again."

Darwin Hartley snorted and leaned forward. "If you care so much, Sheriff, maybe you could catch the guys who keep ransacking our camp every few nights."

Chu put a hand on Hartley's chest. "Easy."

"What are you talking about?" Simon asked.

Hartley's eyes narrowed. "Like you don't know."

"Enlighten me."

Chu sighed. "For as long as we've been here, every few nights we get locals messing with us. It started out with little drive-bys, them honking their horns, waking us up. But it's gotten worse."

"I'll say." Hartley's arms dropped to his side, and his voice rose. "They've vandalized our vehicles, stolen our electronics. A few nights ago, they fired off rounds and threw cherry bombs into our camp like grenades. We put out the fire they started, but a couple of our people got burned."

"We started off thinking it was just some kids playing pranks, but now . . ." Chu shrugged. "It could be frackers, miners, who knows."

"And that's why you keep moving around?" Simon asked.

"Exactly," Chu said.

"Funny thing, though: no matter where we go, the locals always manage to find us." Hartley turned to Donohue for the first time. "I wonder how."

She shook her head. "I haven't—"

"Right," Hartley said. "I'm sure you haven't tipped off any of your local friends like you tipped off the sheriff here." He took a step closer, until they were inches apart and he towered over her. "You're the worst kind of traitor, you know? You think there's some big peace to be made with these people. There isn't. They'll kill the land; then they'll kill you. They're not smart enough to see their nose in front of their face, and if you're in with them, then neither are you."

Donohue didn't shrink back from Hartley, but I thought I saw her hand drift to the butt of her Glock the same way mine had already found the Sig.

"I want to stop the fracking as much as you do," she said, her tone even and calm. "But once the frackers leave, there's still going to be people here. We need to work with them—"

"There *is* no working with them," Hartley shouted. "They're all complicit!"

Simon stepped between them. "Let's cool it down. We're just talking."

Chu put a hand on Hartley's arm, but the tall man shrugged it off.

"I think Darwin's expressing some of the frustration we all feel," Chu said. "It seems like all anyone ever does around here is talk. We in the Green Way aren't big talkers. We're doers."

In my peripheral vision, I could sense that people who'd been sitting by their own tents had stood now and were approaching. We were being surrounded, which meant this conversation was going to end soon, one way or another.

"Is that an Amplify battery, Mr. Chu?" I asked.

"Pardon me?"

"Seth Walker, sir. I've followed a lot of your work, and I couldn't help noticing the big box everyone is plugged into." I nodded at it. "Is that one of Amplify's?"

Chu squared his shoulders toward me so that I got a clearer look at his face. His expression said he was suspicious but couldn't tell exactly where I was headed. "Yeah, it is."

"Are you still involved with Amplify?"

"When you start a company, it's a little like having a baby," he said. "You don't trust just anyone else to raise it. So yeah. I'm on the board. I still hold some stock."

"Everybody around here know you got a financial stake in their environmentalism?" Devers asked.

"What are you asking? Do my people know I founded Amplify?" Chu chuckled. "I think everyone knows that."

"No," Devers said flatly. "What I mean is, if folks shift from fossil fuels, they're gonna need batteries, and that's money in your pocket. So you aren't exactly doing all this out of the goodness of your heart, are you?"

Hartley and others turned to see how Chu would respond. His mouth hung open for a beat longer than it probably should have. "If you're suggesting I don't believe in this cause, you're dead wrong."

Before Devers could get in another jab, I needed to know something from Chu. "Is Amplify producing batteries for hybrid drones?"

"Excuse me?"

I smiled, trying to show I was nicer than Devers. "Have Amplify's batteries been used in drones with hybrid engines?" I'd been thinking that an electric system with a traditional engine might overcome the power restrictions Hughes had mentioned.

Chu blinked several times. "I don't see how that's any of your business."

Simon stepped forward now, getting in front of Devers and me. "My business," she said, "is making sure nothing bad happens at the new pad opening tomorrow."

"Then tell those fracker friends of yours not to start drilling," Hartley said. His eyes widened, glinting in the light from the campfires. "Otherwise, who knows what might happen?"

"That's a threat right there," Devers said.

"No," Chu said calmly. "He's just pointing out the potential consequences of an inherently dangerous activity."

"Heather, we ought to arrest these sons of bitches right now. That'd keep tomorrow peaceful."

I wasn't sure Devers had noticed how badly we were outnumbered.

"I'm guessing," Chu said, "that if you had an arrest warrant, we wouldn't be chatting like this." He raised his hands, palms upward, and gestured to each side. "We're abiding by all the laws here—you've got no evidence otherwise. You want to arrest us, go right ahead. But you'll get a false-imprisonment complaint from our lawyers, and we'll bankrupt your department."

Hartley leaned back now, crossing his arms again.

The muscles in Simon's cheeks twitched. Through clenched teeth, she said, "Let's go."

"But—"

"Now," she said, glaring at Devers.

As we reached the edge of the camp, Chu called after us. "Have a good night! Maybe we'll see each other again soon."

CHAPTER 8

After the extra-early start that morning and all the excitement that followed, I expected to fall right to sleep. And, with an early wake-up tomorrow to try to catch Chu's people in the act at the new fracking pad, I needed all the sleep I could get. But, thirty minutes after Simon dropped us at our motel, I lay in bed, staring at shadows cast on the popcorn ceiling by light trickling in from the parking lot.

A quick time check on my phone—the room included an unlit analog clock—showed why: it was barely past dinnertime back home.

I flipped on the lamp and sat up in bed, the headboard groaning as I leaned against it. My first thought was to dig out a pad and pencil and sketch some circuits. Although I'd left the business of engineering behind after Clarence's death, my brain hadn't stopped puzzling over everyday problems and how technology might fix them. Cooke had been exactly right: I'd been doing that since I was seven. My very first "invention" had consisted of duct-taping my mom's long-stemmed gas lighter to an old-fashioned ice-cream scoop so I could heat the metal cup and extract bigger scoops from the container.

For a while after leaving engineering for the marshal service, I just sort of doodled. The schematics and block diagrams I drew weren't about staying current or part of some kind of clever backup plan; although the air-marshal gig had started out rough, I knew I'd never return to industry. Instead, I found that fooling around with engineering helped relieve some of the pressure in my brain—I had ideas stacking up, and I had to get them out.

Most of my initial stuff was crappy, but eventually I came up with a couple I thought were good. Better than stuff I was seeing out in the world, anyway. So I found a lawyer and started patenting them. One thing led to another, and before I knew it, not only did I have seventeen patents to my name, but my lawyer was licensing them for me. And real money started coming in: the royalties allowed me to buy my house, to help out with my godkids, even cover medical bills for Emma while her own assets were in limbo.

Tonight, though, I didn't feel particularly inspired to work on my latest design: an AI-based feedback system for the gun range. Although that had been consuming my subconscious back in LA, I now had drones on the brain.

Even after tonight's confrontation with the Green Way, I wasn't completely convinced they'd taken down Appalachian 303. But the fact they were attacking from the air so close to where the plane had encountered trouble seemed too big a coincidence to ignore. If Chu's people—or anyone else, for that matter—had come up with some new kind of drone that was big enough to take down an aircraft, I needed some way to attack it.

From the articles I'd listened to, the theory of overwhelming a drone with radio waves sounded promising. Drone makers had long understood that, for any number of reasons, a drone could get cut off from the signals its operator was sending. Maybe the battery powering the operator's controller died; maybe the drone flew out of range. Rather than letting the drone crash when that happened, the drone makers built in commands telling the drone how to keep flying. Some would level off and hover, awaiting new instructions. Others would return to a fixed waypoint, where presumably the operator could reacquire it.

All that meant, if you could artificially block—or at least interrupt—the control signals from the operator, you had a chance of getting the drone to revert to those default instructions.

As a matter of logic, there were a few obvious ways to do that. You could try to disable the controller sending the signals somehow. You could interfere with the control signals en route to the drone to keep them from reaching it. Or, you could keep the drone from hearing the control signals when they arrived—for example, by overwhelming the drone with a cacophony of other signals. That way, it wouldn't be able to discern its instructions from all the "noise."

The Green Way's operators had been hidden and possibly pretty far removed from their drones. That made neutralizing the controller virtually impossible. The control signals, too, were difficult to interfere with because they were invisible—you'd have to guess at their location in the air, which wasn't super-reassuring.

Ultimately, because you could at least see the drone at the point of attack, targeting and overwhelming it directly made the most sense. While that gave me a theory to work with, the devil, as they say, is in the details. I had no idea exactly how to implement such a jammer—what frequencies I might need, how much power—and I didn't really have time to start designing from scratch.

Fortunately, there was one person who might know something about drones off the top of his head.

Plus, he happened to be a night owl.

Dan Shen's number sits at the top of the favorites list in my phone. He answered after two rings. "How's my favorite client?"

"Relieved," I deadpanned, "to hear that my patent lawyer is working late on my stuff."

"Oh, it's not that late." He laughed. "Plus, I woke up today at noon."

"How's Brian?"

"Off at the studio," Shen said. "Said he was gonna hit Starbucks on the way, so I'm guessing he'll be painting all night."

Shen and Brian own a ranch house in Silver Lake, one of the few places in LA where your neighbors couldn't peer directly into your living room. Since our first meeting, I'd spent countless hours up there, sitting in their outdoor courtyard or at the expansive counter in their kitchen. I pictured Shen in the small office he keeps at one end of the house, leaning back in his roller chair, dressed in his usual uniform of cargo shorts and a golf shirt.

"Where in the world is Seth Walker tonight?"

I chuckled at that. Maybe it was all the time he'd spent in hostile places as an MP, but Shen was the ultimate homebody. Brian, his partner, loved to travel, but I could barely get Shen to drive to Manhattan Beach, let alone onto an airplane.

"Rural West Virginia. Just over the border from Ohio, a little town named New Martinsville."

"West Virginia? Dude, what the hell are you investigating there?"

"A plane crash, believe it or not."

Shen grunted. "Another reason never to fly anywhere with you." He paused a moment, then his voice went businesslike. "I'm guessing you're calling about the '524. I haven't heard anything back yet, but—"

"No, no," I said, rising to retrieve the pen and small notepad from the desk. "I know you've got all the patent stuff under control. I wanted to ask, did you ever work on downing drones when you were in the military?"

"Nah, the Iraqis didn't use drones. Those dudes loved their cell phones, though. They rigged all their IEDs to them—that way they could set the charge, get far away, and then call in whenever they wanted it to go boom."

"Did you have any way to jam their signals or something?"

"At first, we didn't do anything, and even once we started, we didn't do it very well. The early jammer tech was shit."

"How come?"

"Bunch of problems," Shen said. "Some units had too little power. Some would cancel each other out. Some actually fried our bomb-sniffer robots. It wasn't till, like, '07 that the systems got really good. By the time I left in '08, we'd forced them back to pushing plungers again. What's all this got to do with an airplane crash?"

"We think a drone might have taken out the plane," I said. "We're not sure, but it would have to be big, and probably armed." The details of the investigation were technically confidential, but I knew I could trust Shen with anything. Back when I had covert status, Shen was the one civilian I'd told. His history in the army meant he never asked too many questions, and he didn't mind if I held back a detail or two. And, as an attorney, he was used to safeguarding secrets. "If it shows up again, I need to have some way to bring it down."

"Oka-ay," he said. "Do you know the frequency bands they're using?"

"Not exactly," I said, meaning that I had no clue whatsoever.

"Well, do you want to insert your own content signal or just interrupt the carrier?"

Shen was referring to the fact that data transmissions typically had two components. When you tuned your car stereo to a particular radio station, the song you heard was the content signal. That contained frequencies the human ear could hear, but those wouldn't travel over long-enough distances. To transmit the song, the radio station modulated it—amplifying the sound information by a certain multiple—up to a different, higher frequency. That so-called carrier signal traveled long distances through the air and got picked up by the car's antenna. A tuner inside the radio would then reverse the multiplication. "I'm guessing their control signals are going to be encrypted or something."

"Well, if you're not trying to tell the drone what to do, any white noise ought to work. You're going to need to match the carrier signal's frequency, since that's what you're competing with."

Given that whoever had designed the drone could pick any frequency band they wanted, Shen and I started talking through the possibilities—essentially, selecting a set of frequencies to use. But that meant choosing between a series of trade-offs. Longer wavelengths traveled farther and were able to avoid interference from obstacles like buildings and trees, but they carried less information and needed bigger antennas. For shorter wavelengths, the opposite was true. The permutations were almost infinite.

"We're thinking about this all wrong," Shen said finally. "Really, 2.4 gigahertz is where this should end up."

"Why?"

"'Cause that's the spectrum band you don't have to pay for," he said.

"If you're building a killer drone, I don't think you care about an FCC fine."

When carving up the spectrum of wavelengths, the government had licensed the use of certain bands of frequencies to radio stations, cell-phone companies, and others, while a few narrow bands were freely available to everyone. And 2.4 gigahertz was one of those.

"Yep. But those fees are the reason so many technologies have clustered around 2.4. Wireless routers, RC toys—almost everything uses 2.4 because the spectrum's free. So if you want to buy parts off the shelf . . ."

Now I understood what Shen meant: deploying existing technology was almost always considered better than designing something from scratch—it cut through a number of headaches. "All right, so we plan on them being in the 2.4 gigahertz band."

"If these bad guys of yours are thinking at all, they're probably gonna use some kind of spread-spectrum/frequency-hopping technique. Even the Iraqis were doing that at the end."

I scribbled down the frequency numbers, then wrote *frequency-hopping*. That was a technique that had been used since the early 1900s. Tesla had worked on it; the Hollywood actress Hedy Lamarr had invented a system to help direct allied torpedoes in World War II. The idea was pretty simple. To avoid interference—or detection—both a transmitter and a receiver would switch, or "hop," between pre-chosen frequencies inside the particular band the devices used. As long as the changes were synchronized, the two devices could still communicate. I'd need to account for that as well.

"Besides frequency," I said, "the two other variables ought to be antenna and power."

"Power's easy," Shen said. "DC should do it. Get a car battery, dude."

"I was thinking of a lawn mower or tractor battery—a little less voltage, but smaller. I'm gonna have to carry this thing. You think I need some kind of active antenna?"

Passive antennas simply transmitted a signal; active ones helped boost and direct the signal where you wanted it to go.

"That'd be great, but I don't see where you're gonna find one. Heck, where are you planning to get *any* parts for this thing?"

"I'm pretty sure I saw a RadioShack when we were driving around town. And I know there's an auto-supply place." I paused a moment. "Say, when you were in Iraq, did you ever hear of a unit called the Dagger Brigade?"

"Hell yeah. Second Brigade Combat Team, First Infantry Division. Those guys saw some shit."

"Bad combat, you mean?"

"Oh yeah. Patrolling over in eastern Baghdad . . . those guys saw the worst of it. Why do you ask?"

"My partner on this one, that was his unit."

"Well, then, you know he's a survivor, if nothing else."

Although we talked a few minutes more, my eyelids began to sag, and I started doing the math on how few hours remained until Simon would arrive to retrieve us in the morning. I thanked Shen, tucked my notes away, and climbed back into bed.

I didn't even notice the popcorn ceiling this time and was asleep within minutes.

CHAPTER 9

When Sheriff Simon retrieved us at the motel the next morning, she looked as tired as Devers and I did. Still, as we climbed into the SUV, she promised she had some tricks up her sleeve to ensure today's protest would go differently than yesterday's.

I gave up any hope of following our route into the wilderness in the predawn darkness. When we reached today's fracking site, though, seeing wasn't a problem: industrial lamps had been erected at each of the four corners of the compound, painting the entire interior in an artificial white light that bleached the color out of everything.

The light wasn't the only thing assaulting our senses—the noise was nearly deafening. Most of the mechanical humming and clanging and banging seemed to come from the various engines, generators, and pumps around the site, but there was also a flurry of activity around the tower, moving things into place. All the workers wore heavy ear covers to protect them from the sound. We weren't so lucky.

Five deputies wearing uniforms that matched Simon's were waiting for us when we arrived. "My whole crew," she said, yelling to be heard. "The overtime on this is gonna kill me."

As workers were still securing the fence gate with heavy chains and padlocks, the eight of us ducked into a trailer to talk with the site foreman, a bearded guy named Bruce. After thanking us all for coming, he used a hand-drawn map to orient us to the installation.

Unlike yesterday's site, where the vertical drilling had long since been completed, at this site both the vertical and horizontal drilling would be done from scratch by the rig in the center of the complex. The first stage—which they'd budgeted seven days to complete—would be a vertical descent of about six thousand feet, with a stop after they cleared the water table to encase the well in cement. That explained the two cement trucks that had been stationed along one wall, their mixers slowly spinning. We also learned that mud would be pumped into the well to cool the drill—the reason for the large water tanks lined up behind the derrick.

Simon briefly explained yesterday's incident, as well as the Green Way's prior attacks on various companies' fracking sites around the county. "Chu has his folks trained to get in and out quick to avoid getting arrested. They'll have this thing timed down to the second. So, for us," she said, "the trick will be stopping their initial push. If we can just delay them, disrupt their entry for a few minutes, their whole plan should break down, and they'll turn tail."

Given previous Green Way encounters, Simon expected them to target either the back wall of the fence, the front gate, or both as points of entry. Thus, we agreed to split into two teams of four—Devers and three deputies would man the rear of the compound, while Simon, the other deputies, and I would be stationed up front. Bruce offered to spare four men to augment our fence teams, plus he said he'd assign several extra workers to guard the derrick.

"Don't do anything more than you need to," Simon instructed the men. "If you can help us slow these guys down, we'll cuff 'em and arrest 'em so maybe they think twice next time." Since we had only a few sets of metal cuffs between us, she passed out thick plastic zip ties to use instead.

By the time we left the trailer, the sky had brightened to a dull gray—low clouds like those we'd seen yesterday continued to blanket the sky. Brittany Anne Donohue arrived with first daylight. Hair tied into the same long pigtail braids, she led a string of protesters dressed in white up the road.

They lined up just outside of the fence. In addition to poster-board signs, her people carried two folding tables, which they erected and then used to lay out a series of baking dishes filled with everything from deviled eggs to fresh biscuits. It looked like Donohue was using her half-protest, half-potluck approach, her people filling paper plates before beginning to march in a circle.

Simon stepped to the portion of the fence closest to Donohue, and they exchanged a few words through the metal links. Then Donohue turned on a megaphone she'd been carrying and began leading the people in songs and rhyming chants.

When the sheriff returned, I asked, "Did they walk all the way here from town?" The drive had taken us at least twenty minutes, so I couldn't imagine what time the ACES people had gotten started.

She shook her head. "Brittany Anne had them park their vans down the road a ways. She didn't want to get a ticket for parking on private property."

As the minutes continued to tick by uneventfully, I wondered whether Chu had tricked us about targeting this site. His reputation in the tech community had been that of a brilliant but ruthless leader, a CEO who knew exactly where he wanted his company to go, and who would steamroll whatever obstacles stood in his way. But he'd also been charming with the press. In an industry filled with introverts who had problems with public speaking, he'd always been known as articulate and funny. I could imagine him in his command tent last night, joking about us expecting them in the wrong place and wrong time while they attacked some older fracking pad elsewhere in the county.

I also couldn't help but think about Loretta.

It was three hours earlier in California, so she was likely still asleep. But soon she'd be waking, then dressing and driving to a job she needed.

A job she had no idea might be yanked out from underneath her at any moment.

After Clarence's death, I'd left Texas in about as much time as it had taken to pack my bags and break my lease. I'd wanted to be somewhere—anywhere—else, and LA seemed about as different as you could get. Not knowing any better, I'd lined up the air-marshal gig, then found a small studio apartment in West Hollywood.

My first day had shown exactly how out of my depth I was. I'd gotten crushed in traffic, showing up late after the ten-mile drive to headquarters took nearly an hour. MacAlister had been in charge then, back before Lavorgna, and he'd ripped me a new one. The other marshals all followed his lead—it was like the first day of a new school all over again. Plus, it turned out I hadn't filled out the requisition paperwork properly, so they didn't have a badge, a gun, or even so much as a pencil ready for me. When I left at five that night, the two-hour drive home left me wondering what the hell I'd done to myself.

The next morning, determined not to make the same mistakes, I left my apartment by six. The runway lights were still aglow when I passed the airport, and I'd congratulated myself when I saw I was the first car in the parking lot. Of course, thirty seconds later, I realized I had no way to get into the building: they hadn't given me an access badge.

As I stood there like an idiot, wondering if I was staring down the barrel of another hellish day of feeling completely inadequate, a raspy voice sounded behind me.

"You locked out, Walker?"

Surprised by the noise itself, and even more so by the fact that someone actually knew my name, I spun around to find Loretta climbing out of an aging Chrysler Sebring convertible. MacAlister had introduced her to me the day before as the woman who booked all the flights. That seemed like a pretty important job, so while I had no reason to think she'd remember who I was, I'd memorized her name.

"Yes, Ms. Alcott. I'm sorry, they didn't give me—"

"Don't you 'Ms. Alcott' me," she said, shuffling past me to the door. She beeped it unlocked with her key card, then held it open. "I'm 'Loretta' to you, and if you ever call me 'Ms. Alcott' again, I'll bop you upside the head."

Although she gestured me inside, I hesitated. She probably weighed a buck-ten holding her purse, but I felt strangely intimidated.

That's when her lips peeled back into a broad smile. "You know, this door isn't getting any lighter, young man. The least you could do for a woman of a certain age is get inside."

There was nothing to do but shake my head and chuckle.

Once we'd crossed the threshold, she didn't let up. As we were waiting for the elevator, she said, "I don't know what you were thinking, renting a place so far away."

"How—"

"I talked to Judy in personnel." The doors parted, and we both stepped in. "Coming from over there, you're going to spend your entire life in your car. Young man like you, you should find a little place by the beach."

"I can't afford—"

"Come to my cube."

When the doors pinged open, she led me out across the darkened floor to her desk. On a yellow sticky note, she scrawled out a phone number. "This is the number of a friend of mine. She's moving to Phoenix to be near her grandchildren and is looking to rent her house in Venice. It's not much—just a little bungalow—but she's not looking to get rich on the rent. She just wants a tenant she can trust."

"Wow, Ms.—I mean, Loretta—thank you." I reached for the paper.

Just as my fingers were about to close around it, she pulled it away. Her eyes narrowed, and she looked at me over her glasses. "She *can* trust you, right?"

"Yes, ma'am. Absolutely."

The corners of her mouth twisted into another mischievous grin. "I know," she said, releasing the paper into my hand.

"Why are you doing all this for me?" I asked.

"You're different, Walker. All the marshals around here"—she gestured around the darkened floor, her long nails trailing through the air—"these guys look straight through me, like I'm . . . their computer, or something. You," she said, "you see me. I could tell that yesterday." She tilted her head back. "And I see *you*, too."

Forcing a swallow down, trying to push those memories out of my head, I stared at the sky just above the treetops, looking for any sign of the Green Way's drones. I pulled the earpiece out. I never need it when the adrenaline is pumping—adrenaline lets me focus. And I was definitely focused now.

As I continued to scan the sky, though, I found nothing besides a small flock of birds. Unlike yesterday's pad, this site's tree line had been cleared some fifty yards beyond the fences. While that raised the degree of difficulty for a surprise ground assault, it also meant you couldn't see what might be happening off in the forest. It was too shadowy, too far away.

I began to fidget to pass the time, stalking slowly up and down the fence line, scratching at my head—which desperately needed a shave—and fiddling with the zipper of my jacket. A check of my phone showed it was 8:03 a.m. Bruce had said they'd planned to start drilling at 9:00 a.m.

That's when Simon grabbed my elbow.

She didn't yell over the din—she simply pointed.

Above the rear of the compound, six black dots had become visible. As they drew closer, they seemed to split in two, revealing twelve small quadcopters like the ones we'd seen the day before. Each carried objects slung below it—presumably more stink bombs and smoke bombs.

Simon leaned over and spoke directly in my ear. "Now for my little surprise." She produced a walkie-talkie from her pocket and called into it, then inclined her head toward the back of the compound, where a half dozen soldiers in camouflage uniforms were emerging from the trees.

"National Guard," she said, half shouting. "I bet Chu didn't count on me calling in reinforcements."

The soldiers lined up along the exterior of the fence, facing the drones. Each had an M4 rifle, which he or she pointed up at the sky.

This sight caused the advancing squadron to pause in midair. As they hovered, you could imagine their operators discussing whether to proceed, given this new threat.

In my head, seconds ticked by loudly—I wondered when the drones would make their move. But they simply hovered in place.

Simon must have run out of patience as well. "Light 'em up," she called into her radio.

The soldiers began firing three- and four-shot bursts. In the sky, the drones began dancing back and forth, up and down. They took a few glancing blows, but most managed to dodge the first barrage of fire.

The soldiers redoubled their efforts, lengthening their bursts of fire, and as they became more acquainted with how the drones moved, their aim improved. One drone took three shots in rapid succession, then sputtered and fluttered in the air before plummeting to the ground.

That first casualty seemed to spur the soldiers on. Twelve drones became eleven. Then nine. Then eight.

"We're doing it!" Simon hollered over the gunfire, her voice a mix of joy and relief.

Remembering how the Green Way had used the stink-bomb drones as a distraction, I patted Simon's shoulder and signaled that we should keep our eyes out front. She nodded, and we both turned.

What caught my eye wasn't in the air, but in the trees.

Or, I should say, the trees themselves.

The road we'd driven to the fracking site had been cut through a thick forest of oaks and walnuts.

But now something weird was happening. The tops of several trees along the road were . . . fidgeting.

It was impossible to describe it any other way: the branches at the peaks of the trees bobbed back and forth in a motion too quick and too random to be wind driven. My first thought was birds or animals, but the motion seemed to be happening in too many places simultaneously.

I pointed, and Simon nodded, trying to get a better look, but before she could say anything, one of the trees started to lean out over the road. At first it moved slowly, but it quickly gathered speed and slammed to the ground with an impact I felt through my boots.

"They're blocking the road!" Simon yelled.

Two more trees started to fall from opposite sides, crisscrossing in midair as they dropped, each trunk at least several feet in diameter. The fallen giants would require a massive effort to clear, leaving no easy way to resupply the compound. And no way for the workers—or us—to leave.

I glanced back to see if the soldiers had finished off the last of the quadcopters.

That's when I spotted the smoke.

CHAPTER 10

While the National Guard soldiers had been picking off the initial group of drones, two new squadrons had crisscrossed over the compound from the sides and dropped their payloads. Canisters lay scattered on the dusty ground, hissing out heavy, white smoke.

As I reached for Simon's shoulder to alert her, these clouds were already coalescing into a dense fog. In seconds, it enveloped us, reducing my view of the site to a flat mass of white. Glancing back outside the front fence, I couldn't spot Brittany Anne Donohue and her group, and they'd only been a few feet away. Even my hand on Simon's shoulder disappeared; I couldn't see past my elbow.

My fingers dug deeper into the fabric of Simon's jacket, trying to make sure I didn't lose contact with her. Finally, her face appeared just inches from mine. I could read her lips rather than hear her as she yelled, "The drill!"

Holding hands, we dashed blindly toward the center of the compound. We stumbled repeatedly along the way, tripping over holes and rocks and smoke canisters, but somehow, dragging each other along, we finally made it. The metal I beams of the derrick appeared first as a tall, dark shadow, then as distinct lines as we drew closer.

We found a single worker standing before the nearest of the derrick's four stanchions. Simon and I instinctively dropped hands and flanked him, watching the perimeter. Despite all the noise in the air, I heard my own ragged breathing and pounding pulse as we waited for whatever threat might materialize.

For seconds that felt like minutes, nothing came.

It was a maddening feeling, knowing something was happening in the smoke but unable to see what or where. Muscles tensed beneath my skin—my instinct was to dash off into the white and find something, anything, to do. I leaned so far forward, in fact, that I almost lost my balance. When I shifted my feet, though, I noticed something different. The soles of my shoes seemed to have less traction than they should.

Crouching, I touched a finger to the ground. Cold liquid chilled my skin—it was flowing from behind me, and fast. When I drew my finger up, it was covered in goopy, silty mud.

The water tanks.

The Green Way must have breached them somehow. Doing that made some sense—without water, drilling couldn't proceed. But these were no small drums—the metal cylinders were each at least fifteen feet tall. That meant tens of thousands of gallons.

And I'd counted four tanks.

As the back of my brain started to do the math, something powerful struck my legs from behind. My knees buckled, and before I could react, I was flat on my back, being carried away from the derrick by icy water assaulting my bare scalp and hands.

It took a moment to regain my bearings, but even as I flipped onto my stomach and took a stroke against the current, the rushing water disappeared from beneath me, leaving me facedown in the muck.

I struggled up to my feet—soaked, dirty, disoriented. The damp cold continued working its way down through my clothes, biting the skin as it slithered along. I took a single step forward, but drawing my foot up and out of the mud had become an effort: the dry, dusty soil had absorbed enough water that the mud was now at least an inch deep.

I double-checked the Sig in my waistband holster as I looked around me. The smoke had dissipated slightly, letting in enough light that the scene was now a bright, white mess instead of a dark, shadowy one. But the noise level had also changed—the industrial sounds had mostly disappeared, replaced by a lower-pitched din that I guessed came from the disruptors and gas workers clashing in ways I couldn't see.

That's when a gunshot rang out.

Not the controlled, staccato bursts of the National Guard's M4s, but a single, significant blast from a shotgun or a high-caliber rifle.

And it was close.

I struggled back through the muck toward where I guessed the derrick stood. As the cloud continued to brighten, I could see a tall shadow ahead. When I reached it, the worker I'd flanked earlier was on the ground, wrestling with a disruptor over a shotgun. Both were covered in mud, although I noticed the disruptor had the benefit of wearing cleats and had managed to get on top of the fracker.

"Freeze!" I said, drawing the Sig.

Both turned toward me.

"Toss the gun, now!"

The two looked back at each other, then complied, pitching the shotgun several yards away, underneath the derrick.

"Get up off him, slowly."

The disruptor dropped his arms, eased back on his haunches. I reached for my back pocket, where I'd stashed Simon's zip ties.

Suddenly, the worker's head jerked to my left. I noticed it a second too late.

Something struck me, hard. The blow hit under my ribs, sending an electric jolt through my chest. With the slippery footing, I lost contact with the ground and was driven to the right. When I hit the wet earth, I slid for several feet, my attacker on top of me.

As I struggled to buck him off, another wave of water came sweeping across the compound and struck us squarely, knocking the disruptor off and carrying him away. It sent me tumbling, too, rolling and twisting as I slid.

Thankfully, surfing was good preparation for this. When you get hit by a wave, your natural instinct is to tense up, but it's actually better to relax and wait for the pressure of the wave to relent.

Here, that took only a second.

As the water drained away, I struggled upright again, somehow still holding on to the Sig. But now my feet sank down to my ankles, rooting me to the spot.

A noise came from behind me. I turned in time to see the same disruptor charging at me, his cleated shoes giving him just enough traction to power through the muck. He was carrying a long chunk of wood, like a club, with nails or screws or something equally sharp protruding from the end.

I yelled, "Freeze!" but he didn't stop.

I got the Sig up and fired once at his shoulder before he could reach me. At that range, the .357 round hit him like a sledgehammer, twisting his body to the side as it knocked him over.

As quickly as I could, I yanked my feet from the ooze and got on top of him. He was too stunned by the bullet to put up a fight. I got his arms zip-tied behind him quickly, flipped him onto his side so he wouldn't drown in the mud, then trudged back toward the derrick.

When I reached it, the first disruptor and worker were squaring off again, on their feet now. As they sloshed back and forth, I came at the intruder from the side, tackling him as his partner had done to me. We landed together in a heap.

His clothes were slippery, and my hands weren't much better—although I was on top of him, I couldn't get an easy grip. I'd just managed to get control of one of his arms when something struck me from the waist down.

Another wave.

With the soil already soaked, this one seemed to pack more punch than the others. It pitched me forward, over the disruptor's head. As I tumbled away, I took in a massive mouthful of mud and water. When the wave receded, it left me sputtering on my hands and knees. As I tried to cough out the water, something struck my left side.

This was a harder blow, from something solid, and I felt something inside me give way—maybe a rib. As I rolled from the impact, I looked back, trying to determine what it was.

The disruptor.

Somehow, he'd found a length of pipe that he was brandishing like a baseball bat.

Between swings, I got to my feet as quickly as I could, but the guy was on me remarkably fast, swinging the pipe wildly and leaving me to duck and dodge in place. I'd sunk into mud well over my ankles now. Unable to yank my feet free, I fell backward into the muck.

Above me, the disruptor raised the pipe over his head with both hands and swung it down like an ax.

I managed to roll out of the way at the last second, the pipe whistling past me and lodging deeply in the mud. Somehow, I wrapped my left arm around it and used the leverage to sweep a leg through the disruptor's, dropping him onto his back. With a grunt, I raised my leg up and dropped my heel as hard as I could onto his exposed midsection. That left him stunned long enough for me to climb to my feet, draw the Sig, and order him to freeze. We were both panting from the exertion and blows as he raised his hands in surrender.

I caught as much of my breath as I could through the rib pain, then flipped and zip-tied him.

Shivering inside my drenched clothes, I tried to assess the damage my body had taken. My bad shoulder throbbed, but the pain in my side was agonizing. Each time I took a breath, it felt like a knife being jabbed into my side.

I glanced up for a moment—the smoke had dispersed enough, the sky was visible—then I caught something else approaching in my peripheral vision.

It was the fracker, wading toward us. He'd retrieved the shotgun from under the derrick.

"Hey," I said as he drew close, but he didn't react.

The worker was eyeing the disruptor bound on the ground. He raised the gun to his shoulder, the barrel pointed squarely at the disruptor's chest.

I quick-drew the Sig and leveled it at the worker. "Drop it!"

He looked at me in disbelief. "That motherfucker tried to kill me."

"Me, too," I said. "But that motherfucker's going to jail, and that's enough."

From the set of the worker's jaw, I could tell my words didn't satisfy him one bit. He retrained the gun on the prone protester.

I dropped the nose of the Sig and fired at the worker's feet. He jumped back, or tried in the muck, and lost his footing, landing squarely on his ass. He still held the shotgun, but only in one hand and by the pump action—his finger was off the trigger.

"Now drop it," I said. "Slowly."

He cursed as I zip-tied him.

"Be nice," I said. "Assaulting an air marshal can get you eight years, so I'm not someone you want to piss off right now."

When I straightened up, I got my first good look around the compound. Through the clearing haze, the site looked like a war zone. The National Guard soldiers, who'd made their way inside through holes the Green Way had presumably cut in the fence, only added to the effect. The water tanks had all been breached—long gashes cut in their sides that had allowed their contents to leak out and turn the entire site into a swamp. All the generators had stopped running; the cement mixers had stopped turning. Once again, the Green Way's people had made it up onto the derrick, hung a green flag from atop it, and woven another web of metal cabling through the moving parts below.

It wasn't only the equipment that looked worn and damaged. Virtually everyone was smeared and caked in mud. About a dozen disruptors had been cuffed with zip ties, but a handful of workers had been as well—all lying or sitting in various positions around the field.

Simon was on the other side of the derrick, facing the opposite way; her hat was gone, as was one sleeve of her jacket. Devers stood near the rear fence with what looked a bleeding forehead.

When Simon turned and saw me, an easy smile filled her face. "I don't know that that quite went according to *anyone's* plan."

A half hour later, the soldiers had helped us divvy up the various arrestees into two separate circles on the ground. To our surprise, when the disruptors were unmasked, we found Richard Chu himself had been part of the raid. His smug expression from the night before had disappeared, leading Simon and Devers to wear smiles of their own.

Foreman Bruce had passed out bottled water to everyone. I ended up pouring mine over my head in an effort to get the slightest bit clean. My teeth were chattering now, breathing still extremely painful.

Simon glanced around the site. "Question is, how are we gonna get everybody back to jail when they blocked the only road out?"

With a series of phone calls, she and the National Guard commander managed to procure a school bus and a personnel carrier. The vehicles would travel as far up the road as possible, and we'd have to walk the rest of the way out to meet them. The school bus was closer, having already completed its morning route, Simon told me. It would arrive in a few minutes. It would also bring two teams of paramedics from the hospital to tend to people's wounds. Brittany Anne Donohue's people could possibly transport a few people, too—Simon said she'd ordered them back to their vans when the hostilities started, and they were parked past the fallen trees.

After some debate, Simon decided the workers should get ferried first; the ones in custody would likely have their bail paid by the gas company, then return here to help clean up the site. The National Guard would bring the Green Way members to town afterward, ideally arriving after the oil workers had already left, eliminating any chance of confrontations in or around the jail.

The deputies prodded the circle of workers up to their feet and started marching them single file toward the compound entrance. Simon made her way to Chu, who remained seated on the far side of the site. Grabbing him under his arms, she dragged him to his feet.

"What the—"

"C'mon, Richard," she said. "You're on the first ride to town, too. I'm gonna chaperone you myself."

She shoved him between the shoulder blades to get him started. Although he gave her a nasty look, he said nothing more and joined the rear of the procession with Simon.

As much I wanted to get to town to get clean and warm and have my side checked, Devers seemed to need it more. Like everyone, he was wet and dirty, but his clothes were ripped and bloody, a nasty gash above his eyebrow was still weeping red despite the compress he held in place over it, and he was clearly favoring one leg over the other. With a silent nod, we turned and started after the others.

It was a long walk to the front gate of the compound. The workers had a head start, and the gap grew as Devers and I struggled along. The footing was comically bad—like walking in deep sand or snow. With each step, you had to yank your foot out of several inches of mud, then reinsert it into the muck ahead of you as it gurgled and bubbled and oozed. The water had long since seeped through my boots, making my feet so tingly they almost felt numb, but Devers was having a much harder time of it, now dragging his left leg with each step.

We weren't even halfway across the site when I heard it.

A singular buzz that sounded nothing like the drones we'd encountered so far.

I scanned the sky but couldn't see anything. Devers did the same.

When the shots rang out, it sounded like thunder. Loud, echoing booms that reverberated around the surrounding hills before returning to our ears again and again.

Two splashes of mud kicked up by the front gate, and then the workers started to drop. One after another, they and their deputy escorts fell like dominoes.

As the last of the workers fell, I finally spotted it: painted the same dull gray as the leafless trees behind it, this was no quadcopter. This was a fixed-wing drone. Driven by a rear propeller, its wings and tail planes were swept back at an angle like a fighter jet. Its wingspan had to be at least eight or nine feet. And slung under each wing was some kind of machine gun.

I reached for the Sig, trying to recall how many shots I'd fired in the melee.

I didn't get to a number before the drone's guns flashed again. This time, Simon and Chu crumpled to the ground.

CHAPTER 11

"No!" Devers's scream sliced through the air.

I tried to shake off the shock and focus on the armed drone, which was bearing down on us next. Mud and water splattered as bullets ripped the ground at our feet. I started firing my Sig first; Devers joined immediately after.

Between us, we fired about ten rounds but didn't score any obvious hits—the drone's head-on profile was too small. But our return fire seemed to halt the drone's guns momentarily. The craft banked and made for the side of the compound.

When it reached the fence line, I lost the aircraft against the trees—it blended in too well with the forest behind it. The engine hum had also disappeared, meaning that was no help, either.

"You see it?" I asked, still scanning the horizon. "Or hear it?"

Devers shook his head.

"We should take cover."

"The tanks?"

Devers was right—the largest solid objects around were the tall, white water tanks. But the nearest one stood almost a hundred yards away from our position near the back of the compound.

"Can you get there on that leg?" I asked.

"Beats getting shot."

We'd made it maybe a dozen steps when the drone reappeared, silently streaking above the tree line. I raised the Sig again, but instead of coming back at us, it turned for the far corner of the site, heading directly for the seated circle of Green Way arrestees and their National Guard escorts. As it accelerated, the drone's engine began buzzing again.

Hearing and seeing it now, the soldiers took up firing positions and let loose with their M4s. At first, they seemed to have as little luck as we did; none of their shots connected. As the drone closed the distance, several soldiers got a decent view of its underbelly and let off longer bursts on full auto.

It didn't seem to matter.

The bullets flashed and sparked against the drone's fuselage, but it seemed unaffected as it pulled a tight turn and came back around, firing at the soldiers.

Three dropped on that pass.

Then the drone swung around again.

Two of the remaining soldiers stood fast, firing until their magazines were empty.

It didn't help. With two quick bursts, the drone killed them where they stood.

Several of the disruptors struggled to their feet and began running for the holes in the fencing. As quickly as they could, the rest followed suit. That left one soldier as the only surviving figure on that part of the field.

The final soldier made a run for the trailers where we'd met with Bruce. Slipping in the mud, he was still down on his belly, crawling, as the drone came around again. From his hands and knees, the soldier looked up at the craft and raised a hand as if to surrender.

Unlike the previous strafing runs, this time the drone's guns—and engine—stayed silent as it approached. I exhaled the breath I'd been holding, glad he'd be spared.

That's when a four-shot burst ripped into him, dropping him in the mire.

I turned away, wanting to vomit but forcing myself to swallow instead. Devers and I had made it half the distance to the tanks—I needed to get us the rest of the way there, or we'd end up dead in the mud as well.

"Can you go faster?"

"This is . . . about all I got," he said.

The problem was his left leg—he simply had no strength in it. Pulling his foot in and out of the muck was proving too difficult.

"C'mon," I said, moving to Devers's right. Gritting through the rib pain, I swung myself under Devers's right arm and locked it around my neck. Then I grabbed the waistband of his pants with my left hand and lifted the best I could.

Devers's extra weight forced my feet farther down into the mud, but not much. Reminding myself to breathe, I started walking, lifting my feet high with each step. I aimed for the nearest tank and straightest line I could.

"It's turning back this way," Devers said.

I didn't dare look—too much distance remained. Although all my muscles screamed and my side throbbed, I tried to ignore the pain and power through the mud as fast as I could.

"It's going around the back side . . ."

In my peripheral vision, I could make out something moving to our right. Thinking about the geometry of it, realizing the drone intended to circle the tanks, I cut to our right. Back toward the drone.

"What the hell are you doing?"

Dogfighting, I thought, without the time or breath to say it out loud.

The water tanks were each about fifteen feet wide, with an eight- or ten-foot gap between them. I aimed for the second gap.

The engine buzz returned, reverberating around the compound. The drone had finally realized our maneuver and was trying to accelerate to counter it.

With ten yards left, I could see the drone in the gaps between the tanks as it cut across the back side. The timing was going to work.

"It passed the tanks," Devers said. "It's coming back."

I didn't stop beside the tanks but instead darted directly into the gap between them, pulling Devers with me. Bullets from the drone began ripping into the mud behind us, cutting across the path we'd traveled.

I pushed Devers down against the tank wall and turned in time to see the drone flash by. While I worried it might bank and try to attack the gap, it didn't. Instead, it headed for the opposite side of the compound.

Devers blinked at me. "How . . ."

Aircraft dogfighting was all about geometry: how tightly each aircraft could turn, what angles they were taking, which one could reach a particular spot first. We were so much slower than the drone, but once I realized it intended to circle around the tanks and approach us head-on, I'd seen an opening. By cutting back toward the drone, we'd forced it to make almost a complete loop around the tanks to get a bead on us. Meanwhile, the obtuse angle between us and the tanks meant our change in direction hadn't lengthened the distance of our path very much. All the extra distance had neutralized the drone's speed advantage.

"Math," I said.

Devers's eyebrows rose. "What's our plan now?"

Before I could answer, the drone's guns sounded again. We both turned to see it strafing the trailers.

"Are Bruce and the others inside?"

"Dunno." Devers shrugged. "I lost track of them."

It stood to reason that any survivors would have taken shelter in the only structures around, but I couldn't imagine the flimsy walls or furniture inside stopping the drone's high-caliber ordnance.

Unfortunately, the drone wasn't content with making one run. It returned again and again, peppering the trailer roofs with each pass. Once more, I felt nausea sweep through my body. I couldn't imagine anyone surviving the barrage.

Just as I gave up hope, though, one of the doors flew open. Bruce, the bearded foreman, strode out, carrying a shotgun. He pointed the barrel at the sky and scanned around until he spotted the drone, which was finishing a turn at the far end of the compound.

"Is he crazy?" Devers asked.

My muscles twitched, desperate to help Bruce despite the distance. All I could do was scream, "Go back inside!"

But Bruce couldn't hear me or didn't care. He locked onto the drone and held his ground as it made its approach. He waited stoically until the drone had drawn within twenty-five yards, then used the pump action to deliver five loads of buckshot to the drone's nose.

Again, it had no effect.

As the drone passed over Bruce, its guns walked three bursts up his torso and head.

"That's it," Devers said. "We're the only ones left."

As if to prove the point, the drone banked out over the roofs of the trailers and turned our way.

CHAPTER 12

"You got any more equations, Mr. Wizard?" Devers's eyes were locked on the drone headed directly for our position. "You better draw one up quick."

I did have an idea, but it was going to take some work. And some luck.

"C'mon," I said, dragging him around the back side of the tank so we'd be covered against this approach.

The drone cruised by overhead, low enough it barely cleared the tops of the tanks. Then it made a long, looping turn and began following the perimeter of the fence to our right.

"Okay, hopefully that bought us a minute," I said, loading a full magazine into the Sig. "I'm gonna have to climb up on one of these to get a clean shot."

Devers shook his head. "I can't climb, Walker . . ."

"I know. You don't need to."

Once I'd explained the plan, Devers looked less than thrilled, but he didn't have any better suggestions. I patted him on the shoulder, then started up the access ladder.

I'm not crazy about heights, and having Devers watch me climb only made the nervous twinges of vertigo that much worse. The broken rib didn't add to my confidence, but I kept my eyes off the ground and hustled up the ladder. I stopped two rungs from the top—enough I could crouch and still be concealed.

Then I poked my head up over the top and scanned for the drone.

It was still following the perimeter fence, seemingly headed back to the trailers opposite our position. That was where I expected it would turn and make another run at us.

If it didn't, this plan was going to be awfully short lived.

After estimating the drone's speed, I ducked my head back down and waved to Devers.

He stepped out into the gap between tanks, whooping and hollering and waving his arms.

I ran some calculations in my head, estimating how long it would take the drone to cross over the trailer roofs and bisect the compound.

"It's coming," Devers said. "It's turning now."

He continued waving for another few seconds. Long enough to get the drone about midway across the field. Then he stepped back behind the tank, as I'd instructed.

I drew the Sig and pointed it across the gap toward the adjacent tank. And I counted down.

Three . . .

Two . . .

One.

I started pulling the trigger even before I saw the drone. Once it did appear—cutting between the tanks, its top surface tilted toward me as I'd hoped—I kept firing, letting the bullets walk down the length of the fuselage.

I'd fired three shots by the time the drone's tail appeared—that left me nine in the mag. As the drone curved to my left, I followed it with the barrel and dumped everything I had at the tail.

Sparks flew as the bullets hit, but the drone kept coming. I winced, thinking the shots had ricocheted with no effect.

Then the drone's nose dipped, giving me a better look at its rear end: the propeller was mangled and had stopped turning, and the control surfaces along the tail were tattered.

Now the rest of the drone angled earthward, descending until its left wing tip caught the ground. At that point, the entire craft began to cartwheel, quickly shattering into several pieces that rolled, bounced, and splashed in the mud until they came to rest.

I'd already started descending the ladder—by the time I reached the bottom, Devers was waiting, wearing a huge grin. "I'd heard you were a pretty good shot, but . . ." He shook his head.

"Lucky," I said.

"How'd you get a bead on the tail?"

I shrugged. "Math, mostly. Calculating speeds and distances. Now that it's down, we should check . . ."

He grimaced. "I . . . I want to be the one to . . ."

"I know," I said. "You get Heather and Chu. I'll do the others."

I started with Bruce, then checked the final soldier. Both had taken head shots that obviated the need to search for a pulse.

Gruesome as their corpses were, though, the trailers' interiors were worse. While specks of dust swirled in shafts of light shining down through the holes that riddled the ceiling, their motion was a cruel illusion. In reality, the air hung still, thick with the warm, metallic stench of blood. I found eight bodies in all, wedged under desks, shelves, and other furniture. From the looks of it, they'd pulled the furnishings down over themselves to stop the bullets, but when the heavy slugs sliced right through, they'd ended up in traps of their own making. None showed any signs of life.

As I emerged from the second trailer, I put my hands on my knees, and, despite the pain in my side, I sucked as much air in through my nostrils as I could, trying to rid them of the sickly smell. While its intensity lessened, it continued to hang there, coloring every breath I took.

When I finally raised my head, I spotted someone in white curled on the ground just outside the front gate. That didn't make any sense—Simon had told the ACES people to hunker down in their vans. But before I could check on that, Devers shouted my name from the middle of the field, waving frantically.

I slipped and stumbled through the mud, trying to go as quickly as I could while still stepping carefully and minimizing the stabbing sensation between my ribs. As I approached, I got my first real look at the stacked bodies of Simon and Chu. Both had landed on their backs, Simon sprawled across Chu's torso.

To my surprise, she was moving. Sputtering and coughing, she writhed onto her side and rolled off him.

"Heather, you're—"

"Alive? Yeah." Her voice croaked, and she tried to laugh but ended up sputtering.

Devers and I slowly helped her to her feet. Pulling back the flaps of her jacket, she fingered three big holes in her uniform shirt. "Thank God for the vest."

"How . . . how does it feel?" Devers asked.

Simon grunted, which caused more coughing. "Like I got shot three times." She nodded back down at Chu. "Is he . . . ?"

I knelt and pressed my fingers to Chu's throat. I could feel a faint throb beneath the skin. "There's a pulse," I said.

All of Chu's wounds were below the waist—one above his right kneecap, one low on his left leg. Most worrisome, a piece of his left foot had been shot off. "We need to keep him from bleeding out."

Devers checked the nearby workers and deputies while Simon and I used his belt and her jacket to wrap Chu's left leg and foot. My belt went around Chu's right thigh to act as a tourniquet. Between the three of us, we managed to lift him and start carrying him. We took three steps toward the gate before remembering it was still padlocked closed, then changed course toward the holes in the nearest side of the fence. That forced Simon to walk backward and glance over her shoulder to make sure she wasn't going to trip. We'd taken only two more steps before she screamed, "No!"

Devers and I held Chu while she sprinted for the fence, following her as quickly as we could.

I didn't get another look at Simon until we were rounding the outer corner of the fence. She was lifting the collapsed figure in white that I'd seen from the trailer. But as we approached, I saw the clothing wasn't completely white anymore—large parts of it were stained dark crimson.

"Hurry," Simon said, "she's alive."

The figure's head lolled backward in Simon's arms, two long pigtails almost reaching the ground.

CHAPTER 13

A crowd of doctors and nurses were waiting when we pulled into the hospital parking lot in one of the ACES vans. They whisked Donohue and Chu away on gurneys, then brought Devers, Simon, and me in for exams.

X-rays showed that the hit from the pipe had busted two of my ribs. My nurse, a country-strong woman named Daisy, recommended ice and rest. I laughed at that second prescription, which only made my side hurt more. Devers's knee turned out to have an MCL sprain from slipping in the mud. After stitching his forehead, they put his leg in one of those soft, supportive sleeves and wrapped it in bags of ice.

Simon got the luckiest. Although she reported having the worst bruising of her life when they peeled the vest off—"I'm gonna be black and blue till New Year's"—MRIs showed no internal bleeding. Like me, she'd broken ribs—two on one side, one on the other—but those would heal with time.

All three of us were allowed to shower and given clean scrubs to change into. The scalding water felt wonderful—it drove the cold out of my bones and seemed to loosen everything up. The scrubs felt weird, their material so lightweight that I had to keep checking to make sure I was dressed.

Chu and Donohue were in surgery by now, so we requested a private room and gathered chairs around a small table to call Melissa Cooke on my cell.

"Thank God you all survived," she said, after we detailed what had happened during the raid.

"There's nobody," said Simon, her voice breaking. "I mean, I lost . . . everyone." Her jaw quivered, even as her mouth drew into a taut line.

"I'm so sorry, Sheriff," Cooke said. "Mitchell, I'll ask the nearby field offices to send reinforcements. It may take a day or two, but you're going to need more hands."

"I . . . I can ask the state police, too," Simon said.

"Let me handle all that for you," Cooke said. "You have enough on your plate. What's being done with the remains of the drone?"

"We're gonna have to go back and gather up the pieces ourselves," Simon said.

"So where do you think we stand?" asked Cooke.

"You ask me, it's open and shut," Devers said. "The Green Way must have been trying out some version of that thing we faced today. Appalachian 303 was their test run."

Simon shook her head. "I don't . . . I don't see that."

Devers cocked his head. "C'mon, Heather. That thing we fought out there wasn't any quadcopter. And Chu's man Hartley has the skills to fly it."

"What do you mean?" I asked.

"You noticed Hartley wasn't one of the disruptors we snatched inside the compound, right?"

"Yeah." We'd unmasked all the Green Way people, but even if we hadn't, Hartley would have stood out conspicuously, given his height. "So what?"

"You wonder why?"

I shrugged. "Chu led the attack—if Hartley's his number two, it makes sense to leave him out of it, or have him coordinating."

"It's more than that. After the show he put on last night, I did a little digging. Turns out, he was in the Royal Air Force, where he flew combat drones in the Middle East. Once he got out of the service, he raced the damn things."

"Drone racing is a thing?" Cooke asked.

"Apparently there's a whole international circuit. I watched videos of 'em," Devers said. "But get this: Before Hartley came over here and became the Green Way's drone guy, he did the same thing for an ecoterrorist group in England. Somebody died at one of their protests, and Hartley was arrested. He got off, but now we're looking at a pilot with a history of violence and a super attack drone that's armed to the teeth."

"That convince you, Sheriff?" Cooke asked.

"Nope," she said. "It doesn't."

Devers's eyebrows crept up his forehead. "Why the heck not?"

Simon locked eyes with him. "First off, because that damn thing shot Richard Chu."

"It was aiming for you," Devers said. "Chu got in the way—"

"Nuh-uh." Simon shook her head, her voice as forceful as I'd heard it. "I stepped in front of him 'cause I had the vest."

"Well, the rest of the disruptors escaped," Devers shot back.

"But why would they shoot their own leader?" Cooke asked.

Devers grunted. "Who knows? Maybe Hartley wants to run the show and saw the chance to take the boss out. Maybe he's pissed Chu's making money off all this."

"What?" Cooke asked.

"Walker called him out last night," Devers said, explaining the Amplify connection.

"You're saying you told Hartley all that and it got him mad enough to target Chu?"

"The Green Way did *not* do this, okay?" Simon stood abruptly, her chair screeching back on the linoleum floor. Chest heaving, she stared off into space for a moment. "I've seen the Green Way do lots of stupid stuff, but they've had plenty of chances and never butchered my entire force in cold blood. There's only one set of animals I can think that would do something like that."

"Who?" Cooke asked.

Simon glanced between Devers and me. "I told these guys yesterday, I think it's drug smugglers. That pad we were at? It's the farthest north frackers have gone in Wetzel County. The forest it sits in used to be totally empty. If the drug guys think the gas companies are getting too close . . ."

"Seth," Cooke said, "you're awfully quiet."

"Yeah."

"What's your gut telling you?"

"From what happened at the campsite, I would've thought it was the Green Way," I said. "And when the attack started, I still believed that. But something we saw in the compound bothered me."

"What's that?"

"When the disruptors ran away, they didn't do it together."

"What do you mean?" Cooke asked.

"In yesterday's raid," I said, "everything was coordinated down to the second. When that whistle sounded, everyone in black ran at once. This time, when the drone shot the soldiers, it was like the disruptors weren't sure what to do. They looked at each other. Some got up, some stayed put. Then, once the rest decided it was safe, they took off, too. If the Green Way was behind the drone strike and everything was all planned out, why would they hesitate?"

No one spoke for a long moment.

"There was one other thing," I said. "Did either of you notice how the drone's engine kept going quiet?"

While Simon shook her head, Devers thought a moment and nodded.

"I'm pretty sure it was using some kind of hybrid engine. Battery power for when it's coasting, a gas engine for acceleration. Once we see the design and parts they used, that may give us a better idea who built it."

"All right," Cooke said. "Then priority one is you all getting back out to the scene and gathering up the pieces. Seth can see if they shed any light on where the drone came from, and then we can give them to NTSB for comparison against the Appalachian 303 wreckage. I think you ought to go question the Green Way again, too—see what their reaction is to Chu's shooting. Especially Hartley. If there really is some kind of internal struggle going on, he may slip up, or someone on Chu's team may shake loose and be willing to talk. While you three are busy, I'll call DEA and Homeland Security and see if they have any intel."

Everyone indicated their agreement with the plan.

Then Cooke said, "Seth, can I ask you a few questions in private?"

Simon and Devers cleared the room, with Devers shooting me an odd look as he slipped out the door. Once I was alone, Cooke asked, "Is Simon all right? Are you?"

I grunted. "I'm okay. I don't think Simon's used to stuff like this."

"How's it going with Devers?" she asked. "Any issues?"

"No," I said. "He pushed Hartley a little, but that guy was already wound up. And if it wasn't for Devers, I wouldn't have been able to get the drop on the drone."

"Okay, last question: How worried do I need to be that more versions of that thing are lurking around out there? Honestly?"

"Worried," I said. "We got lucky—it turned out the drone had an armored underbelly, so I went after the tail. But that thing had two guns shooting full auto, or close to it. Heavy firepower could have brought it down, but if a copy of it attacks another soft target? You're talking massive casualties."

The silence hung in the air a moment.

"How about the design? You see anything unique we can use to trace it, or stop it?"

"It was built like a small airplane," I said. "Eight to ten feet, wing tip to wing tip. It had a rear prop, but a lot of unmanned vehicles use those because pushing is more efficient than pulling."

"Is it like a military drone, then?"

"No," I said, "this was different. Reapers and Predators have giant sensor arrays packed into a big dome up front. This one's nose was streamlined. Plus, the wing and tail shapes were all wrong. The military builds its drones to soar high and go unchallenged—they've got straight wings, and their tails are just for stability, not steering. This thing was built like a dogfighter: swept wings and extra ailerons and rudders for more speed, more maneuverability."

"So you don't think we're looking at stolen tech?"

"If we are," I said, "it's modified, or something I've never seen before. I'll look again when we pick up the parts. Did you ever talk to DOD?"

"Yes," she said. "And I pressed them as hard as I could. They still swear up and down they didn't have anything deployed near Appalachian 303."

"Then maybe Simon's right. Maybe this is the work of a local drug outfit."

"We need to end this, Seth. *Now.* I can't exactly put every shopping mall in the country on high alert for a killer drone attack." She paused, and I could hear her take a breath. "We haven't talked about the press. They were contained on Appalachian 303, but when they hear a whole police force has been wiped out, they're bound to start a panic. I'm guessing I can beg reporters for twenty-four hours to let the investigation proceed, but that's about all I'm going to get."

"So we've got one more day?"

"One more day."

When Simon, Devers, and I were ready to leave the hospital, we didn't have any transportation, and there was no one left in Simon's department to retrieve us. Ultimately, she persuaded a receptionist at the front desk to ferry us to the police station.

As hard as it was to believe, by the time we got there, it still wasn't quite two o'clock in the afternoon. The sun had poked through the clouds, casting bright shafts of light down in places, but not improving the temperature any. While we wore our mud-stained jackets, the scrubs underneath offered little in the way of warmth, and cold air quickly crept its way up my legs.

Simon disappeared into the stone courthouse building for a moment, then emerged with keys for the SUV and cruiser that remained in the police parking lot. "Take the SUV," she said, dangling one key ring in front of Devers. Her eyes were downcast, shoulders slumped; merely holding out the keys seemed like a massive effort. "You'll need it for hauling that . . . thing."

"Aren't you coming?" I asked.

"I've got a couple of things to do."

Cooke's urgency echoed in my ears. "Like what? We need to—"

Simon's head jerked up, and she glared at me. The usual twinkle in her eyes had disappeared, replaced by an intense fire. Her hands balled into tight fists, even as her eyes filled with tears. "In case you haven't noticed," she said, her voice cracking, "I've got five families and a National Guard commander I need to go visit. I gotta tell all of them that I got their people killed, and they won't be comin' home tonight."

The dull ache from my ribs spread through my chest. "I—I'm so . . . sorry, Heather. I wasn't—"

Simon spun on her heel and stalked off before I could finish. From behind, I saw her wipe at her face with the back of her hand as she climbed into the cruiser and peeled out of the gravel parking lot.

◆ ◆ ◆

Despite his hurt knee, Devers knew the roads better and offered to drive. That left me free to kick myself over how I'd spoken to Simon.

In my head, all I could imagine was how furious my father would have been. At least once a week when I was a kid—sometimes more—he'd come home and fall into his chair. Shoulders slumped, he'd blast the stereo and sip at bottles of beer while staring at the floor. Eventually, I learned he was worrying over trouble his enlisteds had gotten into: one guy had too many speeding tickets; another's pregnant girlfriend had gotten bad news at a doctor's visit. Bar fights, credit-card debt, sick parents, divorces. Everybody else's problems.

Back then, I didn't understand—I was just pissed off he wouldn't pay any attention to me. So this one time, wiseass eight-year-old me told him that he shouldn't worry so much about those other people. I was his kid, and I was right there waiting.

His eyes crept up from the floor and shot me a look that made me shiver. He wasn't angry, exactly . . . more than anything, it was a look of utter disappointment and contempt, like he couldn't even comprehend the words that had just come out of my mouth. In a flash, I went from angry to ashamed—I wanted to dig a hole under our couch and dive into it. After what seemed like ten minutes of him staring at me that way, he finally spoke. "A leader's got to take care of his people, Seth. They're your responsibility. If you don't do that, well . . ."

He never finished the sentence. He just trailed off, shaking his head and looking back down at the floor.

Just thinking about that made the hair on my arms stand on end. It was probably the most disgusted my old man had ever been with me. I'd never forgotten that look. Yet, here I was, violating his number-one rule, as if I'd never learned a damn thing.

After several minutes, Devers hadn't spoken, either.

"What's wrong?" I asked.

Devers shook his head.

My face flashed hot. "I'm sorry about what I said to Heather . . ."

"It ain't that. I just . . . I don't get why you're so damn desperate to bail out our number-one suspects."

"I want to solve this much as you do." Loretta's face flashed in my head. "Maybe more."

Devers turned and glared at me. "Really? I mean, I get Simon. She got shot, saw her people slaughtered—she's not in her right mind. But you? You really think a bunch of backwoods holler boys cooking up packets of Sudafed built themselves that drone?"

"I don't know who built it—I'm trying to figure that out. You're the one who was ready to convict Richard Chu before we flew in. You know, the guy who just got shot by the drone?"

"That's it, right there." Devers jabbed his index finger at me.

"What?"

"That fucking arrogance. All you people think you're so much better, so much smarter, than everybody else. Maybe that's why the idea of Richard Chu doing anything bad hits a little too close to home for y'all."

"What on earth are you talking about?"

"You think I didn't read up on you? I know you were some hotshot techno-something-or-other. You look at Chu, it's like looking in the mirror. Lot easier to assume some dumbass, buck-toothed hicks did it than some engineering guru like you."

"Whoa," I said. "I may not have grown up in Lynch, Kentucky, but do you know how many little bullshit towns we pulled through while my dad was in the navy? I've got zero problem arresting Richard Chu or any of his people for something they actually did wrong. I just don't immediately *assume* they did it."

"You heard them talking last night. They despise everybody around here. Even Brittany Anne Donohue—who's on their goddamn side!"

"That doesn't mean they'd just shoot everyone—"

"They care more about trees than people, Walker—that's all you need to know. Stopping the drilling is the only thing that matters to them."

"You really think the gas companies are gonna stop drilling?"

"They will if this keeps up. I sure as hell wouldn't wanna be working a fracking site tomorrow."

I conceded his point with a nod. "It just doesn't sound like an approach they'd take. Painting a huge target on themselves, I mean. Or making themselves more hated than they already are."

"You're giving 'em way too much credit," Devers said. "Killing's easy, once you don't see the victims as human anymore."

"That sounds a lot more like drug dealers to me."

We stopped arguing as we neared the fracking site. He pulled the SUV as far up the road as he could to the downed trees, and we set about walking the rest of the way. The benefits of the SUV heater only lasted a few minutes—as we crested the hill and the compound came into view, the chill only added to the unnerving sight of the victims still lying exactly where they'd fallen.

"No one's come?" I asked. "You know, to . . ."

Devers grunted. "Wetzel County ain't exactly LA when it comes to dead bodies. The coroner's office is down in Charleston—that's a two-hour drive."

While it seemed hard to believe, it gave me hope that Cooke's plan to delay the press might actually work.

We entered through the holes in the fence near where Simon had found Donohue, then started across the mud. The footing hadn't improved—the limited sunshine had done nothing to dry out the soil, and the cold air hadn't absorbed much moisture, either. Given Devers's injured leg, we forced ourselves to take our time, stepping gingerly.

When we reached the midpoint of the field, I couldn't see the pieces of the drone, and I wondered if we'd mis-estimated where it had landed.

But as we continued on and the far side of the water tanks came into view, it became obvious the wreckage was missing.

Devers didn't say anything. He put his head down and continued plodding toward where the drone had finally come to rest. When we got there, impressions in the mud confirmed we'd found the correct spot. But ribbed tire tracks stretched from that point to the holes cut in the other side fence.

"They came and got it," Devers said, his chin almost touching his chest. "They knew we needed it, so they came and hauled it away."

"I saw ATVs in the camp last night," I said.

"Uh-huh."

We followed the tracks back to the woods, where the mud gave way to drier soil. Even without the tire impressions, we could follow trampled vegetation for several hundred yards. But soon after that, the trail disappeared completely.

Devers growled—a deep, guttural sound rumbling in his throat—and used his good leg to take a furious, sweeping kick through the tall grass.

I tried to think of what Cooke would want us to do. "Let's go back, gather up some of the brass," I said. "If we ever get our hands on those guns, we'll want to match them to the shots fired here."

Devers nodded, and we trudged back into the compound. I headed for the water tanks near where the drone had fired at us. But we found nothing.

Not a single shell casing.

At this point, Devers let out a grim laugh.

"The trailers," I said.

As we made our way across the field toward the rickety structures, I checked every spot I could think of over which the drone had fired its guns.

Nothing.

By this point, the bottom had dropped out of my stomach. I bent at the waist, hands on my knees, trying to wrap my head around it all.

"You still think this was drug dealers?" Devers asked. "You ever known drug dealers to police their brass after a shoot-out?"

I shook my head. "There's still probably bullets in some of the bodies. We'll still have some evidence." But even as my lips formed the words, I could hear the desperation in my voice.

Devers was right: the Green Way had done a number on our case.

Which meant there was only one thing left to do.

"C'mon," I said.

"Where?"

"Back to the Green Way's camp. If they took this stuff, they must have done something with it. Let's go nail them."

CHAPTER 14

Devers was limping pretty badly, so I offered to drive, but he brushed me off and got behind the wheel again.

This time, he stayed quiet, as did I.

In my head, I was still trying to make sense of the Green Way being behind the slaughter. Whoever conducted the attack at the fracking pad had returned to clean up the evidence. But if that was the Green Way, why didn't the rest of their behavior line up? And why had they suddenly escalated their tactics to include mass murder?

It seemed even more of a stretch that they had taken down Appalachian 303. Cooke had told me at the start that no notable passengers were on the flight, but now I wondered if that included members of the fracking industry. Could the Green Way really have chosen to bring down a random flight? Could it have possibly been an accident?

Maybe I was making it too complicated. Not all of the Green Way members needed to be involved, not on the front end anyway. The Appalachian 303 crash could have been compartmentalized, with Hartley in charge. Hell, he could have masterminded the attack as a way to eliminate Chu. While disruptors loyal to Chu might have been angry after their escape, Hartley could have concocted some story to regain their trust. Or maybe because their escape made them look like accessories after the fact, Hartley had blackmailed them all into staying.

Was he that crazy?

Who knew for sure? But hadn't Berkeley taught me what a single crazy person was capable of doing?

The heart tattoo on my forearm seemed to sizzle.

I pulled out my phone. Michael had answered my snowflake emoji with a snowman, his message still visible on the lock screen. That boosted my spirits enough that I sent him back a tent emoji.

Noticing the time, I realized that lunch hour was ending in LA. On impulse, I dialed a number I knew by heart and raised the handset to my ear.

It took until the third ring, but finally she answered. "Loretta Alcott."

"Hey there, pretty lady. It's me."

"Hello, dear. Are you ready to come home already?"

"Oh, I'm definitely ready, but I can't yet. I wanted to hear your voice and make sure everything was all right."

"Oh yes," she said. "We're soldiering on."

"Okay, then. If anything comes up, just let me know."

I tucked the phone away as we were approaching the Jacksonburg firehouse again. When we made the turn, Devers asked, "Exactly how many women do you have on the hook, Walker?"

His tone was softer than before, teasing rather than accusatory. Still, I wasn't quite sure where he was headed. "What's that supposed to mean?"

"I don't know. First Cooke wants 'special time' with you, now you're dialing somebody else."

"That was one of the staff in our office—she's old enough to be my grandmother. And there's nothing between Cooke and me. We just worked a case together before."

"Mmmm-hmmm." He drew out the syllables.

"I'm serious."

Devers's fingers rose from the steering wheel for a moment, matching his raised eyebrows. "You say there's nothing, I'm sure there's nothing."

"If anybody's romantically involved on this case," I said, "it sure isn't me."

Devers's head whipped around, but he seemed to relax when he saw the grin I was sporting.

"I don't know what you're talking about."

I laughed out loud at that. "You and Simon are like an old married couple."

"That bad?"

"Yeah," I said. "But good. When this is over, you should do something about it."

He made a noise in his throat that sounded unconvinced.

"Why wouldn't you?"

"Have you noticed where we are? You seen any other guys like me wandering around?"

I grunted. "Is it really all that much different than back in Lynch?"

"You'd be surprised."

I pressed him with a look.

"Seriously, don't judge the town by the name. Mining's like the army—all you got is the guy next to you. My daddy rescued three guys one time after a cave-in. Didn't matter that two of 'em were white. And you know what? Their families bought me and my brothers Christmas gifts every year."

"So why would this place be any different?"

"Lynch started out with black folks. Here, not so much."

"Still," I said. "You and Simon. Don't sleep on that."

By now we'd almost reached the camp. As we pulled into the parking lot, we glanced at each other.

It stood nearly empty. All the out-of-state vehicles had vanished.

Devers parked the SUV in the same space we'd occupied the previous evening. From there, we followed an identical line up the hill and over the plateau. But as we continued to hike inward, all we found were piles of leaves that crunched beneath our feet. After fifteen minutes of marching back and forth, we finally found vestiges of the campsite: impressions from the tents and the equipment, a few stone-ringed pits where fires had burned.

He crouched over one of these and pressed his hand against a log. "Ice-cold."

Starting at what had been the center of the camp, we split up and fanned outward, looking for any sign that the Green Way had migrated within these same woods. After twenty minutes of fruitless searching, we agreed by text to meet back where we'd started.

We stood at the empty campsite for a minute, neither of us wanting to admit the obvious. With daylight waning and no Brittany Anne Donohue to guide us, the chances of finding the Green Way seemed slim at best. Devers opened his phone and activated the GPS. Facing the camp, we surveyed the map together. On-screen, the forest extended several miles in every direction.

"No way we can cover all this," he said.

"Not by ourselves," I said.

Suddenly, a twig snapped behind us.

Devers and I both whipped around, drawing our pistols as we spun.

Sheriff Simon, now dressed in a clean uniform and new jacket, stood ten yards away. "Jesus, boys," she said, raising her hands, "it's just me."

Both of us lowered our weapons and exhaled.

"Don't sneak up like that," Devers said.

"Don't be so quick on the draw," she said. "What did y'all find?"

"Nothing," Devers said.

"Here, and at the fracking pad," I said. "Everything's gone."

"Well, you'll want to come along with me, then," she said. "While you've been striking out, I found us a lead. And he's waiting down in the car."

Simon had parked her cruiser next to the SUV, while another beaten-up truck I didn't recognize stood empty a few yards away. With the late-afternoon sun having dipped below the ridgeline, the windshield reflected the sky above and concealed whoever was inside.

"Y'all climb in up front," Simon said, trailing us by a few steps. "I'll get in back."

Devers drifted toward the driver's door, so I made for the passenger side. We entered the car simultaneously, then turned around to find a familiar face seated behind us: Harvey Nelson, the old guy who'd been sitting outside ACES when we'd first visited Brittany Anne Donohue.

He glared at me, then turned and gave Devers an even nastier look. When Simon opened the rear door and slid in next to him, Nelson said, "Who are these two? Why they gotta be here? I said I wanted to talk to you—"

"It's okay, Harv. They're Feds, working the case with me. You can trust them."

"You sure?"

"Positive."

Nelson's gaze dropped to the footwell. "I was just . . . sick when I heard about poor Brittany Anne. She and I, we don't agree on much, but I know her parents. She was raised right, and she's a good girl. Always very respectful."

"Do you know who hurt her, sir?" Devers asked.

Nelson's shoulders twitched beneath his parka in something that passed for a shrug. "Not for certain. But I do know who all's been hassling them Green Way people. And I heard they're aiming to do it again tonight." The old man turned to Simon. "That's why I called and asked to meet you, Sheriff. This has gone far enough, now—I don't want to see nobody else get hurt."

She patted his knee. "That's the right thing, Harvey. My colleagues and I are all about stopping the shooting. So you tell us what you know, and we can take it from there. Nobody'll ever know we had this little chat."

Nelson listed off a handful of names that meant nothing to me and seemed to have no impact on Devers, either. Simon jotted them all down in a small pad.

When he was finished, she looked at us. "If we're gonna check these guys out, you two need to get out of those scrubs. We'll give Harvey here a ten-minute head start so no one sees us together, then swing back through town."

The motel was a single-story brick structure whose narrow parking lot was ringed by a wooden rail fence and faced directly out onto Energy Road as it passed through the center of New Martinsville. While Simon parked her cruiser beneath the motel's yellowing marquee sign, Devers pulled the SUV right up to our rooms, the final two bright-blue doors that punctuated the side of the building.

I'd set my room's small heater on "High" the night before, so the new socks, jeans, and flannel shirt I chose from the duffel were all comfortably warm when I pulled them on. After this morning's action, I also made sure to reload the Sig and shove two extra magazines into my pockets.

We all got in the SUV and headed south. On both sides of Energy Road, fluorescent signs were already lit, their harsh whites and yellows darkening the purple sky of twilight. Simon had only guided us a couple of blocks, past the Arby's and the Dollar General, when I spotted the red RadioShack sign.

"Hey," I said, "let's pull in here for a second."

Simon and Devers dropped me off and went to hit the Wendy's drive-through window while I shopped. Although RadioShack didn't have everything I would have preferred (their antenna selection, in particular, was pretty limited, so I bought all they had), I found enough raw parts that I thought I could make them work. The store even had lawn-mower batteries, which meant we wouldn't have to make an extra stop.

When I climbed back into the truck, Devers was munching on a french fry. "You building a transistor radio?"

"Close," I said. "I think I can piece together something to knock drones down, but it's going to take a little work."

Devers turned to Simon. "Do you know the guys Nelson mentioned?"

The sheriff's eyes, illuminated by the string of oncoming headlights, flicked back and forth between the windshield and the rearview mirror as she drove. "Yeah, I know them. They're a handful of miners—young guys, early twenties, most of them. Been in little bits of trouble here and there, nickel-and-dime stuff. I could see them hassling the Green Way, for sure. But now I'm wondering if they're into something even worse."

"So where exactly are we going?"

"There's a bar these guys like. Down past Jacksonburg, in a little town called Archer. We've picked them up on drunk-and-disorderlies there before—I'm guessing if they're planning to get up to no good tonight, they'll go there first and front-load a bit."

Traffic died down as we turned out of town, and the sky released the last gasp of daylight that had been silhouetting the trees and finally succumbed to darkness. After downing a hamburger in just a few quick bites, I emptied my supplies across the back seat in hopes of starting to piece the radio gun together, but there wasn't enough light. With nothing else to do, the silent moments ticked by, and I felt a gnawing in my gut despite the warmth the food provided. "Heather," I said finally, "I want to apologize for this afternoon. I wasn't trying to get in the way of you honoring your people."

She glanced up at me in the mirror. "I appreciate that. They were good men, and I just . . ." She paused for a breath. "Let's just say, nothing like today's ever happened before. Once folks pick a better sheriff in a couple of weeks, hopefully it never will again."

"Nobody could've changed how this morning went," Devers said. "Penis or not."

"Thank you for saying that, Mitchell." In the mirror, I saw her crack a slight smile.

"What do you mean?" I asked. "What's happening in a couple of weeks?"

"I'm up for reelection." Simon grunted. "Not that the result's much in doubt after today."

"You really think people will blame you?"

"Sure will. I'm the first female sheriff in county history, so you can imagine not everyone thinks that's a good thing. Heck, when I started talking about becoming a deputy in high school, my mother pretty much ordered me not to. I think she was dreaming I'd marry somebody rich—become a stay-at-home mom, give her lots of grandbabies, visit her all the time. Once that went out the window, she was hoping for schoolteacher, something quiet like that. She figured me on the police force wasn't gonna go well. My first year or two, there were times I wondered if she was right. All the criminals thought they could beat me up or outrun me. The other guys left packs of Midol and tampons on my desk."

"Idiots," I said.

"They didn't know better," she said. "All that stuff ended up doing was pissing me off, making me want to prove them all wrong. I kept my head down, did my best—plenty of folks respect that. And times change; even some of the old coots like Harvey have come around. But I know enough people in the county who are still skeptical about a sheriff with boobs. Today ain't gonna earn their vote."

"One more reason we need to finish this," I said.

"From your lips to God's ears," she said.

The twisting roads were difficult enough to follow in daylight; at night, you couldn't see much more than a few yards of yellow line in front of the hood. Still, Simon drove well over the limit, anticipating each curve, dip, and rise before it appeared. Several minutes after we passed the Jacksonburg firehouse, though, she let off the gas, and the SUV began to bleed off speed until she turned left onto an unmarked side road.

"Not far now," she said.

A single light shone in the distance. As we approached, it grew into a fluorescent sign that was hung from a tall metal pipe set into the dirt. "The Bowman" was written in fancy, looping script across the top half of the sign; beneath were illustrations of a music note, a beer mug, and a black 8-ball.

Set back from the sign was a dark wood-paneled building that looked like it had been intended to be a two-story house. The ground floor appeared to be devoted to the bar, while wooden stairs stretched up the side of the building to what I guessed was a residence above it.

Instead of pulling into the dirt lot across from the Bowman, where several pickups were already parked, we continued past it, eventually pulling a U-turn farther down the road. As we reapproached the bar from the opposite direction, Simon flipped off the headlights and drew the SUV off the asphalt onto the grass. We gradually crept to a halt, hidden in the shadows cast by the side of the bar itself, as well as an intervening stand of trees. From here, we could see the lot in front of the Bowman as well as the vehicles across the street.

Simon silenced the engine, then spoke in a low whisper. "I see their trucks over there. The black F-150 and the gray Ram next to it."

The dashboard clock said it was just after seven thirty.

Two hours later, not a soul had come to or exited the Bowman. Although the SUV's leather seats were comfortable, Devers had shifted several times.

"Are we even sure anyone's in there?" he asked.

"Trust me," Simon said.

"What if they left in some other truck before we got here?"

"They didn't."

"How can you—"

Simon's head cocked to the side. "Because today's Thursday."

"So?"

"So Thursday-night college football is on. The Mountaineers happen to be playing Oklahoma tonight for the lead in the Big 12. That means every regular at this bar got here at least half an hour before kickoff and planted themselves until the game's over."

"Oh," Devers said quietly. "All right, then."

At five minutes past eleven, men began stumbling out of the Bowman. A series of three groups crossed the road, climbed into vehicles, and departed. Although Simon kept her eyes fixed on the windshield, she didn't say anything.

Several minutes later, a group of five men came out together. Unlike the others, these guys weren't laughing or high-fiving. They quietly glanced up and down the road before heading for the trucks Simon had identified earlier.

"That's them," she said, reaching for her door handle.

A loud thunk sounded inside the SUV: the door locks. Devers put a long arm out in front of her.

"Mitchell?" she said.

"Let's not do this here," he said. "We need to find the Green Way. These guys know where they are—let's follow them, take them down after they lead us to the new campsite."

"And let 'em mix it up? That's asking for trouble," she said. "We haul 'em now, they'll tell us—"

"That's gonna take *time*, Heather," he said. "What do you have them on now, really? DUI? Maybe? Let's let them lead us out there and make it obvious they're about to start something. Then we nab 'em and start in on the Green Way."

Simon turned to me. Even with her face backlit by the lights of the Bowman, I could read her plaintive look. But the only thought in my head was Cooke's comment about shopping malls. Public places, like the ones my godkids visited on a daily basis.

"I agree with Devers," I said. "Job one is getting ahold of Hartley. If he's our guy, he may have more drones cooked up. It's too risky to leave him on the loose."

Even if Simon wanted to argue the point further, the die was cast: the two pickup trucks rumbled to life and turned onto the main road.

I could hear Simon draw a deep breath through her nose. Then she keyed the SUV's ignition and inched it back out onto the road. Keeping our vehicle dark, she started after the pairs of red taillights ahead of us.

"I sure hope this works," she said.

CHAPTER 15

Honestly, I was shocked we didn't crash.

Somehow, either through the tiny amount of starlight that had appeared or by sheer, blind feel after a lifetime spent on those roads, Simon managed to keep our SUV from careening into a ditch or slamming into a tree at full speed. Ahead, the taillights swerved this way and that, disappearing and reappearing every few seconds. Thankfully, the pickups drove more conservatively than expected, but we still ended up twisting back and forth through the pitch black with nothing but the pairs of glowing red dots as our beacon.

I wiped sweat from my forehead at one point and wondered how fast Simon's pulse must be racing as she yanked the wheel to one side and then the other. None of us made a sound, as if noise might give us away. There was only the growl of the engine each time she applied the gas, then the whispered hiss of invisible, passing trees whenever we coasted.

I had no idea how long we drove—after seeing the dashboard clock turn one minute after what felt like ten, I decided clock-watching only made things worse.

When the lead truck finally flipped on its blinker, Simon hit the brakes hard enough that I pitched forward against my shoulder strap. The two trucks quickly pulled ahead, turning at a point in the distance.

"We're up near Wileyville," she said, her voice still hushed. "Center of the county. There's eighty acres of campground up here, but I'm guessing these boys know exactly which secluded little spot the Green Way picked out for themselves."

When we reached the turn, I realized why Simon had held back: the asphalt ended abruptly, giving way to a dirt-and-gravel surface that made a lot more noise plunking up against the undercarriage. The taillights were still barely visible ahead—they'd slowed significantly, too—and we crept along behind them, keeping them at the far edge of our sight. When their brake lights flashed, Simon halted the SUV immediately and killed the engine.

One benefit to the long, darkened drive was that our eyes had completely adjusted. Without a word, we drew our guns and slipped out of the truck, leaving the doors ajar. All three of us stepped to the shoulder, where the trees could mask our outlines.

As we inched forward, Simon in the lead, I allowed myself a quick glance overhead. The clouds had disappeared, revealing a navy sky pinpricked by hundreds of stars. With clear conditions, though, the temperature had plummeted; the afternoon's damp chill had become an icy cold that stung my lungs with each breath.

Ahead, we could hear the group of miners as much as see them: dark shapes rustling around, clunking against the sidewalls of the trucks as they unloaded something from the beds. We continued advancing slowly, allowing the five shadows to pass into the tree line. Instead of following or angling to intercept them, though, Simon veered back out into the middle of the road, circling around to the driver's side so that the vehicles stood between us and them.

When she crouched down at the rear quarter panel of the first truck, I wasn't sure what she was doing. Then I heard a soft, telltale hiss.

Patting Devers on the back, I urged him forward, and we tended to the other truck; between us, we had all four driver-side wheels down to the ground in less than a minute. Simon made a chopping motion with her hand toward the forest, and we followed her single file into the trees.

At this point, the miners had disappeared from sight—given their head start, the only clue we had to their location was rustling some distance ahead. The ground descended slightly as we followed. Bringing up the rear, I did my best to leave a five- to ten-foot gap between Devers and me—close enough I could still make out his outline, but far enough back that if I tripped, I hopefully wouldn't knock him over like a domino.

Without any obvious visual references, it was hard to gauge our progress, but I'd say we'd advanced maybe twenty-five yards into the woods when the first explosion sounded. A large crack, followed by a sharp whistle as a blinding white light rocketed into the sky.

Several seconds later, another one followed.

Devers pitched forward into the leaves. For an instant, I wondered if he'd tripped and somehow set off the flares. But then I saw that Simon, too, had dropped to the ground, so I joined them.

The flares hung high above the treetops, casting flickering light down over a broad area before us. Shadows danced from side to side as the light wavered.

Fifty yards ahead, the five miners stood in a horizontal line, a few feet between them. All were armed with rifles; the two burliest had theirs slung over their shoulders, allowing them to carry heavy-looking plastic canisters that contained some kind of liquid. For a moment, nothing happened, and you could sense the miners' confusion as they remained seemingly frozen in place.

Then the shooting started.

Staccato bursts of automatic fire echoed around the woods, making it impossible to locate their source. Scanning the area, I didn't see any muzzle flashes, but when the miners were knocked backward toward us, I focused in on the forest directly ahead.

Within seconds, an army of disruptors stormed out of the trees. The black-clad figures yelled and screamed as they ran, closing fast on the miners' position. A group at the front toted guns, with more flares crackling and shooting upward like fireworks as they approached.

In the face of the oncoming rush, four miners backpedaled before turning and fleeing in our direction. They abandoned their rifles, the canisters—everything—and just ran.

Sensing their advantage, the disruptors fired another barrage, hitting the miners in the back and dropping them to the forest floor.

The final miner, though, was having none of it. He stood his ground, drew his rifle up to his shoulder, and fired at the nearest disruptor. The single shot sounded dramatically different from the disruptors' guns' high-pitched buzz: a solitary boom. The blast caught the black-clad figure squarely in the chest. From only twenty yards away, the force of the bullet lifted him off his feet and dropped him flat onto his back.

And that's when things got weird.

In response to the rifle shot, the disruptors suddenly halted their charge. Many froze in place; others skittered to a stop, sliding to their knees or tumbling forward onto the ground. The miners who'd been shot while fleeing now rose to their feet, looking as astonished as anyone, and turned back toward their abandoned comrade. For his part, the lone miner shooter lowered his rifle and stared at the body now motionless on the ground.

As everyone remained still for a fleeting moment, I realized what had happened. The miners' backs weren't blood soaked—they were splattered with color. The disruptors' guns had looked like automatics when they were running, but on closer inspection, the magazines were actually air canisters.

They'd been firing paintballs, not bullets.

From the miners' body language, I could tell they'd come to the same realization.

When the action resumed, everyone moved at once—like we'd been watching a paused video and someone suddenly pushed "Play."

Some of the disruptors fled. They simply turned tail and ran back into the woods from where they came.

Others charged the miner with the rifle. While he raised it across his chest with both hands in an effort to block them, he was quickly overwhelmed. A pack of at least ten people in black swarmed him. They wrenched the gun away, clubbed him over the head with it, and then, once he was down on the ground, really started to go to work. Pummeling and kicking him. Jabbing at him with rifle butts.

One disruptor stood at least half a foot taller than everyone else.

Hartley.

I locked my eyes on him, not wanting to lose sight once the flares faded out.

The other miners now stormed back down the hill to join the fray. When they reached the crowd, each of them grabbed one or more of the disruptors and pulled them away. In an instant, the single throng metastasized into five separate fistfights.

One of the bigger miners went after Hartley from behind, seizing him under the armpits and tossing him aside. As Hartley hit the ground, the miner pounced on him, pinned his arms, and pummeled his face with a series of punches.

While his upper body was trapped, Hartley's legs were free, and he kicked them upward, locking them around the miner's neck and wrenching him back. Suddenly, the tables were turned, and Hartley was on top. Instead of using his fists, though, he pulled something from his belt. With a flick of his wrist, Hartley extended a baton and then whacked it against the miner's side.

To my surprise, the miner turned into the blow, absorbing it and wrapping the baton in tightly against his side. Then he kept rolling, dragging Hartley over himself until he was flat on the ground and the miner lay perpendicular across his torso. Without releasing the baton, the miner threw two solid elbows into Hartley's face, then leaned his forearm across Hartley's throat.

Simon, Devers, and I climbed to our feet. Devers started to take off, but Simon grabbed his sleeve and restrained him. She strode down the hill purposefully—not running, but walking. Once she'd covered about half the distance to the combatants, she fired her pistol to the side.

Although the light from the last round of flares was finally fading, the loud *crack* from Simon's Smith & Wesson stopped everyone where they were. As she flipped on her flashlight and panned it across the scene, Devers and I drew our guns, too, covering the crowd as best we could.

"I am the Wetzel County Sheriff!" Simon yelled. Any uncertainty she'd displayed about her position in the SUV was gone now—her voice rang resolute and firm. "Everyone here is under arrest. And, so help me, if any of y'all make another move, we will shoot you."

CHAPTER 16

The disruptor who'd been shot never had a chance—the rifle bullet had hit him squarely in the sternum, ripping through his rib cage and the organs underneath. While none of the other injured fighters on either side were critical, there were far too many to fit in our lone SUV. So, even as we frisked them, read them their rights, and zip-tied their hands, Simon radioed for ambulances.

When the paramedics arrived and began carting people away, Simon insisted on riding in the back of an ambulance with Hartley, leaving Devers and me to search the Green Way's camp before meeting her at the hospital. With borrowed red-lensed flashlights to preserve our night vision, we set off into the forest in the direction from which the disruptors had made their charge.

We came upon the camp quickly—it was staged in a shallow cut a few hundred yards beyond where the fight had broken out. Sunken several feet below the surrounding terrain, the camp was hidden until you stood on the lip directly above it. Within the hollow, the camp's arrangement resembled the one we'd seen earlier: concentric rings of smaller shelters surrounding a larger central tent. Although the place appeared deserted, campfires still smoldered in their pits.

Dousing our lights, Devers and I silently agreed to split up. He disappeared into the brush to our left, while I bore right.

As I worked my way along the lip of the berm, I yanked the earpiece out of my ear and stuffed it down into my pocket. I had enough adrenaline pumping that I could hear my heart pounding in my chest. All my muscles felt extra twitchy.

Once I was within a few yards of the first perimeter tent, I eased onto all fours. My broken ribs didn't appreciate that, but I tried to ignore the stabbing feeling in my side. The leaves littering the ground felt cold and slick against my hands; their sweetly rotting smell pushed its way up my nose and stayed there.

I trained my eyes on the dark arch of canvas ahead and crawled forward. Nothing moved. No signs of life at all.

Identifying the gentlest grade down to the camp floor, I inched toward it. Rocks and roots pressed into my palms and knees, the brush scraped my bare scalp and cheeks, but eventually I reached the slope and crept down the earthen hill as silently as I could. Once I reached the small tent, I drew the Sig in my right hand and seized the flap zipper with my left.

After a cleansing breath, I yanked the zipper down and pushed my way inside in a single motion.

Empty. Although whoever had occupied the tent hadn't had time to clear out their belongings. In addition to an unrolled sleeping bag, a rucksack leaned against the fabric wall, and the contents of a toiletry kit were scattered across the floor.

Over the next few minutes, I popped into a dozen tents in the outer rings and each time found an identical result: the camp was abandoned. Gradually, I wove my way inward, searching every shelter until I reached the rear corner of the central tent. Devers was crouched there in the shadows, waiting.

He raised his upturned palms in a silent, *So?*

I shook my head.

He nodded.

With hand signals, we agreed to check the large tent next. Once I signed I was ready, Devers mimed an exaggerated count of three, then yanked open the door flap.

Unlike the other tents, this one was tall enough to stand inside, so I dashed across the threshold in two quick steps, the Sig at high ready. After clearing the far corners, I stepped to my right, checking back behind objects cluttered in the center of the space.

"Clear," I said, just loudly enough for Devers to hear me.

He repeated the word, and we both flipped on our flashlights.

From the look of it, this tent was still being assembled when the miners attacked. A folding card table lay on its side, only one set of legs extended; another table lay flat next to it. Several reinforced cases were stacked nearby—a quick check showed that each contained one of the quadcopter drones we'd seen before. Briefcases contained a number of laptop computers and their accessories, as well as road maps and paper charts of the surrounding terrain.

"We'll need the tech guys to inspect the hard drives," Devers said, looking over the electronics. "I bet we get some decent info."

"Maybe," I said. "But you notice what's missing."

"No killer drone."

"Not just that," I said. "Nothing even related to one. No parts, no controller. No guns, no ammo. Not even gasoline. Plus, absolutely nothing from the scene this morning."

Devers grunted. "They were just moving in. Maybe that stuff's outside. Or still packed in their cars."

We exited through the front flap of the tent. Other than the massive battery box we'd seen at the previous campsite, the only pieces of equipment visible were two ATVs.

"Here we go," Devers said, panning his light over each one. "Plenty of mud, caked all over the tires and the frame." He snapped photos with his cell phone, then produced a couple of plastic baggies, into which we scraped soil off each of the four-wheelers.

Next, we checked satellite photos on his phone. Some kind of clearing was visible nearby, so we plotted a course and headed back into the woods. When we reached the dirt patch, we found it filled with the Green Way's fleet of luxury SUVs. We went car by car, snapping photos of each rear bumper to get the make, model, and plate number, then used our flashlights to peer through the windows.

"Wish we had a slim jim," Devers said when the dark tint on an Audi's windows obscured what was inside. "But we can always come back tomorrow."

Once we'd reached the end of the line, I said, "Whole lot of nothing."

"They buried it," he said. "Or dumped it in some creek. But we both know the man to ask where."

"Hartley."

By the time we backtracked to our SUV, it was nearly four in the morning. Devers had been doing so much on his injured leg that his limp had grown pronounced. My side ached, giving me a little jab of pain each time I took a breath. Honestly, those jolts helped keep me awake: the adrenaline rush had long since faded, and I'd run out of drone-related content on my player, so the earpiece was now feeding the silky narration of an audiobook into my ear. My eyelids suddenly felt heavy.

Knowing Cooke, she'd be rising soon, and I hadn't forgotten her warning about the press, so when we reached the truck, I shot her a text, asking her to call me first thing.

The drive to the New Martinsville hospital went quicker than I'd anticipated; when the sliding doors parted for us, we found Simon standing at the front desk, leaning against the high counter and talking to the receptionist. After so much time outside, the hospital's white fluorescents seemed extra bright, and as the sheriff turned to greet us, the harsh light etched the lines on her face in deep relief. Devers looked like hell, too—his clothes were dotted in dirt and leaf litter, a red spot had appeared on the bandage across his forehead, and he seemed to drag his leg more with each step. Thankfully, there was no mirror around.

"How are you still standing?" I asked as we drew up to the desk.

She grunted, which caused her to wince. "If I sit, I'm gonna end up asleep. How'd you all do?"

We explained everything we'd done and how little we'd found. "How's everyone here?" Devers asked.

"Chu's stable," Simon said. "The foot was the worst of it: the way it got hit, they had to remove what was left. But otherwise, he got lucky—everything should heal. He's still out from the anesthetic, though."

"Brittany Anne?" I asked.

"Not so good," she said, then pursed her lips. "When they opened her up, she was a complete mess inside. One bullet punctured her diaphragm and lung, another ruptured her spleen. Her pelvis got shattered. Docs thought they'd repaired everything, but she started crashing again, and they had to go back in."

"Is she . . ."

"Alive?" Simon closed her eyes and nodded. "For now. They said they've replaced all her blood. If she's not leaking inside anymore, then the big risk is infection. Nurse told me if she's still alive in twenty-four hours . . . then her chances look better."

Simon's left arm still rested on the counter, and her fingers curled under her hand to squeeze into a fist. The knuckles blanched.

"How about Hartley?" Devers asked. "He tell you anything?"

"Haven't gotten to question him yet," Simon said. "The docs kicked me out when they needed to strip him down, and I sure as hell didn't want to see that skinny piece of grizzle without his clothes on." She sighed. "I just thought I'd be polite and wait for y'all. Let's go see if they're ready."

The three of us made our way down the hall, slowly. After a couple of twists and turns, Simon stopped to ask a question at a nurses' station, then pushed her way through a closed door into one of the patient rooms.

There was one bed inside, its back tilted up at a forty-five-degree angle. Hartley's head popped off the pillow as we entered, but only one of his eyes opened—the other was swollen shut, eggplant purple. Strips of tape were splayed across his nose, while a thick bandage was wrapped from the top of his head down under his chin, reminding me of the way Saturday-morning cartoon characters would treat a toothache. Hartley's arms were draped across the blanket that covered him, one wrist cuffed to the bed, the other wrapped in some sort of soft splint.

Simon avoided the chair next to the bed, instead leaning a shoulder against the wall. "You don't look too good, Darwin."

Although Hartley's lips moved when he talked, the bandage held his jaw closed, making his words come out in a mumble. "You're no pageant winner yourself."

If the insult bothered Simon, you couldn't tell.

"Why don't you tell us about today," Devers said.

"Why don't you bugger off?"

"Because we need answers." Devers limped another step toward the bed.

"And I need my rest."

"We know you flew the drones . . ."

Hartley rolled his eyes. "'Course I flew the bloody drones. I've been flying drones since I was twenty-two."

"Richard survived," said the sheriff. "I'm guessing he's not gonna be too pleased with you when he wakes up and finds his foot missing."

Hartley's good eye narrowed. "When you said *drones*, you meant that thing that shot everyone up. You think I was flying *that*?"

"Of course that's what we meant," Devers said. "And you're gonna tell us where you hid the pieces of it after you came and picked them up."

The parts of Hartley's face that weren't already discolored now flushed pink. He began shaking his head as much as the bandage would allow. "I flew *our* drones, not that thing."

"That thing *was* your drone," Devers said, his voice rising. "Military grade, just like what you flew in the Middle East."

"You got a whole lot to answer for," Simon said. "Starting with all those innocent people who got slaughtered today. But the most important thing to us right now is getting our hands on the wreckage of that drone so nobody else gets hurt."

"Fuck you." Hartley turned to Devers. "And fuck you, too. I had nothing to do with that . . . that thing."

"Darwin," Simon said, "we just need you to tell us where it is. If you do, that gives us something good to tell the prosecutors when they're thinking about offering you a deal."

He closed his eyes. "I want my fucking lawyer. I'm not saying another word."

Simon gingerly pushed herself off the wall. "Suit yourself."

CHAPTER 17

Simon asked the hospital staff for a place where we could talk. A nurse named Nathalie led us to a darkened room near the entrance that contained seating for four around a small table.

We'd no sooner collapsed into the chairs than Nathalie returned with several bags of ice, doses of ibuprofen, and a pitcher of water. "Y'all look like you could use something stronger than this," she said with a wink as she passed out Dixie cups. "But I thought we'd start you out slow."

While we thanked her and washed the pills down, she propped Devers's leg up on the spare chair, wrapped his knee with ice, and changed the dressing on his forehead. As she was leaving, Nathalie turned and said, "I'm off in a couple of hours, but I'll check on you before I go. Hopefully, you'll put your heads down and get some rest."

As the door closed behind her, my phone buzzed in my pocket. I laid it in the middle of the table and activated the speaker. "Morning, Melissa."

"Good morning. I'm guessing there's big news if you're texting me at four."

"Sure is." I explained how the fracking-pad site had been swept clean and how we'd tracked down the Green Way and apprehended Hartley.

Cooke whistled. "You've been busy. Is Hartley talking?"

Simon recounted our brief interview.

"He lawyered up when we pressed him on the attack drone," added Devers.

"All right, then," she said. "The Green Way has a bunch of ACLU lawyers on retainer—my guess is, one will drive out from DC to represent Hartley. That should buy me a few hours to get there, too."

"You're coming out?" said Devers.

"Definitely. I'd like a crack at Hartley. Chu, too, if he's conscious by then. If we can pit the two of them against each other, who knows what will spill out."

The Green Way guys didn't realize it yet, but they were in deep, deep trouble. Anyone would be, facing Cooke.

"Plus," she said, "I promised the press an interview in exchange for giving us until one o'clock. We'll be able to tell them about the Hartley arrest, but maybe we'll have even more by then."

"Until you get here," I said, "I think we need to keep trying to find the parts of that killer drone."

Simon chimed in. "It's about four miles from the fracking pad to the Green Way's new camp. But that's through pretty heavy woods—searching in there won't be easy. And Hartley and his people had enough time that they didn't necessarily have to straight-line it."

"After we talked, I worked on getting you some more resources," Cooke said. She explained how she'd recruited agents from several nearby offices to come and supplement Simon's manpower. "Now that this search is an issue, we can also call in an ERTU."

Simon blinked in a way that said she didn't recognize the acronym. I didn't, either.

"Evidence Response Team Unit," Devers said. "They've got everything from hunting dogs to helicopters to sniff out hidden stuff."

"I can have an ERTU there in a couple of hours," Cooke said. "I'll make sure they have someone to start working on the computers you seized, but the most important thing is that we don't want anyone stumbling onto the drone by accident. If we start looking by daybreak, hopefully the risk of that decreases." She paused for a moment. "One other thing came up on my end yesterday, although it doesn't sound like it matters much anymore, given what you found."

"What's that?" I asked.

"I talked to DEA," Cooke said. "They recognized a name from the Appalachian 303 manifest."

I straightened in my chair. "I thought you said nobody important was on the flight."

She sighed. "Don't get too excited—I'm not talking about some cartel kingpin. We ran background checks on everyone right after the crash, and the initial results were clean. But it turns out, one of the passengers was apparently on a DEA watch list—someone they were in the process of approaching to see if he might become a CI. Heather, the names will probably mean a lot more to you than they do to me—have you ever heard of Joseph Simpson or Charles Miller?"

Simon groaned. "I don't know that first name, but I sure know the second. State police have been after Chas Miller for three years—half the heroin in West Virginia probably ties back to him one way or another. He and his family control almost all the distribution in the southern part of the state." She paused a moment, then said, "That's kind of weird, though."

"Why?" Cooke asked.

"Well, the airplane was headed for Pittsburgh, right? Everything I've always heard is that Miller's people get supplied out of DC. The drug runners up here get fed out of Pittsburgh, but it's a whole different crew: the Clancy brothers. They're up around Morgantown, but they've got folks on their payroll here in Wetzel County, in Marshall County, just about everywhere north of Route 50."

"I'm guessing the drug dealers up here don't get along with Chas Miller?" I asked.

Simon smiled and shook her head. "Not so much. I mean, it's not like there's some huge war going on or anything—business has been so good, they haven't had much time to fight. They've just kind of divided the state up between them."

"But if Chas Miller was reaching out to the Clancys' suppliers, wouldn't that piss them off?"

"I imagine so," Simon said. "They'd probably see it as a sign Miller was starting to creep north."

"The Clancys might want to send a message, then," I said.

"It's even more complicated than that," Cooke said. "The DEA agents trying to turn Simpson were based in Pittsburgh. So if Chas Miller found out about the meeting . . ."

"He'd have a reason to want to take down Appalachian 303 himself."

Devers groaned. "Did we really just go from one suspect to three?"

I turned to Simon. "If we wanted to investigate the Clancy people, do we know where to find them?"

"I can make a couple of calls," Simon said. "I bet I can narrow it down."

"I can ask DEA, too. It's not like we can do anything more with Hartley until his lawyer gets there," Cooke said from the speakerphone. "While we wait for that and the ERTU does its thing, you might as well check out the Clancys."

Simon and I both turned to Devers. He inhaled deeply through his nose, then glanced all around the room as if he were searching for our sanity hiding in some corner. Finally, he said, "All right, I guess a nap can wait. Let's go find some drug dealers."

CHAPTER 18

Simon said she needed an hour or two to make calls about where the Clancy brothers' people might be hiding. Although everything ached and my eyelids yearned to shut, it seemed like the best use of my time would be piecing together the drone gun.

Leaving Devers to rest his leg, I took the SUV keys and retrieved the components I'd bought earlier at RadioShack. On my way back, I stopped at a vending machine in the hallway. The pickings were slim. Not wanting a candy bar but needing more than gum, I bought out the row of Goldfish crackers.

When I returned to the small office where Devers was slumped across his chair, I plugged in the soldering iron to heat, then ripped open one of the little foil packages, spilling crackers across the table. My initial thought was that I couldn't remember the last time I'd eaten them, but then it hit me: I'd had them the last two Thanksgivings.

By the time my first November in LA rolled around, I'd settled into the air-marshal gig. I'd moved to the bungalow in Venice, learned my way around. Although I was still MacAlister's whipping boy at the office, I'd learned how we were graded and made sure all my numbers were solid.

To earn some goodwill with the other marshals, I volunteered to cover Thanksgiving. I didn't feel right trying to go see Shirley and the kids yet—it was too soon. Working would be easier.

But when the schedules came out, I was surprised to find myself listed as off for that Thursday. I hurried to Loretta's cube, figuring there'd been a mistake.

"There certainly was a mistake," she said. "You can't come to my house if you're working."

"You want me to come over for Thanksgiving?"

She put her hands on her hips and gave me a hard look. "Just because you're too embarrassed to go see your parents in Florida doesn't mean you should be alone."

Suddenly conscious that we were having this conversation amid the open cubes, I glanced around to see who might be watching. Thankfully, the floor seemed deserted. "How—"

"Never you mind that. Dinner's at four. Don't be late." Without another word, she spun on her chair and went back to her computer, leaving me standing in the aisle.

I showed up at their El Segundo house at 3:15 p.m., carrying a tin of the English shortbread cookies my grandmother always bought for special occasions. When I rang the doorbell to the little, blue one-story Craftsman, Loretta answered, dressed almost exactly as she did for work, in a pencil skirt and a flowing silk blouse. Her gold spectacles were propped up on top of her head, letting me see the way her eyes softened as she cocked her head and smiled. "I'm glad you made it, young man. Come in."

She led me back to the kitchen, where the air was thick with hearty smells. A short balding man was bustling about, tending to pots, checking on the oven. He wore a "Kiss the Cook" apron, and Loretta promptly did just that, planting one on his cheek that left a faint lipstick smear.

"Walker, meet Bob, my better half."

He wiped his hands down the front of the apron before shaking mine. "Welcome."

"Let's get out of the way while he works his magic," Loretta said, giving him another quick peck before leading me into the backyard. Under the shade of a large umbrella, a glass-topped table had been set for three places.

"Bob does all the cooking," she said, once we sat down. "Except for one dish I make every year, but that's already in the oven."

The meal turned out to be a tremendous feast. In addition to the turkey and stuffing made with spicy sausage, Bob served us a southern-style corn soufflé, mushrooms stuffed with a tangy mix of Parmesan cheese and ham, and broiled asparagus. Loretta's dish turned out to be mac and cheese, a creamy, gooey bowl of goodness, the top of which was crusted in crushed Goldfish crackers.

"That's the secret ingredient," she said. "Gives it the right crunch." She was right.

After we'd eaten and talked for a couple of hours, I stood and started to clear my place.

"Bob will get those," Loretta said. "Just sit."

"I want to help."

"You're the guest. Sit."

"I'm happy to—"

"Sit your behind down in that chair, young man, and stop arguing." Although she was grinning, I raised my hands in surrender and sat.

She and Bob cleared the table; then she returned, planting herself back into her chair and patting my hand. "I'm glad you came tonight. I was worried your deep, dark secret would make you chicken out."

I did a double take, wondering again what she knew and how she could possibly know it. My face flashed uncomfortably hot, and I shifted in my seat. "What are you even talking about?"

She looked over her glasses at me. "Those other guys at the office treat me like a potted plant, Walker. Don't you do it, too. I told you before, I *see* you."

"I don't have any—"

Her stare silenced me. "Whatever it is, they won't be as mad as you think. Your family."

My stomach, which had been teetering on the edge, finally dropped out. She didn't know my father. Or what had happened. I couldn't face him after what I'd done to Clarence—he'd ask questions, he'd see right through me. If he found out the sin I'd committed . . .

I stood, my eyes darting around the yard for an exit.

Loretta rose, too. "You can't avoid them forever. You're going to have to—"

I shook my head and forced a swallow down, hoping it would keep my voice from cracking. "You don't know. You don't—"

She shushed me. "That's right, Walker, I don't." She circled the table and wrapped her arms around me. "And I don't need to."

Devers was eyeing my crackers as I began building the drone gun. I offered him some, but he refused. Instead, while I worked on the device, he decided to follow Nurse Nathalie's instructions and sprawled himself across his chair, resting his head in one hand. Once I was done soldering, I followed suit. Although I almost always leave my phone on vibrate, I switched the sound on in case Cooke or Simon tried to call or text. I set the handset a few inches away, then tucked my face down into the crook of my bent elbow.

The darkness across my eyelids was all it took—I didn't notice anything until Simon's voice said, "Rise and shine, boys."

I glanced up and saw the clock above the door was ticking its way toward 7:00 a.m. "You learn anything about the Clancys?" I asked, yawning.

"I did, as a matter of fact. Talked to a game-warden friend of mine. He was up along the northern edge of the county at dawn—he'd heard folks had set some illegal fox traps up there. Said he was patrolling on foot when he saw campfire smoke in the distance and heard a buzzing noise, like those ultralights I told you they use to fly heroin. He went to check it out—nobody's supposed to be up there, certainly not burning anything—and found the fire extinguished. There'd been a camp, though, and he found tracks leading away from it. Enough for four or five people. And a four-wheeled ATV."

Devers and I glanced at each other.

"Your friend follow the tracks?" Devers asked.

She shook her head. "He's just one guy, works alone. Said he had a feeling they were up to no good and didn't want to get himself in too deep. That's why he called me."

"And all this happened this morning?" I asked.

"Fifteen minutes ago. I'm thinking we should get up there ASAP."

The drive started out resembling the others we'd made through the county—Simon headed north through town on Energy Road, exactly as we had that first morning, before turning east. But where the other roads had traced the valleys cut by creeks or streams, this one rode along a series of hillsides so that the land was always sloping up to one side of us and dropping off to the other. While we passed some obviously inhabited sections—one particular farm seemed to stretch for a couple of miles—the dwellings we encountered mostly came as a surprise, appearing unexpectedly out of the trees or as we rounded a bend. Most of the route consisted of seemingly empty wilderness, the only hint of civilization being the road beneath us.

And even that proved unreliable. At one point, the double yellow line ended abruptly, leaving us with nothing but a single lane of asphalt.

The surrounding woods were the thickest we'd seen—trees interwoven overhead, with impenetrable ivy overgrowing their trunks.

As I was beginning to wonder exactly how much farther we could realistically go, Simon navigated a series of hairpin switchbacks, then turned north onto a dirt track.

In the back seat, the rough road surface bounced me around enough to make me wish I'd swallowed a few more ibuprofens before leaving the hospital. The jolts were so bad, I moved the drone gun into my lap to try and shield it from some of the pounding.

But the terrain only worsened from there. The "road" shrank from a car's width of dirt down to two tire tracks' worth separated by a thick patch of weeds. Puddles filled with rainwater hissed against the doors as we splashed through them.

Finally, even the dirt disappeared, and Simon pulled the SUV to a stop on a steep incline, where she set the emergency brake.

"This is it?" I asked. "Really?"

"Yep." She pointed out the passenger's window past Devers. "My buddy left a ribbon."

Sure enough, a thick piece of yellow "Caution" tape wound around a nearby tree trunk, tied into a large bowknot.

"He said the camp was about a half-mile hike in."

Climb would have been a better description than *hike*, as the land sloped upward at nearly a sixty-degree angle from the road. Here, the dense foliage actually helped: with the trees spaced only a few feet apart, we were able to use them as foot- and handholds to help tack our way up the hill. Even that wasn't perfect, though. In addition to solid oaks and maples, there were plenty of sycamores and red pines whose bark would slough off in long peels or thick chunks if you grabbed a trunk the wrong way. All of the reaching and stretching stung my ribs, so I switched the lawn-mower battery to that side, although with the added weight, it didn't help much.

Thankfully, although the sun barely penetrated the leaf canopy overhead, the temperature had moderated such that my scalp and ears didn't feel so chilled. As the climb continued and I started to sweat, I was even able to unzip my jacket for the first time I could remember in West Virginia.

Upon reaching the summit, we found a steep downward grade that was even more difficult to navigate. Devers, in particular, had problems. His gimpy leg wasn't always strong enough to support his weight. He slipped and slid his way down as much as climbed.

When we reached the bottom, Simon produced a compass and pointed the way. The land sloped upward again, but not so steeply this time. Once we cleared the second ridge, we came upon the encampment Simon's contact had located. Consistent with his description, there was an extinguished fire and ATV tracks. But what was most interesting to me was the relative openness of the clearing in which it sat. Shaped like a circle, maybe fifty yards in diameter, with no trees, it was the only spot we'd seen where a person could conceivably land a big drone or ultralight.

"Where exactly are we?" I asked Simon as she crouched to test the remains of the fire.

"Northern edge of the county is a straight line about thirty miles long," she said. "East-west, we're about halfway along it. Maybe a mile from the line, maybe a little less." Rising, she stepped over to the ATV tracks. "And these head straight north. They may be jogging back and forth across the line on purpose."

Devers grunted. "My jurisdiction crosses the line, even if yours doesn't. Let's go finish this."

The fresh ATV tracks were easy to make out: two dark lines of disturbed earth stretching into the distance. The terrain flattened, allowing us to make better time as we followed them, although we still kept it slow for Devers's leg and to avoid creating too much noise in the fallen leaves. After one particularly loud crunch, Devers paused and winced.

"One of the reasons these guys like it out here," Simon said.

After fifteen minutes of walking, the ground began gently tilting upward again. Not long after, Simon's head jerked to one side as if she'd heard something. She raised her hand in a stop signal and stepped behind the nearest tree.

Devers and I followed suit. We stayed there a long moment, frozen in place. The only movement I made was to pull out the earpiece. I suspected things were going to get more intense, not less.

When Simon finally motioned that we could move again, she pointed in a direction perpendicular to the ATV tracks. We began taking turns, leapfrogging from one patch of cover to the next. As we approached the peak of the rise, Simon dropped to her belly and began crawling forward.

I helped Devers ease himself down to the ground before joining him. Both of us inched ahead into positions on either side of the sheriff. I had to use a kind of sidestroke motion, pulling ahead with my right arm while keeping my left tucked against in my side, both to drag the drone gun and battery along and to minimize the pain in my ribs. Although the leaf litter was thick here, we moved slowly enough that the rustling sounded like nothing more than the rummaging squirrels we'd seen all along the way.

Once I reached the edge, I saw we were lying on the lip of another sunken cut in the ground. This depression, much deeper than the one in which the Green Way's camp had been erected, was surrounded on three sides by a curving, crescent-shaped stone formation that rose to at least twelve feet high at the peak. While the circular area inside was devoid of trees, the mouth of the crescent directly across from us was shielded by a thick stand of oaks broken only by a single dirt path. With just the one obvious entrance/exit, the crater formed a near-perfect hiding spot.

And someone had realized exactly that. Two fiberglass trailers—one white, one green, both draped in camouflage netting—had been pulled inside and parked parallel with their doors facing one another. From our position, we were looking at the hitch of the green trailer on the left and the rear window of the white trailer on the right. A single four-wheel ATV occupied the alley between them, along with some crates and barrels.

Several minutes ticked by silently. Enough time that I began to notice the features of the ground—roots, rocks—that were poking and prodding me in various places. The cold soil had also begun to suck body heat away; my thighs and chest, in particular, felt the chill. As much as I wanted to shift positions, I warned myself not to. The lone concession I made to the discomfort was to glance down toward my hip and check on the drone gun.

As I did, I noticed Simon's head moving. She motioned with her chin out past the trailers.

A skinny man in camouflage fatigues had stepped into view at the far end of the alley, his back to us. He carried what looked like a modified AR15 slung across his body in a patrol-carry position, the barrel angled down at the ground to his left. Although he kept shifting his weight, stepping to one side or the other impatiently, he remained focused on the tree line and the mouth of the dirt path in front of him.

At various points over the next twenty minutes, four other men emerged and journeyed back and forth between the two trailers. Each wore a smock, rubber gloves, and some kind of gas mask that hid his nose and mouth—I cataloged the quartet by their hair: Blondie, Brownie, Baldy, and Mohawk.

Finally, a sixth man appeared.

Like the guard at the far end of the camp, this guy wore camo, along with a baseball cap turned backward. After stepping down from the doorway of the white trailer, he removed his gas mask to reveal a thick black beard. When he started in our direction, my right hand slid back toward the Sig.

But the man wasn't looking up at us. His rifle remained casually slung over his shoulder. When he reached a spot below our position, he began rummaging around in his pockets until he produced a pack of Marlboro reds and a lighter.

He drew a butt out with his lips, lit it, then shoved both the lighter and pack back down into his pants. With the rock wall's shadow draped over him, the tip of the cigarette glowed bright yellow as he took a deep drag. We were so close, I could see detail in the ash. After holding his breath a moment, the man removed the cigarette from his mouth, tilted his head back, and blew a tight cloud of blue-gray smoke skyward.

The acrid smell wafted up to us, drowning out the sweeter scent of topsoil and tree sap.

While I couldn't see down past the man's face, when he fiddled with his pants again, the sound of his zipper going down was unmistakable. For several seconds afterward, we could hear the stream hitting the rocks and spilling down into the grass on the crater floor. Then his head bobbed, and we heard the zipper again.

The camouflaged man remained below us for another few minutes until the cigarette burned down to its filter. Finally, he dropped the butt, crushed it under his heel, and returned to the alley formed between the trailers.

I exhaled slightly. While I couldn't see Devers, I thought I heard Simon do the same.

And that's when my phone let out a loud ping announcing the arrival of a text message.

CHAPTER 19

When the ping gave away our position, my brain kicked into overdrive. Even before the adrenaline could surge, I started cycling through all kinds of thoughts simultaneously.

I felt ashamed—of all fucking things, the electrical engineer forgetting to silence his cell phone was about as dumb as you could possibly get. Even more, I felt guilty. Anything bad that befell Simon or Devers would unquestionably be my fault. A part of me wondered how I could have made such a basic mistake while another part pointed to the obvious answer: lack of sleep.

Each of these thoughts spawned several more of its own. Some were downright trivial: Who was calling me at this hour? What was the quickest way to deactivate the sound? Others were . . . weightier. I pictured Sarah's face, and Clarence's. I thought of my late girlfriend's parents, the hate and scorn they'd so rightly shown me for letting harm come to their little girl. I saw Shirley and the kids, none of whom knew the truth of how badly I'd damaged their lives.

With each multiplication of thoughts, the noise level inside my head rose. The main part of my brain recognized what was happening and did its best to shout the other parts down, to try to regain control. In a panic, I realized I'd pulled the earpiece too early. Attacks from my condition can render me completely helpless, functionless—not something I could afford right now. Not if I wanted to live. Not if I wanted to help dig Devers and Simon out of the hole I'd just created.

Finally, a jolt of adrenaline kicked in: I could feel my pulse pick up, my skin start to goose-pimple. That helped quiet all the voices at the periphery until a single thought remained: *Get through this.*

As I snapped back to attention, I saw that the camouflaged guard below us had spun around. He'd obviously heard the ping, and now in one motion, he had the rifle raised to fire.

The muzzle flashed, and a string of bullets sprayed the trees above our heads. Splinters and wood chips rained down onto our backs.

I drew faster than Simon or Devers: by the time their hands touched their pistol grips, I was already pulling the trigger. With no idea whether the guard was wearing body armor or not, I aimed for the little V-shaped notch above the top button of his shirt.

Two trigger pulls, two hits.

At that range, my .357 slugs knocked him back like he'd been struck by a speeding car. We wouldn't have to worry about him anymore.

The others, however, were a different story.

At the sound of the first shots, the tree-line guard ducked behind the far end of the green trailer. I couldn't see whether he was preparing to return fire or starting a move into the woods to our left.

A second later, rifle barrels poked through the rear window of the white trailer and the side windows of the green one and began spraying lead in our general direction. It was obvious they couldn't see us—the shots were too randomly spaced—but the volume and speed of the barrage was enough to pin us down.

We couldn't stay put, I knew that. We needed to move before we got outflanked.

My drone gun wasn't built to take any kind of pounding—even if I tried to cradle it as I ran, it would no doubt end up in pieces. The heavy battery would slow me even more. As much as I hated to leave the contraption behind, I laid it ever so gently in a pile of leaves. Then I rose into a sprinter's crouch.

When the gunfire from the white trailer finally paused—most likely reloading—I took off. At a dead sprint, I dashed to my right.

I can speed-reload the Sig in about three seconds. That's at the range, in perfect conditions. It had taken dozens of hours of practice to get that fast. But in a darkened trailer, worrying about return fire? I guessed the shooters would need as much as ten seconds to switch magazines. I should be safe taking five.

One one thousand.

While dodging trees, I tried to follow the curving lip of the berm as closely as I could.

Two one thousand.

A downed log lay ahead. I considered using it as a launching pad but hurdled it instead.

Three one thousand.

My ribs stung with each pump of my left arm. My lungs burned, already begging for oxygen.

Four one thousand.

I started scanning for a place to stop. Ten feet away—three steps— sat a thick maple, its trunk wide enough to shield my shoulders.

Five one thousand.

I dropped to my hip and let my momentum carry me the rest of the way. The slide was nothing my Little League coaches would have been proud of, nothing the Dodgers would be interested in signing. But it got me down and behind the tree.

Two panting breaths later, the gunfire started again.

The barrel that had protruded from the end of the white trailer now extended from one of its side windows. That reduced the barrage being thrown at Simon and Devers, and I allowed myself a slight smile of relief at the tiny bit of progress.

Now who's going to distract them for you, *genius?*

As if to emphasize the point, a string of bullets smacked against the maple's trunk. I ducked behind it, then took a quick peek to confirm my position: I'd gotten midway down the length of the white trailer. Another five-second sprint and I could reach the end—that'd get me a view of the far side of the compound, maybe a line of sight onto the second guard.

The trailer shooter began spraying longer, more randomly targeted bursts, giving me hope they weren't exactly sure where I was hiding. At the next pause, I took off again.

I could hear bullets whizzing and crackling against wood behind me—apparently, the shooter wasn't reloading. I cut my five-count short and slid again, this time behind an oak whose trunk split into a V. That let me squat behind it and peer through the gap.

Although I hadn't quite cleared the end of the white trailer, I was close enough to see into the space between it and the line of trees marking the edge of the camp. From my position to the lip of the berm was maybe five yards; the trailer sat about an equal distance away from that. The rock formation was lower here, too, only three feet off the crater floor.

One more good sprint would do it.

A burst of shots from the window forced my head back down—they had a bead on me. If I could just get down to the front corner of the trailer, the angle would work against the window shooter and let me check on the camouflaged guard. But I had at least thirty feet of open space to cover. After I crossed the lip of the berm, I wouldn't have any protection at all.

As I was trying to estimate when the window shooter might pause again, a burst of semiauto fire erupted from the trees back where I'd started. I poked my head up and saw the barrel facing me withdraw from the window.

That was all the break I needed.

I launched left behind the oak, crossed the distance to the lip in three quick steps, and leaped.

Knowing how exposed I was, the jump seemed to take forever—I hung in the air way longer than I wanted. But once I landed, I hit the ground running with the Sig up until I reached the corner of the white trailer and cleared around it. No sign of the other guard—he'd disappeared, presumably into the woods on the far side. I'd have to leave him to Devers and Simon. Continuing along the front side of the white trailer, I stepped over its hitch, then advanced to the next corner, where I flattened my back against the wall.

After two quick breaths, I spun out into the alley, crouching to reduce my profile.

My first look was across to the door of the green trailer. It was ajar, and I barely had time to register Mohawk standing there, aiming at me, when bullets from the woods tore into him from the side. Blood spattered against the siding, and I knew he was done.

Continuing to sidestep my way down the alley, I swung the barrel of the Sig back to the door of the white trailer. Blondie was stepping out through it and firing into the trees.

It must have taken him a moment to realize I was there. His head whipped around first, his eyes locking with mine. But, being right-handed, he had to bring the barrel of the AR-15 back across his body to aim at me.

That was a long way.

I fired twice. The first went low, intended as a center-of-mass shot. Instead, it clipped Blondie's arm and made him drop the gun. The second was a head shot that painted the door behind him with blood and brains as he slumped to the ground.

I finished crossing the alley and recovered at the corner of the green trailer. There, I paused a moment. Baldy and Brownie were still inside one of the two trailers, likely aiming at the doorway to take down whoever entered.

That gave me an idea.

Reaching around the corner, I grabbed the lip of one of the barrels in the alley and spun it back to me as quietly as I could. I set the steel drum below and to the side of the window on the front of the trailer, then climbed up onto it and pointed the Sig through the tinted glass.

There was no one inside.

Whatever furniture had adorned the interior had been removed in favor of tables that lined both sidewalls. I could see chemistry equipment, jars of chemicals, and powder they must have been bagging up. But no people.

As I hopped down from the drum, I glanced across the alley. Simon had now crept down from the trees and was straddling the same trailer hitch that I'd climbed over earlier.

I held up two fingers, then pointed at the white trailer next to her. She nodded.

With hand signals, I said I'd cover her as she advanced to the door.

Kneeling in the shadow cast by the corner of the green trailer, I trained the Sig on the windows across the alley, looking for any silhouettes, any motion. Simon crept forward, hunched beneath the windowsills, her pistol pointed at the doorway.

The fifteen-foot journey seemed to take about twenty minutes. But still I saw no movement in the glass panes above her. When she reached the door, it had closed but not latched. She was able to get a hand around it and whip it open while covering the doorway. She leaned inside, then called, "Clear!"

I relaxed slightly and took a step out into the alleyway. I whispered, "You two deal with the other guard?"

She nodded. "Devers nailed him trying to flank us."

"Did the other two duck out while I was around back?"

The look she shot me said she understood what I was thinking: Brownie, Baldy, or both could be hidden inside—in a closet, or someplace else we couldn't immediately see—waiting for the right moment to pop out and ambush us. We'd need to inspect the interiors inch by inch.

Simultaneously, both of us began moving back toward the open mouth of the crater, to the cover afforded by the ends of our respective trailers.

"Can I come down?" Devers called from the woods.

"Sure," I said loudly. "And bring my drone gun, would you?"

Devers appeared on Simon's side a minute later. She waved at him to hurry the final few feet across the clearing, then pulled his shoulder down so she could whisper into his ear. As she explained the situation, I saw recognition flash across his face. He gave me a steely look.

I silently signaled that I'd come over to them. I checked the windows of the white trailer—still clear—and when they indicated the way was safe, I sprinted across.

Whispering, we agreed that Devers would cover the green trailer from here while Simon entered and searched this one. I'd climb up on another steel drum and try to nail Brownie or Baldy from an angle they wouldn't expect.

Devers moved into position first; once he had eyes across the way, I edged out into the alley and climbed onto a barrel. While I was still hunched below the bottom of the window, Simon crept forward to the door and grabbed hold of it. Once all three of us had flashed each other "ready" signals, I started counting down on an outstretched hand that both of them could see.

I held one finger out.

I pulled my hand back; then I held two fingers out.

As I pulled my hand back to count three, a large boom echoed through the camp like a thunderclap, and something erupted behind me.

CHAPTER 20

The noise and force behind me pitched me off the steel drum.

When I hit the ground, all my weight collapsed on my left side, making it feel like I'd been stabbed in the chest by something sharp and hot. The pain was so intense, white light flashed in my eyes, blinding me momentarily.

Once the air left my lungs, I found it almost impossible to force any back in. Inhaling felt like a blade sliding slowly between my ribs.

As I tried to shake off the pain and blink away the afterimages, I managed to roll onto my back. A round opening, several inches wide, had been ripped into the side of the trailer next to where I'd stood.

Honestly, it looked like the biggest bullet hole I'd ever seen. And, although my brain was still foggy, I realized that was what it was: the mark left by some kind of giant slug—.50 caliber or something crazy like that.

But who'd shot it? And from where?

Inside the trailer? Outside?

I glanced around frantically for Simon and Devers. Finally, I found them—they'd retreated behind opposite ends of the white trailer. Their eyes were elevated, scanning the trees.

I grabbed another breath, which hurt slightly less than the last one. That was good—I couldn't stay here out in the open.

Glued to my side, trying to ease the pain, my left arm was mostly useless, so I rolled to my right, trying to use that arm to force myself up onto my feet. I rose and took one step before stumbling, dropping to my knees and then flat on my face.

That bit of clumsiness probably saved my life.

Behind me, another impact sounded. When I glanced back, another huge hole had been cut into the side of the white trailer, this one chest high. If I'd still been standing, the bullet would have ripped me in two.

From the angle of the shots, I realized that whoever was manning the .50 cal must be somewhere in the woods directly ahead, somewhere behind the green trailer, shooting over or around it. I started crawling forward, figuring the flimsy structure would still be the best cover I could get. Even if its fiberglass walls wouldn't block the huge rounds, at least they would keep the shooter from seeing me.

Although it felt like I advanced an inch at a time, I gradually managed to push and drag myself to the edge of the green structure. Despite the pain it caused in my side, I sat up and pressed my back against its side wall.

Both Simon and Devers were staring at me from across the way, wearing concerned looks. I nodded as best I could. Then I just sat for a moment, trying to get as much oxygen as possible, hoping the cool air would filter down into my lungs and suck away some of the heat searing my ribs.

I didn't get much time. Almost instantaneously, four more booms echoed around the camp. With successive cracks, new holes appeared in the side of the white trailer next to Devers, followed by a patch of earth in front of him exploding into the air.

On my right, Simon started shooting. I couldn't tell whether she'd actually seen something or was firing blind, but she gradually emptied a whole magazine over my head. Devers took the opportunity to lunge forward, sheltering himself behind the parked ATV.

Another .50-cal round struck the four-wheeler, popping its rear tire and carving its way into the chassis.

Energized slightly by a few breaths, I rolled to my right again, pressed myself up onto my knees, and then my feet. I staggered to the corner of the green trailer, then peeked around it with the Sig.

Boom. Another round struck the ATV behind me. But I still couldn't see a muzzle flash to aim at.

Boom.

Still nothing in the trees.

I let off a couple of shots to bait the sniper into showing himself.

Boom.

The ground erupted inches to my left, peppering my leg with dirt and gravel.

I retreated around the corner, pressing my back against the wall. Devers remained behind the ATV, but Simon had advanced to the opposite end of the green trailer, shielding me. We exchanged confused looks, then turned back to the woods, aiming into the trees.

None of us expected what happened next.

Another boom thundered through the camp, and the ATV was struck by another round. This one hit the headlight, ripping through the handlebars and into the front suspension.

From that angle, the bullet could only have come from the center of the stone ledge ringing the camp—near our original position. But it had landed only a handful of seconds after the previous shot. There was no way someone could run from my twelve o'clock to my nine o'clock carrying a .50-cal weapon, reestablish themselves, and fire.

Were there *two* snipers?

"Devers, get out of there!"

He was moving before I finished yelling—scrambling to his left, crouching behind the rear bumper of the ATV. As he reached it, the earth where he'd been sitting erupted.

Suddenly I realized how exposed Simon and I both were: standing along the side walls of the two trailers, the second sniper likely had a clean shot down the alley at both of us.

I ducked and covered behind some drums and crates—I wasn't confident they'd block a direct hit, but I hoped staying low and out of sight would be enough for the moment.

From my new position, I could still see across the alley to Devers, but I had no idea where Simon had gone. No time to dwell on that— my thinking had switched from how to outflank a single concealed shooter to how the three of us might possibly escape being hopelessly pinned down by two of them.

The dirt path that the original guard had been monitoring seemed to be the only way out. To reach it, though, meant a long run across wide-open terrain. The new sniper, the one facing the ATV head-on, would be looking directly at our backs, while the original shooter would have clear profile shots.

I tried to think about distractions, cover, camouflage—anything that might get us to safety. But I didn't see any obvious way for us to avoid getting cut down.

I checked Devers, wondering what he was thinking. Before I could attract his attention, another boom sliced through the air.

This time the shell ripped into the trailer wall above my head.

CHAPTER 21

When I realized where the latest shell had struck, I was totally confused.

Not only was my hearing fucked-up—the only sound was a loud whine in my ears—but the firing angles didn't make any sense. There couldn't possibly be *three* different snipers out there trying to kill us. Yet there was no way one or even two gunmen could have maneuvered to shoot from yet another cardinal direction on the compass.

What was I missing? I'd run through these woods—it wasn't easy. The trees were dense, the ground uneven, you never knew what lurked beneath the leaves. No human could cover so much ground so fast. We weren't fighting Superman here, for chrissake—it wasn't like they could fly.

Fly.

The word tickled my brain for some reason, and suddenly I realized I'd been thinking about all this completely wrong.

Gathering myself up onto my feet, I sprinted across the alley to the white trailer. Along the way, I dashed past Devers, who was nervously anticipating the next shot.

A .50-cal round ripped the ground to my left, but with only a couple of yards remaining, I ignored it. Instead, I dived headfirst into the dirt at the base of the trailer, trying my best to land on my right side. I slid forward several feet and ground to a stop next to what I needed: the drone gun.

Of course, now that I wanted to use the damned thing, I saw how fragile and rudimentary my design really was. The lawn-mower battery powering the system was the heaviest part; even though I'd specifically bought the smallest one they had, it was a dense plastic brick, taller and thinner than a car battery. I'd rigged it by cables to the PCB board, while another thinner set of wires connected the board to the antenna. Clutching the battery's handle in one hand and the antenna in the other, I let the board dangle precariously in between.

Fragile or not, I prayed it would work. As I flipped the system on and started projecting, I scanned the sky for any flying target I could see.

No matter where I looked, though, I couldn't spot any kind of drone or other aircraft. No glints in the sun, no shadows or silhouettes. My ears still weren't working properly, but it wasn't like I'd heard engine noise before .50-caliber gunfire began.

With nothing to lose, I raised the antenna at a forty-five-degree angle and began sweeping slow circles around the sky, hoping I'd hit something.

A telltale boom sounded—I could feel it more than hear it—and a bullet careened into the white trailer behind me, ripping through the fiberglass. I whipped around and pointed the antenna in the direction from which the shot must have come. I still didn't see anything. What was the effective range of a .50 cal? I didn't know off the top of my head, but visibility was good enough that if the drone could see us, we ought to be able to see it.

Another boom, and this time the ATV took another hit, the handlebars and instrument panel twisting beyond recognition.

I wheeled around again, holding the antenna in front of me. With nothing to see, I waved it in a figure eight, hoping I might hit whatever was out there.

The shots started coming in quicker succession now, shattering the air with a heavy drumbeat that resonated in my chest: boom, boom,

boom. Bullets started walking across the ground in my direction, kicking up dirt and gravel and making a bigger vibration through the soles of my boots. As the impacts drew closer and closer, I stayed put, pointing the antenna in the only direction that made sense. But the radio gun seemed to have no effect at all.

After a round struck two feet in front of me, something yanked me backward. For an instant, I thought it was the force of the shell—then I felt the tension on my jacket collar. As I stumbled backward, I spun to find Devers pulling me away.

"C'mon!"

A glance back over my shoulder showed the bullets were continuing to follow us, and I decided not to argue.

Turning ahead, I saw Simon standing at the green trailer door. She was holding it open, her free arm waving frantically at us to hurry. I could feel the concussions drawing closer behind us, the dirt pelting our backs as the slugs ripped the earth.

With maybe ten yards to cover, I knew I could run faster than Devers on his bad leg. But not when weighed down by the lawn-mower battery. Ripping the leads away, I dropped the heavy block, shoved the electronics into his hands, and then wrapped my right arm around his waist. I seized hold of his belt and lifted him the best I could. Four strides got us close enough to the door that I could hurl him forward.

The throw was supremely awkward, but it gave Devers just enough forward momentum that he landed in front of the door on his good leg and sprang inside.

I piled in after him, landing squarely on top of him in a heap. Before I could roll off, something heavy fell on top of me. With my face buried between Devers's shoulder blades, my last thought was that the extra weight was from Simon.

From the outside and above, the green trailer draped in camouflage netting tended to disappear against the forest floor below it. But the stream of bullets peppering its side were already locked on target. They walked up the sidewall of the trailer in rapid succession, each leaving a fist-size hole in the fiberglass. Then the angle of the bullets changed, striking the rear of the trailer before progressing onto the opposite side. After three dozen slugs had peppered the small structure, puffs of black smoke began to leak out of the holes and drift skyward.

The bullets continued following the perimeter of the trailer, eventually reaching its nose, where two small propane tanks had been installed on either side of the vehicle's hitch bar. The .50cal shells closed in until one of the tanks exploded.

The force of the first propane explosion rocked the trailer violently. In addition, pieces of the first tank ruptured the hull of the second, whose contents immediately detonated like a bomb. This blow crumpled the front of the green trailer inward.

Flaming embers from the propane explosion stuck to the camouflage netting that adorned the trailer, even as bullets continued to riddle its hull. The fiery yellow tongues grew longer, licking their way up the sides of the structure and onto its roof. These flames added to the black cloud now pouring from every opening.

Smaller explosions could be heard inside the trailer, along with breaking glass. Jars of chemicals spilled their contents and ignited. The burning liquids raised the temperature inside, almost instantly reaching the flash point for the artificial paneling on the walls, the shelving, everything.

The blaze inside the trailer now seemed desperate to break free. Jagged daggers of flame smashed through the windows, their points jabbing skyward. These continued to heat the fiberglass walls until they, too, began to combust and melt.

Ravaged by bullet holes, the blackened walls provided little structural support, and the two-thousand-degree temperature quickly claimed whatever remained. One sidewall yielded first, collapsing under the weight of *the roof. The other sidewall lasted only seconds longer before it succumbed to the same fate.*

At this point, the shooting ceased.

As the fire raged on, smoke billowed above the wreckage, coalescing into a black column that rose high into the sky. Driving the smoke upward were waves of heat that disturbed the air like mirages on a desert highway.

Fifty feet off the ground and a safe distance from the blaze, a similar rippling effect could be seen. Like the fire, it distorted the image of the scenery behind it. Indeed, much like the heat, it gave the impression of oscillating waves rippling outward from a central point.

But this was no thermal illusion: when the optical disturbance ceased, a large quadcopter drone replaced it, hovering in midair for a moment, its guns and cameras all pointed at the smoldering site. Then, its rotors tilted. The machine began a long, slow turn around the blaze.

The drone circled the scene three times, climbing and descending slightly, examining the debris from every angle. Once its third pass was complete, the rotors leveled off and accelerated with a noticeable whir. With the additional lift they provided, the drone rose two hundred feet above the scene.

At that point, the air around the machine began to ripple once again. The drone gradually disappeared behind the refractive distortion, until nothing remained but the sound of its rotors.

Finally, those, too, trailed off, until the only noise in the clearing came from the crackling wreckage on the ground.

CHAPTER 22

"What the bloody *hell* was that?" Devers asked. "How'd it just . . . vanish?"

Although we were fifty yards from the camp, tucked into the tree line, he kept his voice to a tense whisper. Only his head and neck protruded from the tunnel entrance, his hair and skin smeared with a grimy mix of sweat and sandy-colored soil; the blood-stained bandage on his forehead was filthy.

Having pulled myself out of the earthen hole just ahead of Devers, I was now sprawled across the ground next to him on my back, propped up on my elbows. When I glanced down over myself, I realized I was in equally bad shape, or worse. Although my hearing had mostly returned—the ringing had softened to a low hum—that was about the only good news. My left side still ached from falling on my broken ribs, and every breath was a painful effort. It also seemed that I'd picked up some other injuries in the firefight: my back and neck muscles felt oddly stiff; I touched a hot, throbbing spot on my head and found blood trickling from it.

Of course, none of that mattered after what we'd just witnessed. Unlike Devers, I had a pretty good guess how the drone had pulled off its disappearing act before flying away. And that was why I knew we needed to warn Cooke about it immediately.

I pulled out my phone and, ignoring everything else, dialed her number. To my surprise, though, it rang through without an answer. I didn't leave a voice mail. Instead, I jammed the phone back down into my pocket and retrieved my earpiece. With my pulse slowing and the rest of my senses starting to dull, when I popped it back in, the voice on the audio player made a peppy contrast to my pain and fatigue.

At that moment, Simon appeared in the trees to our left. "No sign of 'em," she said.

When we'd been trapped inside the green trailer, Simon had been the one who'd noticed the trapdoor: a narrow hatch tucked beneath one of the shelves. She'd clambered off me and down through it just as the shooting had started; Devers and I had followed as quickly as we could. It had led to a darkened tunnel that dropped three or four feet straight down before bending toward the forest. Pitch black inside, filled with thick air smelling of dank earth, the passage had felt extremely claustrophobic as I'd wriggled my way through it. The engineer in me kept doing calculations of how much the earth above us must weigh and wondering whether they'd reinforced the walls sufficiently. By the time I'd reached the end of the tunnel, Simon had disappeared, presumably chasing Brownie and Baldy.

"Did you . . . ," Devers began. "Did you see?"

Simon shook her head again. "See what?"

His expression remained frozen as he blinked several times. "The drone, it just—"

"Wait," she said, "that was a drone? Like the one that shot me and Chu?"

"Different model—a quadcopter," I said.

Devers continued. "It just . . . evaporated. Into thin air."

"Not really." I slowly rose to my feet.

He scowled at me. "We just watched it."

"No," I said. "It cloaked itself."

Simon cocked her head. "Cloaked?"

"You mean, like in *Star Trek* or something?" Devers clearly thought I was joking.

"That's pretty much exactly what I mean."

He winced. "Oh, c'mon, that's—"

"Science fiction?" I asked. "It's not. Researchers have been working on cloaks for the military for a long time."

"How would something like that even work?" Simon asked.

"You know the stealth planes the military uses? The ones that can't be seen on radar?"

She nodded.

"Radar systems shoot out a wave of energy, then listen for the reflection when that energy bounces off something. Stealth planes are shaped in certain ways and built out of special materials so that they don't reflect the radar waves back to the operator."

"Okay."

"Light's a wave, too," I said. "We see an object when our eyes receive light that's reflected off it. If you can absorb the light waves, or bend them so they reflect in a different direction, you can make something invisible."

"How hard is that to do?" Simon asked.

"Really, really hard. I've read about some breakthroughs they've made here and there, but I've never heard of a fully operational cloak before. Whoever built that drone must have access to some truly cutting-edge tech."

"The Green Way," Devers said. "They got the cash, and they're plugged into all the techie people through Chu."

"But he and Hartley are both stuck in the hospital," Simon said.

"Doesn't mean it wasn't someone else in their group," he said.

"Why would the Green Way want to attack a drug lab hidden out in the middle of nowhere?" Simon asked. "How would they even know about it? And why wait until we're here?"

"You're thinking it was that Charleston crew?" Devers said. "The one Cooke told us about?"

"They've got a lot more reason to take out the Clancys, that's for sure." She turned to me. "What do you think?"

"I think that drone was watching us for a lot longer than we realized. And we need to warn Melissa. The drone we took down yesterday was bad enough. But that thing . . ."

"Could've taken down an airplane," Simon said.

"Exactly." The list of targets an invisible gunship could attack washed over me, giving me chills. "I just tried her, but she didn't answer. We can keep calling on the way back."

I'd only taken two steps in the direction of the SUV when Simon said, "Hey, Walker, you're bleeding."

"I know," I said, tapping the spot on my head. "It's just a scratch."

"No, not that." Simon grabbed my shoulder and stopped me. "Back here."

I glanced back over my shoulder the best I could and saw her fiddling with holes in my jacket.

"Take this off," she said.

As I tried to remove my arms from the sleeves, my neck and trap muscles objected. In addition to their stiffness, they ached; of course, so did just about everything else. After a minute, I managed to twist my way out of the coat. Immediately, I looked to Simon's face, trying to read her expression about what was going on back there. "What is it?"

"You got hit," she said flatly.

Craning my neck, all I could see was a dark stain on my shirt. "A bullet? I didn't feel anything." I couldn't imagine taking one of those .50-caliber shells without noticing. Still, Devers's expression concerned me.

"Looks like something else," he said. "We ought to hurry back and get you to the doctor."

"Fine," I said. "We can call Cooke from the car."

The hike out from the trailer camp was draining, to say the least. But with Devers carrying the remnants of the drone gun and both of them stealing glances at me every few steps, I didn't want to say how tired I felt. I just kept pushing one foot out in front of the other. When we finally reached the SUV, though, I found that my shoulders had tightened up even more.

"Hey, Walker," Simon said, "maybe you wanna lie down on your stomach, to avoid pressing on your back."

"Huh?"

"Heather's right, man," Devers said. "You should lie down."

I didn't really understand the need—wasn't putting pressure on a bleeding wound a good thing? But I felt too tired to argue. I curled myself onto my side as best I could in the back seat.

Simon climbed behind the wheel, and as she eased us back out toward the road, Devers dialed Cooke on his own cell and put the call on speaker.

Cooke answered without any kind of greeting. "Sorry, I saw Seth called. I've been on the phone nonstop since I left Quantico, but I'm almost to Morgantown." There was a hum in the background and a slight echo as she spoke.

"Means you've got about an hour and a half left," Simon said.

"Hartley's lawyers said they wouldn't leave DC until two at the earliest," Cooke said. "That should give us at least a couple of hours together before they arrive."

With some effort, I managed to lift my head enough to check the dashboard clock. Amazingly, despite all that had happened, it wasn't quite noon.

"Listen, Melissa. We've got a new problem."

"What now?"

I let Devers provide most of the details.

"Thank God you're all alive. But you don't sound right, Seth. Are you okay?"

"Yeah. We're heading to the hospital, but I'm a little dinged up. The important thing is the cloak—"

"What does that even mean?" Cooke asked.

"It's super-new tech," I said with some effort. Talking loudly enough for the speakerphone was tough. Deep breaths hurt a lot more than shallow ones. I'd have to speak in small chunks. "Until today, I didn't know anyone . . . could actually pull it off."

"Even if you can't see it with your eyes, would it still show up on radar?" Cooke asked.

"Airport radar? Probably not," I said. "More finely tuned systems? Maybe."

"So I go back to the question: Do we know who's doing this? Or why?"

Simon answered. "I don't think we know any more than we did before going out there."

"Oh yes," I said. "We do." At least the pain of speaking helped me fight against the fuzziness that was starting to creep over things.

"What's that, Seth?" Cooke asked.

"The fracking-pad drone. That was military grade. This thing was . . . a whole other level of tech. You don't let just . . . anybody drive those things."

"You've got Hartley in custody," Cooke said.

"Exactly. And of the . . . handful of people . . . qualified to fly these things . . . there's only one other nearby."

"You mean Wesley Hughes?" Devers asked.

"Yep."

"Wes wouldn't be helping drug dealers," Simon said. "He's had a rough time, sure, but—"

"Did you ever think . . . he'd hold a gun on you?" I asked. "Or that he'd . . . booby-trap his family's farm?"

"What are you saying?"

"Just that Wesley . . . may not be . . . the same guy you remember."

"But we all saw Hughes," Devers said. "He's not exactly living at the Ritz. You really think he's flying multimillion-dollar drones when he ain't eating?"

"Good question," I said. "I hope I'm wrong. But I think we . . . at least need to . . . interview him again."

Although Cooke spoke next, I couldn't quite make out the words. It wasn't a return of the ringing in my ears; I was simply too tired. I tried to keep my eyelids open, but they kept sliding shut on their own.

Finally, they stayed that way, and the darkness took over.

CHAPTER 23

I woke with a start.

Although I was lying facedown, I could tell I wasn't in the car anymore. Whatever was underneath me now was more comfortable and less cramped than the SUV's back seat. Everything was quieter. Brighter.

And it felt like someone was stabbing me in the shoulder.

I flinched—turning my head to the side, trying to rise. A hand pressed gently against my back, and a woman's voice I didn't recognize said, "You don't want to be moving too much right now."

"Who—"

"It's okay, Seth."

That second voice, I knew. "Melissa? Where—"

Cooke stepped into my vision. Her arms were crossed against her chest, making her look even more serious than usual, but her face cracked into a slight smile. "Why is it every time you and I work together, I end up visiting you in the hospital?"

I grunted. "Shouldn't I be asking you that question?"

I'd just gotten the words out when whoever was working behind me did something else. Suddenly, my left trapezius muscle burned so hot that I couldn't help squeezing one eye closed. After a quick breath, I asked, "What's going on back there?"

I heard a metallic clunk, followed by wheels squeaking as they rolled. A woman's face slid into view, eclipsing Cooke behind her.

"I'm Dr. Vernon." Her glasses had special lenses mounted on them that made her look more like a jeweler than a doctor. She flipped those up to reveal warm brown eyes.

"The sheriff told me about all the excitement you had this morning," she said. "Some jagged pieces of fiberglass hit your back and wedged themselves in. I've been numbing you up as I go, which may be why you're feeling a little uncomfortable. When I'm done getting everything out, you're going to need some stitches."

I glanced down at my left arm, which dangled off the side of the bed, pointing down at the floor. Through the fog of waking up, I'd noticed something weird about it—now I saw a plastic tube protruding from my elbow. "And that?"

Laugh lines crinkled at the corners of the doctor's eyes. "If you were a truck, my husband would say you were about two quarts low. Blood loss is why you passed out on the way in. That IV will fill you back up."

I gave her a nod.

"By the way . . ." Vernon extended her left arm and slid back the baggy sleeve of her white coat. Just above the wrist, her forearm was decorated with a small tattoo of the snakes-and-staff medical symbol. "You've got some beautiful art back here. I'm going to do my best not to muck it up with these stitches." Then she gave me a wink and moved out of my line of sight.

Although I hadn't realized it before, I now noticed my shirt was off. I suddenly felt cold, the skin on my arms puckering up into goose bumps.

Cooke leaned in, as if she could tell I was uncomfortable. "Do you want me to leave?"

I thought a moment. "Nah. You've seen me a lot worse than this." And that was true—Cooke's one of the few people who's seen me after an attack of my neuro condition. That memory caused me to turn my attention to the audiobook playing in my ear. "Did you tell them about the earpiece?"

She nodded. "Learned my lesson the last time."

The anesthetic must have been taking hold. As Vernon did something to my back, it didn't hurt; this time it felt more like pressure, as if she were rubbing a kink out of the muscle.

"How long was I out?"

"It's almost four."

"So we ran out of time?"

Cooke shook her head. "I gave a quick interview to the press. I was able to say we'd already arrested suspects for the deaths of the deputies, so that bought us some more leeway. At least till tomorrow morning. Other than that, the Green Way's lawyers are still en route, so I haven't been able to question Hartley or Chu yet. I've got evidence teams out working the scenes of all the shoot-outs you've managed to have in the last forty-eight hours."

Even I had to crack a smile at that one.

"I told Simon and Devers to get some rest while you were unconscious. And I had DOD pull Wesley Hughes's service records."

"Anything helpful?"

Her eyes rolled. "Not much more than we already knew. Enlisted out of high school, became a drone-sensor operator. While he was stationed at Creech Air Force Base in Nevada, he earned his college degree on the side so he could get commissioned and fly."

"Was he a good pilot?"

Vernon must have started stitching—I felt my skin getting tugged in one direction, but thankfully no pain.

"By all accounts, yes. If anything, maybe too good—he seemed to enjoy flying more than politics. Hughes turned down a promotion at one point that would have cycled him back to a DC desk job.

Then he got passed over on the next review cycle, and that's when he got out."

"Simon said people around town thought Hughes might be suffering from PTSD. Any sign of that in his records?"

Cooke cocked her head, the muscles in her face tensing.

"What does that look mean?"

"His psych exams weren't significantly different than most other drone pilots'."

"So . . . ?"

"So these guys are under tremendous stress. They're flying remotely, so they're expected to work crazy hours. They're subjected to an intense amount of stimuli—the sensors on these drones are so good, they've actually had to scale back the amount of information fed to the flight crews to avoid overwhelming them. They'll sit and watch the same people day after day, week after week. And then . . ."

"Then, what?"

"They kill them. A lot of them, Seth. I mean, a *lot*. Guess how many kills Hughes was credited with?"

If it weren't for Vernon working on my back, I'd have shrugged. "No idea. Twenty?"

She stared at me.

I thought of the little symbols they used to paint on the sides of fighter planes when a pilot shot enemies down. "Fifty?"

"Eighteen hundred and fifty-seven."

"Wait, what?"

Her mouth drew into a grim line as she nodded. "Almost nineteen hundred people."

My eyes drifted away from Cooke's face as I remembered what Hughes himself had said: "Drones kill. That's all they do, just watch and kill."

Before this case, I'd shot a few people. When I was protecting Emma, we'd faced a small army of gun-toting soldiers; the Berkeley case, too, had ended in a shoot-out. I didn't lose much sleep over either of those, and sometimes I wondered why. Usually, I told myself it was because I shot bad guys. And that was true—in every case, they'd hurt me or someone else before I pulled the trigger.

Deeper down, though, I had enough other demons to give me nightmares. While things had improved, not a week went by without the ghosts of Clarence or Sarah visiting me at least once in my sleep. Reminding me of the blood on my hands.

I tried to imagine that times a thousand.

Pilots like Hughes saw their targets depicted as images on a screen. If they used night vision or infrared, the targets probably wouldn't even look human. When you shot a remote target like that, or blew it up, did you feel . . . anything?

A cold sensation prickled its way across my skin, and this time it wasn't from the hospital air-conditioning.

A hand patted my shoulder, snapping me back out of my thoughts. I turned my head the best I could and saw Vernon standing next to the bed.

"I'm done stitching you," she said, taking a step toward the IV stand. "Now, let's check your oil gauge." After a moment, she bent at the waist so that our faces were just inches apart. "I'm not stupid enough to think you're actually going to stay in bed and rest, Mr. Walker. And we've pushed enough fluids into you that you're probably good enough to go. But I'll warn you: If you're going to be active, be careful. It's pretty easy to rip those stitches out, and then you'll be right back here to see me again."

I thanked Dr. Vernon for her help, and she left the room.

Cooke watched the door close, then turned back to me. "Now that she's gone, I can ask: Is Simon okay? I mean, can we trust her if we're going after Hughes?"

I considered the question as I slowly rolled over onto my back. "I think so."

"When you raised Hughes as a suspect on our call, she pushed back pretty hard."

"Yeah, she went to high school with him. You can tell she cares about him. But when we went to his property the first time, she didn't hesitate to stand up to him."

"Then once you're dressed, we can wake her and Mitchell. I want to go grab Hughes for questioning as soon as possible."

Although I mentioned the drone gun to Cooke, when she heard it hadn't worked at the drug camp and would need fixing, she decided that time was too precious. She rode with us from the hospital in the SUV; before we left, she called one of her evidence teams and told the Special Agents to meet us at Hughes's property for extra manpower. Funny thing: the farm's address was remote enough, GPS didn't recognize the location. Cooke had to hand her cell phone to Simon so she could narrate directions to the other agents, old-school/analog-style.

We made two stops before heading out of town on Route 7. First, at the motel, Devers and I reloaded our weapons and grabbed extra magazines. He emerged from his room wearing a bulletproof vest over his clothes. I didn't have one of those, but I'd at least traded out my latest scrub top—the doctors had commandeered my shredded jacket and shirt, both blood soaked—for a flannel shirt and fleece jacket that helped take the edge off the cold.

Next, we hit the police station. Simon ducked inside alone and emerged a few minutes later. She'd clearly bulked up with a vest of her own beneath her satin jacket. She also carried another vest slung over one arm and a shotgun tucked beneath the other. The gun went into the trunk. While she didn't make eye contact, she handed me the vest.

"This belonged to Matthews," she said quietly. "He was about your size."

The sun that warmed the woods in the morning had now disappeared. Not only was dusk approaching, but the clouds had coalesced into a heavy gray blanket draped across the hilltops. Halfway to Hughes's farm, Simon had to switch on the wipers—the dots striking the windows began as rain, but the drops gradually grew larger, with solid, crystalline centers that melted upon contact with the glass.

Despite the weather, Simon leaned heavily on the gas until we reached Hundred. There, she pulled the SUV through the switchbacks and up Hughes's narrow road. A white van with Pennsylvania plates and a Pittsburgh Penguins sticker in the back window sat idling a hundred yards short of Hughes's rusted gate.

Cooke jumped out of our truck before Simon could put the SUV in park. She stalked to the passenger side of the van and said a few words at the window. Exhaust stopped streaming from the van's tailpipe, and its doors flew opened, allowing four men and one woman to spill out, all in distinctive blue FBI coats with yellow lettering on the back.

Moving deliberately, Simon silenced the SUV's engine, slid down from the driver's seat, and circled around to the trunk. After retrieving the shotgun for herself and a couple of flashlights, she whistled and waved Cooke and her team back toward us.

"Wesley's got the driveway booby-trapped and lined with cameras," Simon said as the agents approached. "You don't wanna go near that gate."

"You know a different way in?" Cooke asked.

Simon's eyebrows rose as a small grin spread across her face. "Let's just say, when Wesley and I were kids, sometimes we wanted to visit without our parents knowing. I doubt he'll have the *whole* place rigged—c'mon." She spun on her heel and started downhill, retracing the road back the way we'd come.

With daylight gone, the temperature had plummeted. My scalp seemed to tighten against the cold air, and I could feel the sting of each bit of sleet as it hit my skin. Even as I drew the collar of the fleece up and plunged my hands into my pockets, I had to admit the chill added a certain beauty to the scenery. Our breaths emerged as clouds of tiny twinkling crystals, while the ground and trees were now covered by a fine, silvery sheen. Plus, the precipitation had killed off the sulfur smell we'd noticed on our first visit; the air now smelled crisp and clean.

We walked maybe a quarter mile downhill—far enough that Cooke was shooting Devers and me questioning looks—until Simon crossed abruptly over to the fence. The wires here wrapped around a tree whose trunk forked about five feet off the ground. Because of that, the top wire had been strung extra high, leaving a large space between it and the middle wire. Simon stepped through the gap, then waited until we'd all joined her inside before lighting her flashlight and heading into the trees.

Generally speaking, our course curved slightly back to our left, following a faint trail that gradually wound uphill. Rocky outcroppings had forced their way up through the soil at various points, forming walls or chutes that we had to navigate. Simon continued cautiously, leading the way while our pack fanned out in a rough triangle behind her.

The leaves carpeting the ground here had lost their color and had begun the slow decay into mulch. That, together with the moisture from the storm, helped dampen the sound of our footsteps. And it was a good thing: although we were all on alert, the dense foliage made it impossible to see far ahead, even with the flashlights' help. No matter which direction you looked, the tree trunks blended together into a hazy mass of gray.

We trekked cross-country for ten uneventful minutes. Although Simon stopped us on several occasions with hand signals, we resumed moving each time after a short pause. The injections in my back had mostly worn off now, leaving me with a stiff soreness in addition to the jabbing pain in my side. Darkness continued to fill the gaps around us, making it harder and harder to see the others in our party. Still, everyone stepped lightly, and no one said a word.

As the moments continued to tick by, it seemed we might continue hiking into the darkness forever.

That was, until one of Cooke's agents stepped somewhere he shouldn't have, and a brilliant-red fireball erupted to our right.

CHAPTER 24

When the explosion triggered, I turned toward it.

Bad move.

The light and heat and force all hit me squarely in the face. Even from a dozen yards away, the blast was powerful enough to knock me on my ass. In an instant, the bare skin on my cheeks, nose, and forehead went from feeling nearly frozen to flash fried. The initial flare was so bright, it blinded me, my eyes seeing nothing but floating, white afterimages.

Although every instinct screamed at me to get the hell out of there, my brain overruled them. Rushing off and triggering another booby trap was exactly what Hughes would want us to do. We needed to think our way through this mess.

"Who's hurt? Who got hit?"

Cooke's voice came from my left, toward the front of our formation. I heard rustling around me.

"Don't move!" Now that our noise discipline had been broken, I screamed the warning. "Everyone, stay put!"

There was a chance, I knew, that Hughes was out in the darkened woods somewhere, lining us up with an infrared sniper scope like the one he'd used that first day. But it seemed wiser to risk the chance of him picking us off one by one than all of us dying simultaneously in another explosion.

I cupped my hands over my eyes, blinking as rapidly as I could and trying to regain at least a little bit of my sight. When the ghostly halos started to fade, I glanced around.

The male agent who'd stood farthest to our right had completely disappeared, while the two agents closest to him writhed on the ground. Everyone else seemed intact. Devers, Simon, and the other agents from the team had drawn their weapons and now faced outward to guard our position.

Thankful for the cover, I turned back toward the source of the explosion. Although I hadn't noticed it before, I could see now that we'd been nearing a jagged rock outcropping on that side—the agent had moved to circle around the rock when he'd triggered the booby trap. One medium-size tree near where he'd stood had been reduced to a burning stump, while others surrounding it had bent or broken outward. A black blast mark had been etched on the rock.

Hughes must have rigged a trip wire to the tree rather than using some kind of land mine.

"Seth, my people are hurt!"

I glanced over and found Cooke on all fours, every muscle in her face taut, her eyes glinting in the flickering firelight.

"I can't just sit here," she said in a hiss. "I have to get to them!"

She was right, of course. The question was, how to do that without blowing all of us up. As I shifted positions, tension built on the cord attached to my earpiece, forcing the hard plastic against the inside of my ear in a painful way. I realized I could pull it out—I didn't need the audio distraction with my heart pounding like a jackhammer.

But as I did, an idea struck me.

"Heather," I said, focusing my eyes past Cooke on Simon, who remained at the front of the formation. "Pass me your shotgun, will you?"

The sheriff looked confused, but she placed the gun on the ground and slid it back to Cooke, who relayed it to me. "What's that for?" she asked.

"Just give me a second." I popped the earpiece out of my ear, unplugged it from the audio player in my pants pocket, and drew the cord out the neck of my fleece. As quickly as I could, I tied the plug end of the cord around the barrel of the shotgun. Then I rose to my knees and pointed the gun out in front of me like a fishing pole with a short line.

Sure enough, the earpiece functioned as a small weight, giving the cord some tension as it dangled toward the ground. It wouldn't be any help against pressure-pad triggers, but at least I could spot any trip wires.

I glanced over at Cooke. "Get right behind me. Shine a light in front."

Crouching so that the earpiece hung just above the ground, I started toward the injured agents. As I inched forward, my eyes locked on the cord; it seemed to take an hour to cross the short distance. My pulse continued pounding the whole way; despite the temperature, I was now openly sweating. Through it all, though, I knew I needed to keep the end of the shotgun steady—I locked my elbows in against my sides to help brace against any shakes.

When we finally reached the downed pair, we saw the extent of the damage. The side of one agent's face was badly burned, while another had an inch-thick branch protruding from his side, just above his waist.

Cooke looked up at me after quickly inspecting the wounds. "These are too serious—they've got to be evac'd."

I nodded.

"I'll radio an ambulance," Simon said. "Have it meet them out at the road."

Cooke assigned the two remaining agents from the evidence team to carry the one who'd been impaled. Together with the burned agent, they set off back the way we'd come.

So much for the extra manpower. And the light—we'd brought three flashlights into the woods, but after letting the ERTU team take two, we were now down to one torch for the four of us.

Once we were alone, Cooke, Devers, Simon, and I huddled together against the outcropping. "How much farther?" Cooke asked.

"Not much," Simon said. "Another couple hundred yards, over the next ridge."

"The way Hughes set that trap," I said, "it looks like he was expecting people to pass this way, close to the rocks. Does that make any sense to you?"

Simon blinked twice. "After the next clearing, there's a narrow chute between the rocks. That's the last thing before you get to the barn and house."

"Driving folks to a choke point," Devers said. "Ambush 101."

"Is there any way of getting from here to the buildings without going through that little pass?" Cooke asked.

Simon thought a moment, then nodded. "The way I'm thinking, though, the last bit is gonna be really hard. It's steep, and with this"—she held open her palm, catching one of the wet snowflakes that were falling—"it'll be extra slick." She shot a concerned look at Devers.

"Slick beats the hell out of dead," he said flatly. "I can make it."

Cooke and I nodded our approval, and then we set off.

Armed with the shotgun/earpiece trip-wire detector, I took the point position. Simon followed behind me, hand on my shoulder, providing light and giving me directions. With his gimpy leg, Devers trailed Simon, while Cooke brought up the rear.

I'd only made it two steps before the earpiece cord snagged on something invisible.

I halted everyone, then dropped to my knees. Simon panned her light around from different angles until finally I saw it: a section of thin, clear fishing line. With no way to mark the wire, I helped the others clear it, then stepped over it myself before resuming my position at the front of the pack.

We had to repeat that process three more times in rapid succession, but once we were able to take ten, fifteen, and then twenty steps without encountering another wire, it seemed like we'd gotten past the range of Hughes's traps. Eventually, I removed the cord from the end of the shotgun, pocketing the former and handing the latter back to Simon. Still, I had to assume Hughes knew we were coming by now. Although I hadn't seen any trap cameras, it seemed a given that he would have rigged them here like he had along the driveway.

While we were able to increase our pace, the terrain prevented us from moving too quickly. As Simon had warned, the ground began dropping off to our right until we found ourselves on a steeply angled hillside. We worked our way across it, using the bases of the trees as stepping-stones until finally we reached a point where the ground transitioned from leaf-strewn dirt to smooth, solid rock.

Simon stepped forward and panned her flashlight over it—we would need to cross about fifty yards of slick stone without any trees or other foliage to hold on to. As if the forty-five-degree slope wasn't challenging enough, when she swung her light to the right, we saw that not only did the rock face continue all the way down to the base of the hillside below, but we stood at its flattest point. A few yards to our right, the angle increased sharply—not quite a vertical drop, but close.

One slip and you'd be headed on a very quick trip to the bottom.

I stuck one foot out and dragged the toe of my boot sideways along the stone. There was some traction there, but the sleet had made it slippery.

Simon turned back to us and held the flashlight under her chin. "Gotta go real slow. Mitchell," she said to Devers. "You stick with me. I'll help you—"

"I can make it," he said.

Her eyes narrowed. "Don't give me any of that masculine bullshit right now. You'll break your neck if you fall from here." She pushed past us, back into the trees, then returned with a long, straight branch. "You're gonna use this in one hand and keep your other arm around me. We'll take every step together." Simon turned to Cooke and me and handed us the shotgun. "You two might want to do the same thing."

Cooke and I locked eyes and nodded. Because of my ribs, I moved to Cooke's left and draped my right arm across her shoulders. Holding the gun in her right hand, she wrapped her left arm around my waist. Without a flashlight like Simon's, I activated the light on the back of my phone. It would ruin our night vision, but at this point I figured we needed every bit of help we could get.

"We'll call out each step," Cooke said. "Left, right—okay?"

"Sure."

Ahead of us, Devers and Simon appeared set, with him similarly standing on her left. They exchanged a long, meaningful look before Simon peered back over her shoulder at us. "Let's go."

After allowing them a small head start, I raised the phone and turned to ask Cooke if she was ready. Her face, just inches from mine, was closer than I'd expected. Her eyes, normally so steely and determined, had softened. "I don't know about this," she said in a more vulnerable tone than I was accustomed to hearing from her.

"I know," I said, trying hard not to think about the height of the hillside or imagine what the drop would look like if I was staring down over it. "We'll get through it together."

She gave me a curt nod.

"Left," she said, and we both took a baby step forward.

"Right." Another.

"Left." And another.

On the third step, when my boot touched the ground, it started to slide. My weight shifted as I tried to pull it back and maintain my balance. I squeezed Cooke's shoulders for support and found Simon had been right: a second person did help.

Once I'd secured my footing, Cooke asked, "You ready?"

"Yes," I said.

"Right."

We took three more steps before our next stumble. This time it was Cooke's turn, as her right foot started to skitter downhill. She bent her other knee, trying to crouch before she lost the support of her right leg. Sensing what she was trying to do, I followed her down. She pulled herself in against my waist, and I returned the effort, giving her a chance to pull her fully extended leg back into line.

I felt her take and release a deep breath as we stood upright together.

I pointed my light off toward the distant trees we needed to reach. Compared to the seven baby steps we'd traveled, they seemed impossibly far away.

"See," I said, "we're almost there."

Cooke snickered, and I felt her relax slightly.

"Left," she said. "Right."

As we inched our way forward across the slippery expanse, I glanced ahead to check on Simon and Devers. They'd already made it nearly halfway. If anything, they seemed to be having too much success: rather than pausing between steps, their rhythm had accelerated so that now they were walking at a nearly normal speed. In the brief moment I watched, they took four steps.

On the final one, though, Devers turned his plant foot the slightest bit.

And that was all it took. In an instant, he'd hit the ground and started sliding past Simon on his belly.

Simon immediately dropped to a squat and shot her arms out toward his hands. The two grabbed each other, and somehow her boots held fast against Devers's momentum, even as her flashlight and stick tumbled away, clacking loudly against the rock until they disappeared into the darkness.

Cooke and I sped up our pace, my phone in front of us, its diffuse light enough to illuminate the strain and concern on Simon's and Devers's faces. They'd locked eyes in addition to hands, and I swear I could see their lips moving, saying words to each other that were inaudible from our position.

Seconds raced by in my head, but I had to remind myself not to go too fast, or to reach too far forward on any given step.

Simon winced and squeezed her eyes shut. Holding the prone Devers must have been taking an incredible effort. Cooke and I shuffled ahead, still several feet away.

One set of their hands came apart, and Devers shifted several more inches downhill. Simon recovered and grabbed Devers's remaining arm with both hands, but this left her leaning precariously over her boots.

We had only seconds left.

Our deliberate stepping got us there just in time—as Cooke and I moved to either side of Simon and seized Devers's arms, she pitched forward onto her knees and collided with him. For an instant, I worried the impact might pull all of us over the edge.

But a second went by, and we remained in place. Then another.

Everyone took a breath, and we started to untangle ourselves.

Once we'd helped Simon and Devers up, the four of us stood in a tight circle, facing each other. Our chests were heaving. Simon was smiling and crying simultaneously, and she might not have been the only one. We all embraced for a moment, squeezing each other's shoulders hard and bowing our heads into the huddle, before breaking back into pairs to start walking again.

The remainder of the rock crossing was nerve-racking but uneventful. When we finally reached the trees on the far side, we paused a minute to catch our breaths.

Simon took the lead when we resumed hiking. Although we checked for more traps, they seemed to have disappeared; Hughes must have decided the combination of the rock-chute ambush and the sheer hillside would be enough to claim anyone coming this way.

As we continued, the ground leveled off quickly, and soon we didn't even need our phones to illuminate the way: several steady lights appeared at the edge of our vision. Our pace slowed, but as we drew closer, I could see that they were mounted on the back side of two separate structures. One, off to our right, I recognized as the Hughes farmhouse. The other—a larger, darker building that loomed directly in front of us—had to be the barn.

Simon crouched when she reached the edge of the trees, and the three of us lined up alongside her. The building sat ten yards away, across a grassy clearing illuminated by floodlights mounted on the rear corners of the roof. As rickety and downtrodden as the farmhouse had seemed on our visit, the barn was exactly the opposite: windowless, built from concrete with a metal roof and a heavy wooden door, the building looked like it could withstand a tornado.

Although the barn appeared taller than normal, I was surprised to see that it consisted of only one level. As if reading my mind, Simon whispered, "It's built into the earth. The bottom floor opens out to the field on the front side of the house." She settled into a prone position as her eyes swept Hughes's property.

Devers, Cooke, and I joined her on the ground, watching every shadow but seeing no activity. Wet flurries continued to drift down from the sky, but there was no wind to shake the trees—no animals roaming or bugs chirping. If we hadn't almost died several times over the last hour, the quiet scene might have seemed serene.

Now that we lay on the ground, though, the cold had a chance to settle back in. Precipitation trickled down my scalp again. Heat seemed to spill from my belly and legs into the earth. That left me moving occasionally to keep warm while simultaneously trying to stay as still and quiet as possible.

I noticed the others fidgeting, too, and after what must have been fifteen or twenty minutes with no activity, Simon rose slowly to her feet.

As she took a single step out into the grass, the rest of us winced and watched tensely, as if some other booby trap might be waiting. But nothing happened. No one came running, no guns blazed or alarms sounded.

The three of us got to our feet, silently shaking out our stiff muscles and drawing our guns. Forming a circle with Simon in the lead facing forward and the rest of us covering the other directions, we carefully crossed the grass toward the barn door.

Although I was covering our left flank, I stole a few glances ahead. Unlike the rest of the structure, the ten-foot-tall barn door had been built from thick wooden planks with wheels mounted along its top edge to fit into a horizontal track that allowed the door to slide back and forth. I didn't see any visible lock, only a simple handle: a heavy metal loop that looked like it had been forged from bent rebar or something similar.

When we reached the door, Cooke, Devers, and I each took a knee, continuing to cover our respective fields of fire. That left Simon to deal with the handle. From behind me, I heard the metal wheels creak, and she said, "If Wesley was storing something big, like a drone, this'd be where he'd hide it. There's plenty of room down—"

The sheriff's voice disappeared, interrupted by the sound of a shotgun blast.

CHAPTER 25

All three of us turned in time to see Simon's body fall. A split second later, we'd wheeled around and aimed our guns at the space just inside the barn door.

But that's all we found: space.

Empty air, and a shotgun mounted on a ladder step at roughly eye level.

Lowering the Sig, I turned to find Devers collapsed on his knees at Simon's side. His face was buried in her chest, his shoulders and torso heaving. My eyes moved up her body until they saw what I dreaded most—there was no question about Simon's condition this time. The shotgun round had removed almost the entirety of her face; the sheriff had died the instant she'd opened the door.

Despite the cold, I stripped off my fleece and laid it over her head. Devers shouldn't have to see that again.

Cooke and I forced ourselves to turn away and clear the barn's interior, then scan the landscape around us. If Hughes were still here and somehow hadn't detected us yet, then the shotgun blast would either bring him running or send him fleeing. As empty seconds continued to tick by, we saw and heard nothing except for Devers's sobs. While Cooke tried to console Devers, another thought occurred to me.

Hughes had booby-trapped so much around the farm, he was clearly trying to protect something. Even if he wasn't physically here, he might have some way of remotely destroying whatever it was that we'd suffered so much to discover.

"We need to hurry and search the barn," I said, directing my comment at Cooke.

Devers exploded to his feet and started for the door. "I am going to kill that emaciated motherfucker . . ."

I reached for his arm, but he slapped my hand away.

"Don't," he said, wheeling around and jabbing an index finger at me. His eyes were blazing, as fiery as I'd seen them. The moisture on his cheeks shined brightly in the floodlights.

"Wait a sec, Mitchell," said Cooke. "God knows what's inside, but I doubt it's Hughes. Rushing in is only going to risk us ending up like Heather."

Devers swung around and opened his mouth, but no words emerged. His hands balled into fists that started to shake. Then his whole body shuddered—he ended up doubled over, tears streaming from his eyes. Squeezing them shut, he hung his head silently.

"Seth, you lead, and I'll follow you in. Mitchell"—Cooke put her hand on his shoulder—"you stay here with Heather. Make sure no one hits us from behind."

I grasped the Sig in both hands and stepped to the doorway. After re-clearing it, I ducked through, keeping myself tight against the wall. From what little I could see, I was standing at the base of a U-shaped balcony, the arms of which stretched forward to matching sets of stairs leading down to the ground floor. While this upper level was darkened, dim yellow light filtered up from below, painting the far wall of the building and silhouetting the railing ahead of me. Thick beams overhead supported the ceiling, while the floor was lined with plywood planks. The air, just as cold as it was outside, smelled of sawdust and hay but lacked the telltale odor of animals.

What I noticed more than anything, though, was the silence.

As I started moving to my left, I wondered how much give the floorboards might have—two steps later, I found out when one groaned loudly beneath my foot. From then on, I tried to locate the nails marking the planks' attachment points while also keeping an eye on the staircase ahead of me.

I'd reached the corner of the building when Cooke slid through the door. I signaled her that I would continue left while she went right.

At the top of my side's staircase, I finally got a better sense of the layout. Each stairway consisted of two sets of open risers connected by a small, square landing. They descended to a large open area that stretched from the lower level's concrete floor all the way up to the ceiling. A pair of tall, sliding wooden doors stood closed on the far wall—based on what Simon had said, I assumed those led into the meadow I'd seen in front of the farmhouse on our first visit. While a single utility lamp lit the open area, two darkened hallways stretched back beneath the loft that we would need to clear.

I waited for Cooke to reach her staircase, and we both started downward, weapons trained on the shadowy passages awaiting us at the bottom.

As soon as my foot touched the concrete floor, I crossed to the side of the nearest hallway entrance and braced myself against the wall. On the opposite side of the room, I saw Cooke had done the same.

I peeked quickly around the corner. Just enough light penetrated the passage that I could make out doorways on either side of it. While I assumed these little rooms were originally intended as animal stalls, both sliding doors stood ajar. Again, no sound or smell suggested anything was alive back there.

Cooke signaled that we should each check the hallway on our respective side, and I gave her a nod. Once again using my phone as a makeshift flashlight, I turned the corner in a crouch, with the Sig ready.

The door on my right was closest, a few feet farther down the passage. I advanced to the edge of its doorframe, took a silent breath, then spun into the room. A check of each corner showed it was devoid of people but full of tools: all sorts of wrenches and saws hung from hooks drilled into the concrete; a pair of large industrial-size toolboxes you'd find in a garage or machine shop had been rolled against the walls.

Returning to the doorway, I covered and watched the entrance across the hall for a moment, then darted over to it in two quick steps.

This room was also uninhabited and equally full. The middle of the floor was covered by a pallet supporting a few bags of what I assumed was fertilizer, while the walls were lined with modular shelves that held various cans and bottles.

Back in the hallway, I used my phone to illuminate the floor and saw it continued around to my left, presumably to link up with the passage Cooke was investigating. More stalls lined the wall now facing me.

I moved to the doorway of the first one, cleared it, and stepped inside.

None of the light from the front of the barn penetrated this far back, but as my phone flashlight cut through the darkness, I saw that Hughes had removed the walls between stalls here, turning what had been a series of small rooms into a single elongated chamber. And he'd needed the extra length: along the floor lay several sets of drone wings. Another portion of the room held two fuselages.

I knelt beside one pair of wings to examine them. Unlike the machine-gun drone I'd shot down in the field, these weren't swept, angled wings; they were straighter, more like the ones on traditional military drones. Given that they'd be better suited to soaring than dog-fighting, part of me wondered if these had served as some kind of early prototype.

As I was considering that, something rustled at the far side of the room. I aimed the light and the Sig at the noise all in one motion, and found Cooke standing at the farthest door.

"You clear everything?" she asked.

"Yeah, you?"

"Yeah."

I angled the phone down to illuminate the wing I was holding. "Look at these."

"So Hughes was flying the drones."

"Sure looks that way," I said. "I found a tool shop and a bunch of chemicals in the other rooms. How about you?"

"One stall is an armory, full of guns and ammunition. The other . . . You should see that one."

Cooke led me to it. When I stepped inside and panned the light around, I couldn't help but whistle. One wall was decorated with framed medals and certificates Hughes had received from the air force, along with a poster of the soldier's oath to the Constitution that seemed like it belonged back in the farmhouse. The rest looked like it could have been my own garage workshop back home.

"I take it you know what this stuff is?" she asked.

"Sure," I said. "Oscilloscope, signal generator. Radios and antennas. Materials to build circuit boards and a workbench. Everything Hughes would need to rig up his own custom electronics."

I had to hand it to him—the setup was almost as good as mine. Almost.

As I panned my phone around the room and called out components, in the far corner, back behind the workbench, something glinted and caught my eye.

I circled over to it. A roll of material stood on end amid spools of wire and solder. More than anything, it looked like glittery wrapping paper. But, nearly a quarter inch thick, it was made from a grid of interlocked, perpendicular plastic strips, the sparkle coming from metallic spots inside the honeycombed matrix.

Cooke must have noticed my preoccupation with the shiny stuff as I unrolled the sheet slightly and bent down to study it, shining my light onto it from a number of angles.

"Do you know what that is?" she asked.

"Oh yeah," I said. "I know exactly what this is. It's the kind of metamaterial you'd use to make an invisibility cloak."

CHAPTER 26

"Meta-what?" Cooke asked.

"Meta*material*. They're engineered to have properties you don't find in nature. Look in here," I said, shining the light so she could see down into one of the tiny channels. "Each of those shiny little dots is its own little circuit. When you pump electricity through all of them, they'll interact to create a field that'll distort electromagnetic waves in a distinct frequency range."

I glanced up to find Cooke staring at me blankly.

"They bend light instead of reflecting it."

"How'd Hughes make something like that?" she asked. "It must have taken forever."

"That's the thing—you can't just make this stuff yourself, even in a fancy workshop like this. Metamaterial has to be precision fabricated."

"So Hughes had help."

"He had to," I said. "I can't imagine how much this stuff cost. Metamaterials aren't supposed to be magnetic, so the original ones were made with gold or silver—I can't tell what they used here, but whatever it is, this little piece probably cost tens of thousands of dollars."

"Is there any way to trace who made it?" Cooke asked.

"Maybe your labs could. There are probably only a handful of places in the world capable of fabricating something like this." One end of the workbench was cluttered with papers—I riffled through them quickly. Lots of technical information, but nothing that indicated the metamaterial's origin.

"Did you see anything in the other rooms that might suggest who's supplying him?" Cooke asked.

"No, but I only got a quick look. You want to go back over it all?"

She nodded. "If Hughes has a backer, who knows how many other pilots like him they've equipped with this stuff?"

I started to gather up all the workbench papers to go through them later, but Cooke stopped me. "That's evidence," she said, so I settled for pictures of the documents instead.

Then Cooke led me to the armory. When we entered the narrow stall, she pointed to a switch on the wall. "Think it's another trap? Or just the lights?"

I panned my phone flashlight over the switch box—it looked routine enough. Encased wiring led from it up the wall and across to a pair of fluorescent tubes on the ceiling. But there was one way to be sure it was safe.

"Wait here a sec." I backtracked to the tool room and retrieved a screwdriver. After removing the faceplate from the switch box, I checked the wires inside. They were run correctly, and I saw no sign of a trap. I flipped the switch, and the tubes flickered on.

Cooke exhaled, releasing a small cloud of mist. We gave each other a grim smile, then turned to examine the contents of the room.

One whole wall had been dedicated to racks of long guns. Hughes clearly had a thing for AR-15s—there were four on the wall, and empty slots for two more—but he also had two Bushmaster C-15s, a Smith & Wesson M&P15-22, and a DPMS Mark-12, along with a series of shotguns.

The middle wall contained Hughes's handguns: a collection of Glocks, Sigs, and S&Ws with two more empty slots.

Shelves on the third wall held ammunition, neatly arranged and organized by caliber. The boxes were so rigorously organized, in fact, that you could tell several boxes of 9mm bullets had been removed. Conspicuously absent were any .50-caliber rounds, but one entire shelf had been emptied.

"Wherever he is," I said, "it looks like he's packing."

"I thought you guys said Hughes was scraping by, eating squirrel."

"He sure looked like it," I said. "Simon even joked about bringing him some food when the case was over."

"Well," she said, gesturing around with her hand, "this collection alone cost a small fortune. He could have fed himself with that."

"He might have accumulated it slowly," I said.

"Maybe. We'll need to try and trace the purchases."

After the armory, I brought Cooke back to the tool room. Again, she noted how much the assembled material must have cost, but otherwise, that stall's contents didn't seem to hold any clues. When we entered the chemical room, though, Cooke's face blanched.

"Those bags," she said, nodding at the pallet. "What's in them?"

"Fertilizer, I think."

We pulled one off the top of the stack. I watched her eyes tick back and forth across the label of ingredients. Then she swallowed hard. "This is potassium chlorate."

"Is that bad?"

"It's the chemical they use to make match heads," she said. "It was also the favorite explosive for IEDs in Afghanistan." The muscles in Cooke's jaw clenched until finally she turned to me. The steeliness had returned to her eyes. "Let's hit that last room."

The elongated room where we'd found the wings—I was calling it "the hangar" in my head—didn't have as obvious a light switch as the other stalls, but eventually Cooke found one mounted in the middle of the sidewall. I checked the wiring again, just to be safe, then flipped it on.

I think we were both surprised.

My eyes were drawn to the concrete floor, which had a lot more parts strewn across it than I'd seen in the dark. In addition to the larger hull pieces, I saw propellers and shafts, engines in various states of assembly, landing gear. I moved from pile to pile, trying to determine whether Hughes was building more drones or cannibalizing pieces from existing ones.

Something in the back corner caught my attention.

It was a fragment of fuselage. Dark gray, there was a noticeable white mark across it, like someone had nicked it with a piece of chalk. Shaped something like a comet, the rounded end of the mark contained a small dent.

On a hunch, I took out one of my extra magazines, slid a single bullet from it, and held it up to the dent.

There was no way to know for sure by eyeballing it, but the two seemed to match.

"I think this is a piece of the machine-gun drone we shot down." When she didn't respond, I turned and found her standing at the far wall. I stepped over to join her.

Large squares of paper had been tacked up around the room. Cooke stood before one of them, staring at it silently from a few inches away, as if she were a visitor in a museum examining a painting. "It's a map," she said.

"Not just a map," I said. "A VFR chart."

"VFR?"

"Visual flight reference. It's a map for pilots of what they'll see from the air."

Like a topographical map, the chart depicted land features in different shades of green based on their height and water features in blues depending on their depth. But VFR charts also contained all sorts of other symbols and colors. Highways and railroads were shown with different kinds of lines—cities were colored yellow, restricted areas white. Upside-down V's—"Λ"—denoted obstructions, while circles depicted the airspaces around airports and provided navigational information. Numbers were printed everywhere, identifying everything from ceiling and floor altitudes for different classes of aircraft to the maximum eleva-tions of obstructions in a given area.

This particular chart was a sectional, the basic level of detail pilots used. Two sets of concentric circles overlapped, with patches of yellow all around and between them. The innermost circle on the right was white, meaning it was restricted.

"This is DC," Cooke said.

"Yep, here's Dulles." I pointed at the left-hand set of circles. "And Reagan." I moved my finger to the right.

I took a step to the left and examined the next maps mounted along the wall: terminal-area charts for each of the two Washington airports. I kept moving down the wall, checking each chart as I went.

"We've got to put everyone on alert," Cooke said. "If he's bringing explosives to DC on a vehicle we can't see . . ."

"It's not just DC," I said.

"What do you mean?"

"Here's Pittsburgh," I said, pointing to the next sectional. "He's also got Cleveland, Columbus, Cincinnati. And this last one is"—I leaned in to read the airport code—"Louisville." I turned back to face her. "That's a lot of airports. What the hell is he after?"

Cooke's eyes took in the series of maps as she shook her head. "No way to know, and in some ways, it doesn't matter. We just have to stop him." Then she looked up. "If he's already on his way, though . . . If there are others working with him . . ."

"C'mon," I said. "Hughes had a truck out front. All of these places are drivable from here."

We took the barn stairs two at a time. Devers was waiting where we'd left him outside the door. After filling him in on the full extent of the threat, we left Heather Simon's body and moved toward the farm-house slowly, testing each inch of the way for every type of trap we'd seen. At last we came upon the chicken coop I'd seen on our earlier visit.

From there we could see that the gravel area at the side of the house was empty—the truck and horse trailer were missing.

"Where was it parked?" Cooke asked.

"Right there," I said, pointing to an empty spot on the ground.

"The gravel's an even color," she said.

She was right—if the vehicles had shielded the ground from the sleet, they hadn't done so for a while.

Cooke pulled out her cell phone, then turned the screen toward us. "No signal. We need to get out to the SUV," she said. "Get on the radio and call DC. Call everyone. Put out an APB for his truck and—"

"What about . . ." Devers gestured back over his shoulder. "We can't just leave her."

Cooke's face fell. "I'm so sorry, Mitchell. But we don't have a choice right now."

Devers's mouth straightened, and his lips pursed. After a moment, he nodded grimly.

The three of us started up the driveway. Devers had the hardest time because of his leg, but we kept up a pretty good pace despite navigating the booby traps Devers and I had seen during our original visit.

When we finally reached the gate at the road, it stood unlocked.

"That's changed," Cooke said. She shot me a look that seemed to question whether our detour through the woods had been necessary. Without another word, she took off for the SUV.

Devers and I followed until, suddenly, she stopped, turned, and kicked the side of the truck in anger.

The SUV rested on its rims on the pavement—all four tires had been shot out.

CHAPTER 27

We ended up calling for an ambulance. Truth was, if we were going to helicopter our way out of New Martinsville, we'd need to use the hospital's helipad anyway. Plus, Cooke wanted to check on the status of the ERTU members who'd been hurt in the woods before we left.

While we waited at the base of Hughes's driveway, Cooke worked the radio. Over a fifteen-minute span, she called seemingly every alphabet agency in Washington, and although it was now the middle of the night, they all swung into action. By the time she'd finished, DHS had issued an alert through the National Terrorism Advisory System, the FBI had triggered an arrest warrant for Hughes and a nationwide APB for his truck, and the FAA had raised the security status at all of the airports whose charts we'd seen. The FBI, NSA, and DHS were all now sifting through every 1 and 0 available to them in cyberspace, trying to uncover everything they could about Hughes. Even DOD was involved—she'd asked them to scramble fighters over every targeted airport, as well as send three military choppers, one for each of us.

"Each airport will have manpower spun up now," she said afterward, "but they won't know what to look for. You two are the only people alive who've seen this thing—we'll have to split up. Dulles is a four-hour drive; Reagan's slightly farther. Depending on when he got on the road"—she checked her watch—"he could be just a couple of hours away."

Between the DC airports' proximity to Quantico and the need to assist all the government agencies bringing their resources to bear on this, it made sense for Cooke to cover them, while Devers would head home to Pittsburgh and could coordinate Cleveland from there. That left me with the three airports to the west: Columbus, Cincinnati, and Louisville. Columbus was closest, about one hundred fifty miles away, so the plan was that I'd set up there and handle the other two remotely.

While Cooke was still busy outlining contingencies and pressing her contacts for updates, I sat in the back seat of the SUV, thinking.

Planning how to intercept Hughes was all well and good, but at some point, someone was going to have to confront his cloaked drone. Sure, the authorities might catch him en route; Hughes might do something stupid. But he hadn't yet. He'd been clever enough to remain one step ahead, so I had to think that he'd have dreamed up a way of avoiding detection now, whether that meant changing vehicles, hiding out, or something else.

We had to assume his drone would reach his target. Which meant we'd have to take it down.

Except, how could you stop something you couldn't even see?

I kept returning to the pieces of my drone gun sitting back at the hospital. While it had proven to be a colossal dud the first time, I chalked that up to being unable to aim. When Shen and I had talked through the idea, we hadn't known about the cloak. Now that we did, I wondered if there was some way to adapt to it.

The problem was, to overwhelm the drone, you needed a pretty focused beam. I couldn't aim the gun everywhere at once; there wasn't enough power. Even if I could overcome that limitation—by rigging the system up to a giant generator and some kind of industrial antenna, for example—there was no guarantee the signal density would be enough to interfere with Hughes's control signals. Plus, if we cranked the noise up too far, that could cause other problems: knocking out every radio at an airport would leave a pretty big mess.

No, I had to aim right at Hughes's drone. That was the only way.

I closed my eyes, trying to replay the scenes at the drug camp over in my head. I thought maybe, if I could walk through the cloaked attack step by step, I'd spot some weakness—some tell—in the device's behavior.

But when I shut out the world, I couldn't picture the trailers, or the little crater encampment. I didn't see the sky, or the trees. None of the firefight. No matter how hard I tried to visualize the action from that morning, the only image that would form behind my eyelids was Heather Simon's face after the shotgun blast.

I should say, I'm not crazy about blood and guts—as an air marshal, you don't get exposed to them very often. In my new job, I've met police who are totally desensitized; they could eat a rare steak at a crime scene without a second thought. I'm not that numb. But it's not like I've never seen a gunshot wound, either. I've shot enough people, and been shot at enough myself, that violence generally doesn't shock me anymore.

This was different.

This was personal. Almost as personal as the shotgun blast that had killed Clarence.

Clarence . . . my engineering mentor, my godkids' father. With his thick, almost cartoonish glasses, deep dimples in his cheeks, and pudge around his belly, he'd looked like a big nerdy kid.

He'd acted like one, too: always quick with a joke, he'd loved nothing more than to laugh. Not *little* chuckles, either. Big, throw-your-head-back kind of belly laughs that often went on a second or two longer than they maybe should have.

Clarence was the kind of guy you immediately knew had gotten teased and mocked and beaten up as a kid. Changing schools every year as a navy brat, I'd had some experience with that myself. But where I'd learned to carry a chip on my shoulder, single out the biggest bully, and convince him I was too dangerous to pick on, Clarence had none of that edge.

I don't know whether being a target made him gentle, or being gentle made him a target, but either way, Clarence had one of the softest hearts I've ever encountered. Unfortunately, becoming a successful engineer hadn't made Clarence immune from ridicule—certain higher-ups told him he was "weak," that he couldn't "do the hard things"—but his compassion, his kindness, was one of Clarence's best traits. It was the thing his wife, Shirley, loved most about him. It was the reason his kids ran to him and threw their arms around his neck when he got home each night.

It was why he'd cared about my career. Why he'd been thrilled instead of resentful when I'd gotten promoted over him. He'd taught me many things about engineering, about electronics. But more than that, Clarence had cared about me as a person, frequently sharing life lessons drawn from his own experiences as well as having an uncanny understanding of who I was. He openly worried that I was lonely—he said I needed a home. So he'd opened his and done everything he could to make me part of the family.

And while he was closer to me than he was to our other colleagues, almost everybody in our laboratory had a story about how Clarence had helped them, supported them, or recommended them, even when doing so diminished how much credit he got.

That's why we were all so shocked when Clarence arrived at work carrying a shotgun.

He didn't even know how to carry the damn thing: he clutched the very tip of the barrel while letting the stock hang down around his ankles, as if the weapon were some kind of bizarre walking stick. When we questioned him about it, his face reddened until it resembled a swollen strawberry. Reluctantly, he explained that the gun had belonged to his father, who'd died the week before. He'd inherited the gun, and while he couldn't bring himself to sell it, he didn't dare leave it around the house because of his young children.

For eight months, the shotgun stood in the corner of his office, gathering dust behind a coatrack.

As the boss, I should have said something. In the end, after I didn't, I was the one who found him.

I'd come into the office extra early, so I'd been surprised to find light poking its way out from his door. When I knocked and got no response, I pushed it open with my knuckles.

The feeling was unlike anything I've ever experienced, before or since. All the air seemed to disappear from the room. I couldn't breathe for what seemed like minutes; even now, when I have nightmares about that day, I wake up gasping for breath.

I dashed over to him, dropping to my knees at his side. Stupidly, I fumbled around, trying to find a pulse, trying to think of a way to save him when even a quick glance above his shoulders said any efforts would be futile.

It looked, quite simply, like a bomb had exploded inside his mouth. Any structure, any rigidity, in his lower jaw was gone; his tongue and the rent skin of his face hung down limply. The few remains of his teeth stood stark white against the raw red of the exposed muscle and tissue. I could even see the bloody floor below him through the exit wound in the back of his head.

Strangely, seeing his eyes was the most disturbing part. They were intact and open wide in a look of shock, yet they seemed improperly small. It took me a while to realize that he'd removed his glasses. They sat folded on the desk.

I came out of that office covered in Clarence's blood. It soaked into my clothes, it stuck to my skin. I must have washed my hands a hundred times, yet it seemed like I could never get the stain out from under my nails.

With everything that was going on at the company, I should have guessed what might happen. I'd known Clarence better than anyone—I should have seen it coming. If only I'd thought ahead, I could have stopped him by taking the gun after he'd left one night, or encouraging Shirley to come retrieve it and lock it up.

For a supposedly smart guy with a brain that spins in a million directions, I have no idea why it never occurred to me. Not that saving Clarence would have absolved me from the other mistakes I'd made, the other wrongs I'd committed. Not even close. But my friend would still be alive. My godkids would still have their daddy.

On the long list of ways I'd failed Clarence, that was the final one.

That's why I couldn't go home—why I couldn't face my old man. And that's what folks like Cooke misunderstood about my tattoos: the formula on my back, the heart on my forearm. They all assumed the ink was some kind of reminder, as if I could somehow forget Clarence, forget Sarah.

I didn't need reminders.

I needed *warnings*.

I was still thinking about Clarence when the ambulance drew up behind the SUV.

Its LED flashers shot staccato bursts of light into the cab, the flashes snapping me back to attention. Unfortunately, I wasn't any closer to a solution on how to detect—or fight—Hughes's invisible drone, but I needed to come up with something quickly. Otherwise, catching up to Hughes wasn't going to help us in the slightest.

CHAPTER 28

Since there was no other traffic to compete with, the ambulance crew returned us to the hospital in record time.

With the military helicopters due any minute, Cooke dashed inside to check on her people as soon as we pulled into the driveway. Devers announced he wanted a few moments alone. That gave me the chance to retrieve the drone gun. I found it on the table where Devers had deposited it.

Or, what was left of it after being crushed by the weight of three bodies and dragged through the drug traffickers' escape tunnel.

I checked the PCB board first—thankfully, the components seemed to have survived intact, maybe because their profile was so small. The wiring I'd ripped apart when ditching the battery would obviously need to be replaced, but that wasn't too hard.

A bigger issue was the battery itself.

Where was I going to find another battery at this hour?

My immediate thought was that I should have cannibalized the battery from the SUV we'd abandoned at Hughes's property. Although it wouldn't have delivered all that much more power than the lawn-mower battery despite its larger, heavier frame, it would have been better than nothing. Distracted by my memories of Clarence, I just hadn't thought of it before the ambulance had arrived.

The ambulance.

Now that was an interesting thought. Collectively, the flashers, the lights inside the rig, and all the medical equipment had to draw a ton of amperage. And the paramedics couldn't risk the vehicle not starting from cold weather or other stress.

As quickly as I could, I shuffled back out to the ambulance bay, where the rig we'd arrived in was still parked. I found the driver behind the wheel. While he wouldn't part with the battery the ambulance was actively using, he said he had a spare in the garage and offered to retrieve it.

I almost groaned out loud when he delivered it: the heavy-duty block was significantly larger than a normal car battery. The paramedic— a burly-looking guy—was straining to carry it. I could only imagine the strain that was going to put on my side.

Still, now that I had power again, I turned back to the gun itself. To keep the PCB board secure, I lashed it onto the antenna setup with some smaller zip ties. That meant the only loose wires were those connecting the battery and the board. There was nothing I could do about that, and they'd be the easiest to reattach if they became dislodged. Finally, I daisy-chained a few more of the zip ties together into an elongated strip. By fastening the ends to the antenna, it created a kind of strap that could go over my shoulder or suspend the gun around my neck. With the extra weight to worry about, having both hands free seemed like a good idea.

Realizing I was likely out of time, I jammed the remaining spare parts into my laptop bag with my computer. With that bag slung over one shoulder, the gun over the other, and the battery in my right hand, I was ready to go.

When I emerged from the office carrying that load, Cooke was approaching from down the hallway while Devers stood nearby, leaning against the wall.

"Just heard the first bird's five minutes out," he said.

"Good." Cooke looked me up and down. "What's all that?"

"The drone gun I told you about."

"I thought you said it didn't work."

Before I could explain the changes I'd made, a male nurse dashed around the corner. When he saw us, he stopped and doubled over, hands on knees. "Are you all the agents working with the sheriff?"

My eyes instinctively flew to Devers, whose face stiffened.

Cooke answered. "Yes, that's us."

Relief spread across the nurse's face. "I work in the ICU. Brittany Anne Donohue just woke up and is asking for Sheriff Simon. Says it's important."

I quickly reminded Cooke who Donohue was. She told Devers, "We can handle this. You go ahead and take the first helicopter."

Devers shook his head. "No. I want to hear what she has to say."

The nurse led us down a maze of hallways to a room in the back corner of his unit. Inside, a single bed dominated the center of the room, surrounded by all kinds of medical equipment and a tangle of tubes and wires connected to Brittany Anne Donohue.

She looked even younger and more petite than when I'd first seen her at the ACES center. Although Donohue had a good decade on Emma, my head filled with images of the teenage singer when she'd lain in a similar bed toward the end of my last mission.

Donohue's long pigtail braids were gone—her dark hair was pulled messily over to one side. The pink hue in her cheeks had also disappeared. Her eyelids drooped enough that I wondered whether she'd fallen back asleep.

"Where . . . ?" she asked, her voice emerging as a raspy croak. "Where's the sheriff?"

Our expressions answered her question.

"She's dead . . . isn't she?"

I nodded. "You should know, though: She was the one who found you. She carried you in here herself."

Donohue's face cracked, tears streaming from the outside corners of her eyes. "She was always . . . so . . . nice to me."

I stole a glance back at Devers, who was fighting tears himself. "You both only had brothers, right?"

She nodded weakly.

"Sweetie, the nurse told us you wanted to tell Sheriff Simon something," Cooke said. "He seemed to think it was pretty important."

"I . . . I know . . . who was flying the drone," she said. "The one that shot me."

Cooke stepped forward and put her hand on top of Donohue's. "Who's that?"

Donohue sputtered like she wanted to cough but didn't have enough breath to do it. "I wish . . . I wish the sheriff was here. She's the one I should tell."

"Is that because it's someone she knows?" I asked.

Donohue closed her eyes and nodded.

Although he'd remained near the door, Devers now circled around me to get to the opposite side of the bed from Cooke. He bent at the waist until his face was just inches from Donohue's. "I knew Heather—Sheriff Simon—pretty well," he said in the most tender tone I'd heard him use. "She'd want you to help us if you could." Then he reached for a water cup resting on a table and held the straw to her lips so she could get a drink.

"There's a man," Donohue said after several small sips. "In Hundred. Wesley Hughes. He used to—"

"We know about Hughes, and we know what he did in the military." Cooke squeezed her hand and leaned down to lock eyes with her. "Why do you think it was him?"

Donohue's gaze drifted up to the ceiling. She inhaled sharply through her nose and held it for a moment. "I'm . . . not that religious.

But I believe in God, you know? 'Specially now. I think he made the Earth—not in, like, seven days exactly . . . but I think he's behind everything."

When she didn't continue after a moment, Devers prompted her. "And?"

"And, so . . . people know me, know about the Center. A few times I got invited . . . to go to this church."

"A church in Hundred?" Cooke asked. "Which one?"

"Not church like a building," she said. "Church like a bunch of people who worship together."

"What's it called? Where do they meet?"

Donohue leaned toward Devers and took another sip. "The Church of the Holy Stewardship. When it's warm, they put up a tent outside. They move it around the county, trying to make it close to everyone. In winter, I think they rent a meeting room at one of the hotels."

Cooke still clung to Donohue's hand. "So you actually attended their meetings?"

"Only one."

"Why's that?"

"They were a little too"—Donohue's face contorted—"hard-core for me."

"Hard-core, how?" I asked.

"I mean, some of what they do isn't all that different from my Center," she said. "Everybody brings some food to share, if they can. Folks bring their kids—they're running around the whole time."

"A potluck picnic doesn't sound very 'hard-core,'" I said.

Donohue took a breath. "I was raised Catholic. I'm used to mass; Bible study doesn't even bother me that much. This is more like . . . like people giving testimony, you know?"

"Testimony about what?" Cooke asked.

"What folks think is happening to the earth. Climate change. Overpopulation, extinctions. These people think nature, the earth, is a gift directly from God. I mean, I think that, too. But they believe we're supposed to protect it. Mining and fracking and chemicals—they believe all that's a sin. Like, a mortal sin. Like abortion. It's murdering the earth, and if we keep going, it'll bring about the Rapture."

"And you saw Hughes there, at the church meeting?" Cooke asked.

Donohue nodded once.

"How'd you know it was him?" I asked.

"I've seen his picture in the paper. I knew who he was—everyone did."

"Wait a second," Cooke said. "I thought Wesley Hughes had become some kind of recluse or something." She stared at me.

"He looked . . . pretty rough," Donohue said. "I've seen poor plenty, but he was . . . bad, even for around here. And he didn't seem comfortable—from what folks said, it was his first time there, too. Everyone clapped for him, though, when he got introduced."

"Because of his service?" Devers asked.

Donohue nodded. "Everyone knows what he had to do to serve his country. The fact he's so down and out now . . . it just makes people feel that much worse."

"Okay," Cooke said, "so Hughes comes out of seclusion, goes to church, and gets an ovation. What about that makes you think he was behind the drone attacks?"

"It was what he *said*."

CHAPTER 29

"Wait," Cooke said, "Hughes *spoke* at the church, too?"

"Yes, ma'am. He stood up, and everyone clapped. Then he kind of shuffled up front. He talked about ten minutes. He got real upset in the middle, speaking about his mom, but everyone understood that."

Cooke glared at me again, her eyes demanding some kind of explanation.

"Heather—Sheriff Simon—told us Hughes's mother died not too long ago," I said. "But when we were at the farmhouse, he wasn't exactly the chatty type. You pretty much had to use a crowbar to get a word out of him."

She turned back to Donohue. "What did Hughes say at the church, sweetie? Start at the beginning—every little bit might be important, okay?"

Donohue nodded and closed her eyes, trying to picture it. "He started out saying how he'd never been one to give speeches, but how hearing everyone else's testimony moved him. He went around the room and pointed out people who'd talked, what they'd said.

"After that, Hughes said he'd been thinking about God a lot. He said he'd read the Bible as a child but didn't really understand it until he was a soldier." Her eyes still closed, Donohue smiled. "I remember that line, because a little boy ran through the tent right at that moment, screeching. Everyone laughed. Even Hughes smiled. He said he'd started going to Bible study as a pilot, and the Word of God had eased his mind. Given him strength.

"But then he'd come home. Hughes said he hadn't known about the fracking pad near the farm, that his mom had sold off the rights without telling him. Money had been tight, and she hadn't wanted to worry him. The gas company had come and made their typical promises—she gave them a split estate so they could drill on the land, and she'd make a little every month.

"Hughes said that when he came home from the air force, he was in a selfish mood. Said he didn't have a plan—didn't know where he was gonna go, what he was gonna do. He just figured he'd been gone so long, he'd spend a little time at home. But when he got there, everything changed. Even just driving up to the house, he said he noticed the smell. It got up into his nose and gave him a headache."

"When we visited the farmhouse, we could smell it," I said. "Like rotten eggs."

Donohue nodded. "He talked about seeing his mom when she came to the door. He said she'd lost some weight, and he thought it might be a good thing, like she'd been exercising. He complimented her, and she thanked him, but didn't say what was different. And then he started noticing things. Little things, he said, like she'd go to eat something, and she'd flinch when she bit down. He assumed she had a toothache, but it was open sores in her mouth. He saw her grabbing her stomach—she said it was cramps. But she was barely eating."

Donohue's eyes flicked open. "That was about the point when Hughes started losing it. Choking back tears."

"What else did he say?" Devers asked.

"He said that he saw his mom go into the kitchen and pour herself a glass of water. He chuckled when he said it, because the glass was a Tweety-and-Sylvester one from a set they'd gotten at Bob's Big Boy when he was a kid."

Donohue swallowed deeply, then shut her eyes again.

"Hughes said that when she filled the glass, the water was yellow brown, like if you mixed dirt into your lemonade. He said he watched her take a drink, and he pulled the glass right out of her hand. They had a well, and the water had never looked like that before. He said he sniffed, and it stank."

"So what'd he do?" Cooke asked.

"He asked her how long it had been like that, and she said 'a while.' He made her see the doctor. It took a couple of weeks to get the appointment and all—by the time they brought her in, she was less than ninety pounds. The doctors found intestinal cancer—it had spread all over inside her. She died within a month."

Donohue had started crying herself now. Lighter, more softly than before—no sobbing, just silent tears slipping down her cheek.

Devers's phone beeped, breaking the silence. He checked it, then held it up for Cooke to see. "First chopper's here. Others right behind it."

"Tell them we'll be right there," she said, her eyes locked on Donohue. "Did Hughes say anything else, honey?"

Donohue nodded. "His voice got quiet. I could barely hear him. He said that he missed his mother every day. He said that he'd been proud to go out and wear a uniform and fight our enemies like his ancestors had, because the war was important. But what the church was doing—trying to teach people, trying to save them, trying to save the environment—he thought was even more important. He said that, as a soldier, he never thought our greatest enemy might already be inside the country, killing us from within. But it was. He said a terrorist might kill a few people—a hundred, or a thousand. But that was nothing compared to frackers poisoning the earth. He said that would kill us all."

"That it?" Cooke asked.

Donohue nodded.

Cooke thanked her, and I did, too. Devers leaned over to her and said, "This helps."

"Does it?" she asked quickly.

"A lot," he said. "Heather would be really proud of you."

For the first time since we'd entered the room, Donohue smiled.

"You get some rest now," he said. "We'll take it from here."

With that, her face and shoulders relaxed. She seemed to sink down deeper into the mattress, and her eyelids closed. She'd fallen back asleep before we made it through the door.

Once we reached the hallway, Cooke's strides lengthened. I had to work to keep up, while Devers limped along behind us.

When we reached the office that I'd used as a workshop, I paused to grab my gear and the drone gun. Cooke continued all the way to the sliding door before stopping and turning around to wait for us. I could see dread and determination in her expression.

"You okay?" I asked.

"Oh yeah. Great." She sighed. "Maybe the highway patrol will pick Hughes up for a busted taillight or something."

Devers grunted. "C'mon, boss. You know we ain't that lucky."

CHAPTER 30

Before I could finish strapping into the Black Hawk helicopter, the pilot added power and began a vertical climb into the clouds. While the headset for my seat came equipped with heavy earphones that muted much of the engine noise, I could still feel the vibration and power of the rotors through my legs and back. Outside, the reflected glow of the chopper's belly lamp came and went as it blinked, but otherwise the window was filled by a blank wall of gray mist.

That view lasted until we finally emerged from the top of the cloud bank. At altitude, the nearly full moon was out, painting everything in silvery-white light that seemed particularly gentle after the fluorescents we'd left below. The brightest stars pinpricked the royal-blue sky overhead, while the clouds receding beneath us came to resemble a frothy white sea that extended to the horizon, broken only by small black islands created by the tallest hilltops.

Without warning, the chopper banked left and swung us around to the west. As we turned, I caught a glimpse of Cooke's bird, barely more than a blinking light now, already dashing east, while a third Black Hawk approached, flaring its nose and dipping its tail into the clouds. Before it submerged completely into the mist, our pilot angled our chopper's nose down and accelerated away.

On the horizon, the trailing edge of the cloud front came into view, looking like the jagged fingers of foam the ocean casts up on the shore.

We raced across that threshold, then dived down to only a few hundred feet of altitude. Ultimately, we followed a lush valley, tracing a set of railroad tracks and the stream that paralleled it.

Once we'd settled into a steady cruise, voices began chattering in my headset, soon joined by Cooke's. "Seth, Mitchell, are you both airborne?"

"I'm here," I said.

"Me, too," came Devers's drawl.

"I checked in with Quantico—no sign of Hughes from local authorities," she said. "So we can keep our fingers crossed, but we have to plan for him to reach his destination.

"I've been thinking through the story Donohue told us," she said. "From what Hughes said at church, it seems like he's out to make a statement. If we extrapolate that out to the geographies we know he's interested in, Reagan and Dulles airports make sense as targets in and of themselves. Terrorists love attacking DC, and there's enough traffic in each of those places to cause a significant body count. Some of the other airports, though, don't make as much sense. So I just asked CIRG to look for any significant fracking- or energy-related events or people in proximity to those cities.

"The first thing on the list that really jumps out is going to be yours, Seth: Ohio State is hosting a four-day conference on the future of fossil fuels. The CEOs of several big oil companies are supposed to attend, and the head of the EPA is slotted to give the keynote address. Now, given the administration's deregulatory agenda since taking office, Hughes might see eliminating the EPA chief as a blow against fracking, plus there should be plenty of media there to cover the speech. But that's not the worst part."

"What's worse than that?" Devers asked.

"The head of the EPA graduated from Oklahoma State. They're slotted to play Ohio State tonight in football—"

"Tonight?" I asked.

"Hard to believe it's Saturday, isn't it?" Cooke said. "But yes, tonight. Ohio State's stadium seats a hundred and five thousand, so if you were looking for the place to attack the administrator while also inflicting the largest number of casualties, that's it."

"I think I'm glad Pitt sucks at football this year," Devers said.

"You're not off the hook, Mitchell. Not by a long shot."

"Great," he said. "What am I looking at?"

"To start out, the engineering school at Carnegie Mellon is having a competition for renewable fuel designs."

"Hughes should love that," Devers said.

"Normally, I'd agree with you," Cooke said, "but it's being put on by BP, Shell, and Exxon, three of the biggest oil companies. A bunch of environmentalists have been calling it a sham and are planning to protest. Then there's the NFL tomorrow . . ."

"The Steelers?"

"Steelers, Browns, the Bengals in Cincinnati. Even the game here. Every single NFL game in each of our cities has some kind of connection to the oil-and-gas industry through the owner's business holdings or in some other way. Those stadiums are huge targets—the FAA puts no-fly-zone caps over them, but we know that's not going to stop Hughes."

As Cooke continued talking, getting into the details of various contingencies and listing the agencies tasked to assist us, I found myself staring out the window. Despite our airspeed, my eyes caught flashes of detail—leaves on the moon-soaked trees, glimmers on the surface of the water, individual ties crossing the black rails.

Throughout the trip, I'd been struck by the local landscape. It was so . . . wild, so feral, compared to the manicured palm trees, strip malls, and freeways I'd grown used to back home. So much of my life—riding on planes, traveling through airports, making my patents—deals with technology and development. I think that's one reason I enjoy surfing so much; it's a chance to connect to something natural. Looking out over the wilderness here, I could understand why people like Hughes were so protective of their land. This valley probably looked exactly the same today as it did fifty years ago. Or a hundred. Hell, with the railroad in place, it probably hadn't changed since the Civil War.

The Civil War.

That tickled my brain.

Hughes's ancestors had fought in the Civil War. They'd fought in all the country's wars, as we'd learned at his farmhouse.

But there was something different about the Civil War.

When Devers had asked about that, it was the one time Hughes had really gotten talking. But he hadn't dwelled on any of the other veterans in his family. Only the ones who'd served in the Civil War.

Closing my eyes, I tried to picture the military memorabilia in the Hughes farmhouse. There was so much—keepsakes like that had obviously taken generations to accumulate.

The more I thought about the medals and the swords and the news clippings, though, something else struck me.

The way they'd been cleaned.

Everything else in that farmhouse was a total wreck—strung with cobwebs, covered in dust. I could still smell the stench of the kitchen, feel the grime on the table. Hughes was dirty himself.

But not those memorabilia.

They were the only things in his house that had been treated with any care.

Hughes had been living alone for months. That meant *he'd* been taking care of them.

They mattered to *him.*

My mind fast-forwarded to Hughes's workshop in the barn. His air force medals, the soldier's-constitutional-oath poster. He chose to display them where he'd see them every day—their selection had to say something about the man we were searching for. And what his mission might be.

His *mission*.

Suddenly, it all clicked. "Maybe we're thinking about this wrong," I said, not realizing I'd interrupted Cooke until it was too late.

"How's that?" Cooke asked.

"You were just talking about the kind of 'statement' Hughes is trying to make. I don't think that's what he wants."

"Seth, every terrorist is trying to say *something*."

"Not Hughes," I said. "Hughes doesn't see himself as a terrorist."

"No terrorist thinks he's a terrorist," Devers said. "They're all 'freedom fighters' or 'revolutionaries.'"

"Mitchell's right," Cooke said. "Lone wolves, in particular, often see themselves as grandiose figures, carrying out some kind of divine will."

"That's not Hughes," I said.

"What about all that stuff he said at the church?" Cooke asked. "You don't think he believes he's got a divine purpose?"

"He might think God justifies the mission, but I don't think he's looking at himself as some kind of chosen one or anything."

"How do you think he sees himself?" Cooke asked.

"As a soldier," I said.

"Terrorists love to mix religious and military vernacular," Cooke said. "They describe themselves as a 'soldier' in a 'holy war' or—"

"That's not what I mean," I cut in. "Hughes sees himself as a real soldier. The latest in a long line of people who fought for their country. He's not trying to make a statement, he wants to make a *stand*."

"I don't get it, Walker," Devers said.

"Neither do I," Cooke said.

"What's the oath new soldiers take?" I asked. "Devers, I'm guessing you know it by heart."

"I do solemnly swear," Devers said without hesitation, "that I will support and defend the Constitution of the United States against all enemies, foreign and domestic—"

"Exactly!" I said. "Hughes had that posted in his workshop. And what did Donohue say she heard Hughes say at church?"

"That fracking was the greatest enemy," Cooke said.

"The greatest enemy our country faced from within. Don't you see? Hughes thinks he's doing his sworn duty."

"That doesn't tell us what he's going to do, though," Cooke said. "Or where."

"No, but I have a feeling his family history does. Devers, remember asking Hughes about his family's service?"

"Yeah. He talked about Bull Run and Louisville."

"Bull Run—that's Manassas. Right near Dulles," Cooke said.

"Yep," I said. "But the battle of Louisville was the one he talked most about."

"Well, Louisville wasn't really a battle at all," Devers said. "Bull Nelson held Louisville against the threat of invasion by the South."

"Why did that matter?" I asked.

"Louisville was a transportation hub. The railroads coming out of there fed supplies to a bunch of the Union armies—the Confederacy figured if they could take Louisville, they could cut off the supply lines."

"And that's why the stand was so important?" I said.

"Yeah," Devers said. "The Union knew what the South was planning, knew they couldn't give up the city. But their troops were out of position. They had to race to fortify the place, and they got kind of lucky the South didn't attack while they were vulnerable."

"Didn't you notice how Hughes lit up when he was talking about that?" I asked.

"I guess," Devers said. "Hughes was such a dim bulb, I didn't think he lit up all that much about anything."

"But, Seth," Cooke said, "we've looked at everything happening around Louisville. There're no events, no gatherings. The airport's not that big—there's nothing that's a target."

"Did you look at cargo?"

"Did I look at what?"

"Cargo," I said. "Louisville's the third busiest airport in the country when it comes to cargo."

"Give me a second," she said. The line went quiet and stayed that way for a while. The longer the silence went, the more convinced I became.

When she finally returned to the line, Cooke said, "You may be right."

"How's that?" I asked.

"AmerEast has an air shipment of equipment due into Louisville this morning. It's supposed to be transported by rail to West Virginia over the weekend."

"What's AmerEast?" Devers asked.

"The eighth largest oil company in the world," Cooke said. "And the fourth biggest fracker."

CHAPTER 31

Ultimately, we agreed that Cooke and Devers needed to continue on to DC and Pittsburgh—it was too risky not to have them leading the resources deployed to cover the other airports. But I knew Hughes was going to try to make a stand at Louisville, just like his ancestors had. I could feel it.

Question was, now that I knew that, what the hell could I possibly do to stop him?

Cooke had said the plane carrying the AmerEast shipment was due in at 7:05 a.m. The additional distance from Columbus to Louisville was going to add a half hour to my chopper's flight time—it would put me in just before six. I expected Hughes would be there early to set up his ambush—I'd need to intercept him in that hour-and-five-minute window.

But how could you stop something you couldn't even see?

As one part of my brain continued spinning on that and another did time/speed calculations, I noticed an alert on my phone's home screen.

Slightly horrified, I realized it must have been the text that caused the ping at the drug camp—I'd forgotten all about it between the shoot-out, the trip to the hospital, and the hunt for Hughes. When I opened it, I saw it had come from my godson, Michael:

Uncle Seth, you missed emoji of the day yesterday! I'm wondering where you are. If you're lost, send me a signal.

Following the text, he'd inserted symbols suggesting all the different ways I could get in touch. Some were obvious—a phone, a computer. But then he'd also added some cute ones: a signal fire, a telescope.

The message made me smile. I could remember a time when Michael couldn't even spell—now he was texting. But I also felt a small pang in my chest. How much he'd grown up already, and how much more he'd grow before I realized it.

That feeling sharpened and slid down into my gut. Not only was Michael doing all that without a father—because of me—but I couldn't be bothered to keep up with his texts. As the knot in my stomach continued to tighten, I kept my eyes locked on the screen.

Good, I told myself. *Keep looking at it. You deserve the discomfort.*

But as I stared at the icons in his message, my brain suddenly shifted gears: telephone, computer, fire, telescope.

Telephone. Converts sound into electricity and back into sound.

Computer. Runs on electricity, receives wireless and other electrical signals.

Fire. Radiates heat and light.

Telescope. Focuses light or other kinds of radiation so they can be seen from a distance.

Drastically divergent systems, but they all had one thing in common: waves.

Sound waves, electrical waves, radio waves, thermal waves. Each was a different form of radiation with its own wavelength and frequency. Our eyes could see some of those wavelengths—in the spectrum of visible light—but not others. So we'd created detectors to see other portions. Heat sensors "saw" waves in the infrared spectrum. Some telescopes "saw" radio waves emanating from deep space. In each instance we converted one kind of radiation we couldn't see into a different form that we could . . .

That was it.

The metamaterial in Hughes's drone was designed to cloak *visible* light reflections. But the drone emitted more radiation than that.

The most obvious one was heat: virtually everything had some kind of thermal signature. But all the drones I'd seen in Hughes's inventory used some kind of battery or hybrid engine. Electrically powered systems ran notoriously cool, so I couldn't guarantee there'd be much infrared radiation to detect. That wouldn't help.

The drone would also be communicating with Hughes's controller—the radio signals my drone gun was designed to drown out. But what if I used them to find the drone in the first place? If I could see the radio waves, I'd be able to locate not only the drone but also Hughes's transmitter.

If we could lock onto both, we could take both of them down simultaneously.

While that sounded solid in concept, I tried to pump the brakes on my excitement. Seeing radio waves wasn't something you did every day, and whipping up a device to do it from scratch wouldn't be easy. Especially in a darkened helicopter hurtling across the country at 175 miles per hour, with no laboratory or supplies.

I'd need to take it step by step.

To "see" any kind of signal, I'd need to receive it. That meant antennas. Thankfully, I had several. I didn't know exactly which would work best, but I could try them all.

Even if they gave me an eye into the sky, though, I had no idea what to look for. Hughes could be using any of an almost infinite number of frequencies. While Shen and I had done our best to deduce the range Hughes used, the drone gun hadn't worked before—which meant there was no guarantee we'd guessed right. And even if we had gotten the frequency correct, that presented its own problem: the drone gun itself would be a source of interference. Looking for the drone anywhere near the gun would be like trying to see stars in the sky at midday.

My head fell back against my shoulders. If only there was some way to know how Hughes had designed the system . . .

Wait. There was.

I had photos of the papers from his workbench.

I pulled them up and started swiping through them, skimming the text as fast as I could. Some pages were machine printed, some hand-written, so reviewing them was a slow process. After a few, I paused and thumbed out a text to Michael:

Thank you for your text, little man! You saved the day!

Although I couldn't find a lifesaver emoji, I added a blue ribbon, a trophy, and a heart.

It ended up taking almost every remaining minute of the flight, but as I felt the Black Hawk level and slow, I thought I'd come up with a system that might work.

The trick, it turned out, was something Hughes had said to Devers. Devers had asked about drones carrying cameras, and Hughes had noted that video and control signals would be carried on different frequencies. From Hughes's notes, I now knew what those two frequencies were.

Hughes and the drone would be sending control signals back and forth to each other. Those were the waves I needed to track. To do that, I'd zip-tied extra antennas onto the bottom of the drone gun, wired them to my phone, and then lashed the phone to a flat spot along the base of the gun. Using the phone, I'd accessed the internet and found some open-source software written to help networking engineers visualize Wi-Fi coverage in a particular space. They used it to determine whether enough signal carried into an office or a hotel lobby.

I needed to do the same thing, only on a much bigger scale.

The software's visual interface was pretty clunky—it showed transmission waves as lines and arcs, but those became distracting when trying to isolate their point of origin, especially on my tiny screen. Through a few tweaks of the code, I was able to change the interface so that each signal source would be displayed as a blinking light, its color and speed indicating its relative intensity. A red, nearly constant dot would show the strongest signal, while orange and yellow dots, and dots that blinked at a slower frequency, would indicate weaker ones.

Because I'd be looking for the control signals, though, I'd needed to change the noise the drone gun was designed to project so that I wouldn't interfere with my own detection of the drone. Thankfully, Hughes's notes contained the transmission plan for video data from the drone. By bombarding the drone with noise in that frequency range, I ought to be able to interfere with Hughes's vision and force him to fly blind.

While I wished I had time to test the thing, I didn't see how I could. And I saw now that I'd run out of time. A sprawl of airfield lights was growing below us. From the look of it, we'd approached from the east—one concrete runway lay directly ahead, while the rest were set at an angle. To our left, a massive terminal building loomed, with planes evenly spaced along its length. Another building stood to our right, but it looked tiny in comparison. Probably the airport's fixed-base operator for general and civilian aviation.

My clock said it was 5:55 a.m.

The pilot's voice crackled in my headset. "Do you have a preference for where we set you down, sir?"

"I need to get to the highest point," I said. "The terminal doesn't look to have much elevation, though—that's not gonna help."

"The terminal is a single story," he said. "But that's not the terminal at our ten o'clock. The passenger terminal's at our two thirty."

Checking the window, I saw he meant the smaller building at the far edge of the field. "Then what's that giant building in front of us?"

"That's the UPS processing center."

We'd continued advancing across the tarmac, and now I saw what he meant—every plane lined up along the larger building bore the shipping company's brown-and-yellow logo, as did the scores of tractor trailers, parked and waiting to be loaded. But none of that solved my predicament: the airport had no high ground to occupy.

"What's the tallest thing around? The control tower?"

"On the field, that's affirmative," the pilot said. "But there are some taller structures just off-site."

"Can you swing us around? Maybe do a loop of the airfield or something?"

I didn't hear the flight crew laugh, but they might as well have: no sooner had I asked the question than the helicopter banked sharply to our left. We pulled a tight 180-degree turn that pressed my back into the seat. Once we returned to the edge of the tarmac, they banked in the opposite direction to follow it.

Although my insides felt wrung out, I didn't have time to complain about the ride—my face was planted against the window, desperately scanning for anyplace I could set up. The eastern edge of the airfield was bordered by a freeway that separated it from a residential neighborhood and a few small motels. Although the sight lines were clear in that area, I'd need more elevation.

We traced the concrete ribbon north until it fed into a giant knot of over- and underpasses at the northeast corner of the field. The highway running along the airport's northern edge was wider and lined with larger chain hotels. When we reached the next corner and turned south, though, the surrounding construction dropped back down to low-slung industrial buildings, a pattern that continued along the southern edge of the airport.

"Those buildings on the north side," I said, "they seem to be the tallest things around."

"Out past them is Kentucky Kingdom," the pilot said.

"What's that?"

"An amusement park. It's closed this time of year, but it's got some tall towers."

"Can you patch me through to Quantico?"

The radio operators connected me to Cooke, who reported that she'd reached the Dulles operations center. Once I explained where we were and what I was looking for, she had her research people get working.

"Let's see," Cooke said, "the coasters are each about a hundred feet tall. Oh, but there's a Ferris wheel that's one fifty."

"The tallest hotel looked like it was only four or five stories," I said. "Sounds like Kentucky Kingdom's the way to go."

While I was relieved we'd found something tall, the base-instinct part of my brain was already dreading the view from that height.

"We'll square it away with local law enforcement," Cooke said. "I'll see if they can get someone out there to help you. But for now, just get there and do what you can."

"You heard the boss," I said to the pilot over the intercom. "Can you set us down by Kentucky Kingdom? As close as you can to the Ferris wheel?"

I checked the time again as we cut across the field: 6:09 a.m.

The hotels lining the north side—the kind of utilitarian-looking brick-and-glass buildings I'd stayed in a thousand times as an air marshal—were ringed by a shared parking lot. Lights from the highway spilled over a grassy berm, illuminating the front side of the lot and the faces of the buildings. Occupancy looked high: there wasn't an empty spot to be seen.

Once we crossed over the roofs, though, it was a different story. The parking lot on the back side of the buildings stood almost completely empty and was bordered by a grassy field that, from the air, looked to lead directly to Kentucky Kingdom's rides.

The Black Hawk touched down along the line where the asphalt met the grass. I had my bag, repacked with the laptop and supplies, slung around my neck as I hopped down and took the drone gun in one hand and the battery in the other. I hunched over and started away from the helicopter; it rose before I got clear, the rotors kicking up a storm of dust and dirt that assaulted my exposed skin.

Although my injuries had stiffened up during the flight, I started across the field on foot as quickly as I could. The uppermost tips of the towers inside Kentucky Kingdom were painted a jaundiced yellow by light from the highway that cleared the hotel roofs, while the rest of the park, like the grassy field around me, was immersed in dark shadow.

Halfway to the nearest set of rides, a chain-link fence topped with barbed wire blocked my path. Although there was a gate, it was padlocked shut with a heavy chain. Through the fencing, I could see exactly where I needed to get, but while I might have been able to climb over, as banged up as I was, there was no way I could do it hauling fifty-plus pounds of battery. So I started to my right, following the fence line, hoping to find some other entrance.

I'd made it maybe twenty-five yards when the shrill *whoop-whoop* of sirens began to pierce the dull hum coming from the freeway. In the distance, strobing police flashers were approaching along the edge of the field. As they drew closer, one pair gradually spread into two. The silver cruisers screeched to a halt in front of me.

For a moment, I froze. While I hoped Cooke had sent them to help, I realized that wasn't a given. Someone who looked like me, carrying something resembling a rifle in one hand and a bulky load in the other, sneaking around a darkened lot near an airport in the middle of the night? People had gotten arrested—or shot—for a whole lot less.

Thankfully, when the nearest cruiser door opened, the first words I heard were, "Agent Walker?"

I released the breath I'd been holding. "That's me."

"We got orders to get you up onto the Giant Wheel."

I climbed into the back seat of the nearest cruiser, and both cars peeled into a tight Uturn, thankfully without the sirens this time. The dashboard clock said it was now 6:14 a.m.

Although part of me worried about losing time with the cops, the truth was I never would have made it without them. We had to backtrack all the way around to the far side of the park to reach the main entrance. The gates there were padlocked as well, but now another speeding cruiser arrived from the opposite direction. A man in a flannel shirt and jeans jumped out of that one, unlocked the chains, and then yanked one side of the gate back to let us in.

My car sped through first, following a curving access road until we skidded to a halt next to the base of a thick metal piling that extended upward at an angle. As I stepped out from the car, my eyes followed the beam upward: it looked to be one of a pair that met to create a triangular base on this side of the Ferris wheel. A matching pair of supports stood on the opposite side.

The wheel itself loomed overhead, dizzyingly tall. More than anything, though, I was struck by how densely packed the wheel was—two or three times the number of spokes you'd expect radiated outward from the central hub, and I counted at least forty gondolas around the outside ring.

The other cruisers caught up to us now, forming a line along the side of the access road. Several uniformed officers emerged, along with the man in flannel. My driver gestured toward him and said, "Agent Walker, this is Manuel Ferrera, one of the park managers. He's gonna get you up there."

When I went to shake Ferrera's hand, he wore a nervous smile. "These guys pulled me out of bed," he said. "I thought I was under arrest or something."

Despite the clock ticking in my head, I tried to chuckle to help calm him down. "You're not the only one. Help out with this, they might give you a key to the city."

"You wanna be all the way at the very top?" he asked.

I sighed. "*Want* is kind of a strong word. But yeah, higher is better."

"Okay, let's get you in, then I'll fire her up. The lights gonna bother you?"

"Can you run it with them off?" I asked.

Ferrera shook his head. "But there's none inside the gondolas—just on the outside framing."

"I'll make it work." Honestly, at this point, a few light bulbs seemed to be the least of my problems.

A raised boardwalk had been constructed around the entrance to the wheel. Ferrera led me up onto it and then up a slight ramp to the bottommost gondola. It had just enough headroom for me to stand inside on a floor made of textured metal. Rugged fiberglass walls extended only about thigh high, while the rest was open-air, save a series of metal bars that connected to the matching fiberglass roof. The gondola's "door" consisted of nothing more than two metal ovals that latched together across the opening—it seemed awfully flimsy to me as Ferrera shut the clasp and locked me in.

Glancing around, I was slightly dismayed to see there were no belts or other restraints mounted onto the molded seats. The car was wide enough for at least two people to stand on each side, giving me a fair amount of maneuvering room.

I took a deep breath and set the battery on the seat across from me. Making sure I had enough slack in the cable for the tip of the gun to protrude out through the bars on my side of the gondola, I sat down, slipping my laptop bag off my shoulder and setting it next to me.

I'd just activated my phone when the gondola jerked to one side and started to move.

CHAPTER 32

The gondola's sudden motion caught me by surprise; I hadn't heard any engine noise. Despite the size of the wheel, it needed virtually no time to accelerate to speed. I'd traveled nearly a third of the way up before I realized what had happened.

As my car passed the angled support, I could see why: electric motors on the top and bottom surfaces of the beam were driving the wheel around. Another pair were doing the same on the matching support on the opposite side. Mounting the motors so low must help with maintenance.

Now that I got a look at it, the interior structure of the wheel was far more complex than I'd realized. From the outside you saw spokes connecting the outer ring to the hub, but that was a kind of two-dimensional illusion. What I'd thought of as "spokes" were really nothing more than coverings for the real support structure: girders connected by thick metal poles to their counterparts on the opposite side in a dense web of diagonal cross-bracing.

I also saw what Ferrera meant about the lights—dozens of bulbs had been mounted on the outside surfaces of each girder cover and both outer rings that held the gondolas, thick cabling along the insides of the girders powering them. I was riding a giant, glowing target, and that wasn't even the worst part.

As the gondola continued rising, my heart began pounding in my chest, and my stomach started feeling hollow. I told myself to ignore the motion and the height, to focus solely on the job. But that proved easier said than done. Once the car got halfway up, the wind kicked in—not any little breeze, mind you, but full gusts that slapped my face and howled past my ears.

They also caused the car to sway from side to side.

I could feel the cold flash of sweat across all my skin at once. That moisture seemed drawn directly from my mouth and throat, which went bone-dry and constricted enough to make it hard to breathe, let alone swallow. Looking at the floor helped slightly, but I knew I couldn't do that the whole time.

Instead of pulling out my earpiece, I unplugged it from my audio player and attached it to my phone, which was still mounted on the gun. I dialed into the line Cooke had given me and listened as it rang, trying to let the sound distract me from everything else.

"Seth, is that you?" Cooke's steely voice sounded particularly reassuring. "Are you in position?"

"Almost."

"You sound weird," she said. "And there's a ton of background noise."

"Wind," I said. "It's awfully high."

"I forgot—you hate heights, don't you?"

"Yeah," was all I could manage.

When the car reached the very top of the wheel, it stopped with a slight jolt that gave the gondola additional sideways momentum. Although I tried to focus on stationary objects—the metal girder of the outer ring, now above the gondola roof, and the spokes running vertically on either side of the car—it only made the gondola's motion seem more drastic. Every little swing felt like a giant lurch. Through the doorway, I could see to the ground below, which, thanks to the lights on the wheel, was now partially illuminated. I looked away, wishing it were still shrouded in darkness.

"Talk me through what you're doing," Cooke said in my ear.

"I'm in . . . position now," I said, generating what little breath I could. "Top of the wheel. Switching on the scanner to look for Hughes's control signals."

I didn't want to activate the switch on the PCB board and power the jamming circuits quite yet because I had no way of knowing exactly how much time the batteries would give me.

"See anything?" Cooke asked.

"Scanning now," I said. "What time is it?"

"Six twenty-three. You think Hughes will have his bird up this early?"

"He should want to scout around a little bit. He's not worried about it being seen."

I gazed off to the horizon, and that helped a little. The Louisville skyline loomed straight ahead if I sat in my seat correctly. The shadows of different roller coasters and rides were visible to my right and left. The freeway, and the airport beyond it, sat over my left shoulder.

Turning in the seat so that I rested on my left hip, I was able to point the drone gun's antennas out through the bars toward the airport. The software interface appeared on my phone screen, ready to start.

I began by angling the antennas toward the right-hand side of the airport, then slowly moved them back to my left. Talking to Cooke had slowed my pulse enough that I allowed myself a quick glance out toward the runways. Part of me worried they were too far away. But I reminded myself to think in three dimensions—if the drone were circling outside the airfield to avoid air traffic, it ought to pass directly overhead.

"Anything?" Cooke's voice hadn't turned desperate yet, but it was getting closer.

"Nothing," I said. "But it may take a bit to get synced with him." My scanner was cycling through the frequency values in Hughes's modulation scheme—I wouldn't necessarily see him or the drone until we got onto the same wavelength, literally. "Hang on, what's that?"

"What do you see, Seth? Is it the drone?"

I had the antennas pointed to the far left of the field, the side bordered by the freeway. On the phone screen, a yellow dot was blinking.

"I've got a signal," I said. "But it's stationary. Not the drone."

"Is it Hughes?"

"Might be. Give me a second." As I swept the gun back toward the center of the airfield, more yellow dots appeared. Five in all, forming a rough pentagram around the airport's circumference. Not surprisingly, the strongest signal was the closest, which looked to be mounted on top of one of the nearby hotels. "Clever."

"What?" Cooke asked. "What do you see?"

"Five transmitters. He's set them up around the airport—they must help him boost the signals, to make sure he doesn't lose contact with the drone."

"Can you tell which one's him?"

"No way to know," I said.

"How about the drone?"

"Still don't see it." Thinking maybe I was looking too low on the horizon, I raised the antennas up to a thirty-degree angle and started sweeping across the runways again.

I got all the way back to the right-hand side with nothing. "Time check?"

"Six twenty-six."

Was I wrong about something? Hughes's transmitters were out there—why wasn't the drone?

The wind kicked up again, and as the car swayed, any sense of calm I'd achieved evaporated immediately.

Just keep looking, I told myself. *It's got to be out there somewhere . . .*

I raised the antennas another fifteen degrees and swept again. Still nothing.

"Seth, you've got me worried now. We're at six thirty-one."

"I know, I know." While I ran calculations in my head, trying to double-check everything, I raised the antennas as high as I could between the crossbars until they pointed nearly straight up.

"C'mon . . ."

I held it there for several seconds, watching the screen and silently begging for something, anything, to appear. When nothing did, I resigned myself to lowering the gun and starting over.

Before I could, a bright-red circle flashed on my phone's screen.

It slid from left to right, traveling so fast that I barely had time to register it before it disappeared off the edge.

When I tilted the antennas to my right, it reappeared—a large red dot, barely flashing, its signal was so strong. It was still moving, but with the angle now more oblique, I was able to follow it and keep it roughly in the middle of the screen.

Stealing a glance out between the bars, I saw nothing—no lights, no moving craft. Just empty sky.

"I've got it," I said.

"Are you positive?" Cooke asked.

"It's a huge radio signal, consistent with Hughes's parameters, and I've got no visual—I repeat, no visual to match. It's the cloaked drone."

"We're at six thirty-seven, Seth. If you're going to down it, you'd better do it fast."

"I hear you," I said, but my eyes were locked on the screen. The red dot had shrunk in size as it flew farther away, and now it was starting to drift back toward the left-hand side of the screen.

The drone was circling the field, exactly as we had in the chopper.

Given where I was, that meant there'd eventually be a several-second window during which the drone would follow the freeway, heading directly toward me.

"I'm going to activate the jammer when it comes close to me on its next pass," I said.

"You sure you can wait that long?"

"I don't want to spook him," I said. "And I don't know how many chances I'll get. Better to hit him once, head-on, with everything I've got."

"Be sure, Seth," Cooke said. "We need you to be sure."

Keeping my eyes on the phone screen, I moved one hand to the PC board and felt around until my fingers closed over the switch for the jammer.

The drone was making its turn at the southeast corner of the field—that left just one more turn to go.

Even though this wasn't like firing the Sig, I noticed my brain starting to go through my routine shot discipline. My breathing slowed, my eyes narrowed their focus.

The red dot had nearly doubled in size now. From its motion, I could tell it was rounding the turn over the spaghetti junction of highways. Then it held steady on my phone screen and began to grow. Coming right at me.

With the drone gun pointed out the left-hand side of the car, I moved the antennas slightly to line the dot up in the center of the screen. Then I flipped the switch.

A half second after I activated the jammer, the dot jumped on the screen. Where before its flight path had been smooth and steady, now it began bobbing. It wasn't easy keeping it centered in the focus of the beam now, but it was working—Hughes was flying blind. As it grew closer, the dot shook and shimmied.

And that's when the machine guns sounded.

CHAPTER 33

Bullets tore through the fiberglass sidewall of the gondola and ricocheted off the metal girders all around it.

With my whole side exposed, the only thing that saved me was the way the drone was jittering through the air as it approached from my left. If Hughes couldn't see, he couldn't shoot straight—I needed to keep the pressure on.

Cooke was screaming in my ear, asking about the sound of bullets hitting the gondola, but I ignored her, focusing on the drone and nothing else.

As I worked to keep the antennas locked on, though, Hughes had other ideas. The drone whipped by overhead, then circled back, coming at me head-on this time. As it approached, it fired again, another hail of bullets striking the gondola.

Somehow, I still hadn't taken a hit. I made myself as flat as I could, trying to present as small a target as possible while still watching the dot and aiming the gun. As the drone drew closer to the gondola, it received even more energy from my drone gun. At first it floundered and sank slightly; then it almost recovered before dropping again.

"I've got you . . ."

Suddenly, the drone shot upward. The climb was so steep, there was no way I could follow it—the antennas, protruding through the bars, couldn't angle up that far. I worked to pull the antennas back into the car and swing them around, but I was too slow.

Shots rang out behind me.

The drone must have looped over the gondola—it was approaching from the opposite side now, at full strength. Against the dark sky, I could see bright muzzle flashes, and machine-gun fire continued to ring out, each impact causing the car to shift and shake.

Although I rolled onto my backside to keep the antennas aimed at the drone, I knew its bullets would travel a lot faster than my hands. Even as I tried to aim generally toward where the flashes were, I squeezed my eyes shut, bracing to be ripped apart.

I felt one searing slice through my right side, below my ribs but above my waist, followed by a pop in the seat behind me. A superficial wound, but the first of many to come.

Another set of shots rang out. Not the drone's. Different sounds, from a different place—single shots instead of auto-fire.

I opened my eyes in time to see the drone's muzzle flashes angle downward. I rushed to the opposite side of the gondola. Below me, the police officers were stationed behind the doors of their cruisers, firing up into space at the flashes even as a hail of bullets rained down on them.

"No!"

I had no idea if they heard me screaming as the drone's bullets ripped across the hoods and roofs of the cars, sending the officers ducking for cover. I pushed the antennas through the bars on this side, trying to find the red dot on the phone screen. As I was searching for it, the guns fell silent. I turned the antennas in every direction but couldn't reacquire the signal.

Finally, I spotted it.

It had grown small on the screen, seemingly retreating. At its new distance, it appeared to be hesitating, turning. Once it started back toward the wheel, it stayed low to the ground and looked like it was picking up speed.

Another strafing run.

"Get out of there!" I screamed as loudly as I could, but the police only stared up at the sky. Either they couldn't hear me or were too preoccupied to notice.

I continued firing the jamming signal toward the drone, but its effect had diminished. Part of it was likely the distance, but I also guessed I had drained my battery. Without power, I was as defenseless as the guys below.

The dot kept growing, following the amusement park's access road.

I tried to remain calm. To think.

How can I find a power source to replace the battery at the top of a Ferris wheel?

Well, come to think of it, I was standing on one. The whole wheel had electricity pumping through it—it might as well have been a giant battery.

The wheel's electric motors would be the surest bet. Turning this giant hunk of metal required a ton of torque, which required a huge power expenditure. Glancing downward, I saw the motors attached to the support beams below. Probably a hundred feet away, straight down. No chance I could get to them in the seconds I had remaining.

That left the lights.

Each bulb probably didn't draw much amperage, but to light all of them simultaneously had to take a ton of juice. And the cabling ran inside the spoke coverings, a few feet away.

A few feet *outside the car*.

My heart and stomach seemed to move in opposite directions when I realized what I needed to do. My throat closed again while my entire GI tract seemed to want to drop out the other end.

With my hands shaking, I managed to detach the battery cables and drape the drone gun's zip-tie sling over my neck. After a single trembling step toward the door, I told myself I needed to do better than that.

I wasn't sure if my shaking fingers could work the gate latch, but somehow they pried it open. The ovals swung inward on their hinges, leaving nothing separating me from the metal pole except a couple of feet of air.

No time to wait, I told myself. The drone was closing in on the police and Ferrera. Rocking one foot back a step, I launched myself outward.

The initial impact wasn't that bad. The pole struck my chest, feeling solid, and I wrapped my arms and legs around it as tightly as I could. Both my sides burned like crazy—the broken ribs on one side, the new bullet wound on the other—but as I held there a moment, I thought to myself that this idiotic plan might just work.

Then I started sliding.

The pole had been painted with thick industrial paint that felt as slick as ice. With sweat drenching my arms and hands, I didn't stand a chance: I dropped a few inches at first; then, after managing to stop myself by squeezing tighter, I really started picking up speed.

I must have dropped ten or twenty feet—air rushing by my skin, ground rushing up to meet me—when my foot struck one of the cross-braces. Although my boot started to slide outward on the diagonal shaft, I had enough friction to stop myself.

After a moment, I could breathe again, and my heart seemed to restart. Glancing around, I found myself in a precarious position on the pole, but I was stable. The cross-brace was sufficiently solid, and I had enough of a foothold, I could start thinking about retrieving the drone gun from my back and reaching for the electric cabling inside of the girder ahead of me.

The clock in my head told me the drone had to be getting close as I let go of the pole with my right hand. I'd just raised it up to my shoulder to grab the zip-tie strap when a fiery explosion erupted below.

CHAPTER 34

The force of the explosion shook the wheel, and while I held on tight, I wondered whether it had done enough damage that I might end up riding the metal structure down as it collapsed.

After a moment, things stabilized, and I risked a quick look to the ground—one of the police cruisers had been destroyed, and another was burning. I didn't see the policemen or Ferrera.

Hughes's bombs, made from the match-head chemicals in the barn.

We'd half assumed there'd be one large explosive, but he must have equipped the drone with a collection of smaller ones.

Heat rising from below reached me now, and as the air circulated, I noticed things starting to shift. Again, my immediate panic was that some structural defect was about to send the whole thing tumbling, but the motion was subtler than that. Almost imperceptible, but definitely to one side and not the other.

A moment later, I understood: the braking system must have given way, either partially or completely, allowing the Giant Wheel to start listing to my right.

That was just great—I was the only thing upsetting the balance of the wheel. Eventually gravity would pull me around and down, and then I'd end up on my side or completely upside down.

If I survived that long.

The ironic thing was, if I were going to take the drone down, I actually needed Hughes to try to finish me off.

Letting go with my right hand again, I reached back and got ahold of the drone gun this time. With my arm outstretched, I panned the antennas in a wide circle, hoping to locate any trace of a signal.

I finally did, leaning almost all the way back away from the pole. Based on where the dot was and how it was moving, I guessed that Hughes had decided to follow the access road all the way around the amusement park. That would bring the drone back around in a few seconds, maybe a minute, to finish us off.

Was that enough time?

As much as leaning back had hurt, pulling myself back to the pole was worse—it felt like having hot pokers shoved into both sides. Once I got my chest back against the metal, though, I could see the cabling I needed. Locking my left arm around the pole, I wrapped the drone gun's strap around that wrist and passed the gun to that hand. Then I reached out with my right.

Thankfully, the wiring along the girder wasn't tacked down—it had been run loose between periodic junction boxes. They hadn't left much slack, but I was able to get my fingers underneath it. Squeezing it tight, I pulled as hard as I could, trying to use my arm and shoulder instead of my side. Two tugs, and the wiring finally gave way.

The end of the cable was a frayed mess, but I managed to splice its ends onto the drone gun's leads the best I could. A couple of LEDs on the circuit board lit up, meaning current was flowing.

Time for one last shoot-out.

Switching the gun back to my right hand, I began scanning around. That's when I realized how far the wheel had turned while I hadn't been paying attention. I'd dropped from twelve o'clock all the way down to two thirty. That meant the drone was now directly over my head. It also meant more of my body weight was being supported by my arms and legs instead of the cross-bracing.

Lifting the gun up past my shoulder killed my side—I started sweating even more than before. But I told myself to focus on the screen, to block everything else out.

After a few seconds of scanning, I found the red dot again. It had turned around to start its bombing run. That meant I had only a few seconds left.

Of course, I'd dropped almost to horizontal on the wheel now, which meant I wouldn't last much longer anyway.

The drone continued approaching, and I kept that red dot as close to the center of my phone screen as I could. Once it had closed about half the distance to me, the jamming started to have an effect. The drone started shaking again, its flight path growing rocky and imprecise. The lighting cable was giving me plenty of juice. All I had to do was keep the antennas pointed at the target.

I heard crackling, and glancing into the distance, I saw flashes. The drone was firing its guns, but I didn't need to worry about that anymore.

I just needed to hang on.

By the time the drone had halved the distance between us again, it was really having difficulty—the dot was wavering all over the place. The added power was doing the trick. If I could just keep the jamming signal locked on . . .

The drone fired a long flurry of shots that plinked and ricocheted around me, but that turned out to be its last gasp. As it came around the final curve of the access road, the drone clipped something—a tree, a wire—and careened into the ground.

I heard the crash more than saw it, but once the pieces had come to rest, I could see small fires burning.

It had worked. The damn thing was down.

I let out a little grunt. Breathing felt somehow easier, although I had to order my muscles not to go completely limp since I was now perched with my head below the rest of my body.

"Seth? Seth? Are you alive?"

Cooke's voice, in my ear. I didn't know if she'd been shouting the whole time, or whether she could tell something had changed.

"Alive," I said. "And the drone's not."

"Where's Hughes? Do you have a lock on him?"

Oh no.

While surviving the firefight, I'd forgotten about the need to keep track of Hughes's five transmitters. He could be hiding behind any one of them. I guessed I had dropped to four thirty or five o'clock on the wheel. From that odd position, I tried to extend the gun out in the direction of the airfield. But it was so heavy, and my grip on the pole felt like it was giving way.

I tried to adjust, tried to lock my knees and free arm around the pole. Blood had started rushing to my face, flushing it, while the pressure on my arm continued to increase. The sweat on my skin had me sliding on the paint.

"I don't . . ."

"You don't what? You don't have eyes on Hughes? Say again, Seth."

I tried to sneak a breath, to get more oxygen to my muscles, which were screaming for it, as my side protested more than ever. Although I clenched every muscle, I could feel myself starting to slip.

"I—"

Then something changed.

The wheel, which had been drifting downward since the explosion, suddenly jolted to a stop. Almost completely upside down, I craned my neck around, looking all over the place to see what had changed.

Finally, I saw him.

Ferrera.

He'd climbed the access ladders to one set of motors—from my vantage point it looked like he was about fall up into the sky. He saw me and waved, a big grin on his face. I had no idea what he'd done exactly, but he'd definitely stopped the wheel from turning.

With the last bit of strength I could muster, I lifted the drone gun one final time. At this low angle, I was pointing it out into the trees—I didn't know what I'd be able to see.

The screen didn't show all five dots, only three: the closest one, on the hotel, and then one on either side of the airport. They were all glowing like before.

Until one blinked.

The closest one, the one that had been the strongest.

It blinked again. Blinked, then disappeared.

I did a double take, trying to make sure my whole detection system hadn't crapped out. But the other two lights were still there. Only the center signal had disappeared.

"Hotel," I said.

"What?" Cooke asked. "Hotel? What hotel?"

I wanted to answer, but I had nothing left to do it with. Even if I'd had enough power to inhale, my side still burned like crazy, threatening to take away my grip any second. As my face continued to flush and I started to wonder what would happen when I hit the ground headfirst, I saw Ferrera again.

He had some kind of bent metal pole with him—it looked like the key to a giant windup toy. He plugged the pole into the side of one of the motors.

A crank!

He turned the wide end of the pole, and suddenly the Giant Wheel shifted. I moved several feet closer to the ground.

Yes.

Yes!

I wanted to yell, to encourage him, but I had no breath for that, either.

He turned the crank again, and once again the wheel shifted.

Two more turns, and I was completely upside down, my head pointed at the ground. I could see the lines between the boardwalk boards directly below me. I imagined this was as close as I was going to get.

I let go with my knees, hoping my legs might drop and help cushion the blow.

In the end, my feet did end up hitting first. They didn't soften the impact on my back, though, which slammed the ground immediately after them.

Sputtering, coughing, I rolled onto my side. *There might still be time,* I told myself.

I struggled up to one knee, then one foot. As I stood, the ground felt uncertain, as if it might tip out from underneath me at any moment. Shaking off the vertigo, I tried to regain my bearings and find what I was looking for.

The police cars.

I staggered over to the one that remained in the best shape, forcing myself behind the wheel and yanking the belt across my chest. Thankfully, the keys were in it, and when I turned the ignition, the engine roared to life, along with the flashers and the siren.

I stomped on the gas before remembering to shift—when I finally dropped it into gear, the back end fishtailed from the torque. First light had touched the horizon now, and as the car spun, I scanned the sky until I found the silhouettes of the hotels.

Straightening the steering wheel and pointing the cruiser toward them, I pinned the pedal to the floor. I sped along the access road until it started to curve back toward the main entrance. I continued straight, plowing across the grass toward the chain-link fence I'd seen when the Black Hawk had landed.

I didn't even glance at the dashboard. I knew I needed as much momentum as the engine could give me.

The cruiser hit the gate at full speed. The chain snapped, and I barreled through.

As I reached the big parking lot behind the hotels, I scanned ahead, searching for movement. If Hughes had been up on one of the roofs, it would take him a couple of minutes to get down. He had to be here, somewhere.

Finding nothing by the time I reached the far end of the lot, I pulled a hard turn, rounding the farthest building and circling around the front side. Here, a single line of vehicles was parked along the lot's outer edge, facing out toward the freeway. My eyes scanned as far down the row as they could in the dark.

That's when I saw him.

Two buildings away, a tall figure, dashing from right to left and ducking between two cars.

I floored the accelerator again.

As I gained speed, brake lights flashed near where the figure had disappeared, followed by reverse lights glowing white. A car began to pull out of a parking spot—a small hatchback Ford.

It paused momentarily, and its taillights changed color again, shifting into drive.

I let the cruiser drift to the right a bit, then cut the wheel back left. When I made contact, my head flew forward toward the steering wheel. It was like taking the world's hardest punch to the face: for a long moment, everything in my vision turned an impenetrable white.

Gradually, my senses returned. There was pain—a lot of it—and a burning smell in my nostrils. But I'd done it, plowed the cruiser into the driver's side of the hatchback, pinning it against the car occupying the space next to the one the Ford had just vacated. Even better, I'd managed to strike the driver's side door with the corner of my bumper. All I could see of Hughes was the back of his head, but the way the door had collapsed inward, he wouldn't be climbing out that way, either.

Through the fog, I told myself to stay on the gas. I pressed the pedal with whatever reservoir of strength I had remaining, and the scorched smell intensified as tires burned against the pavement. The cruiser's engine howled as it forced both the little hatchback and the neighboring car to the very edge of the lot, and then beyond it.

A deep, grassy ditch separated the parking lot from the freeway, and now all three cars slid down into it. Trees had sprouted at the bottom of the swale, and they acted as a natural barricade, blocking the progress of the neighboring car. Hughes's hatchback continued to be squeezed against that, the weight of my cruiser further crumpling the side of the Ford.

After all three vehicles came to rest, I looked for Hughes—I thought I saw him collapsed over the Ford's steering wheel. I tried to stay conscious, told myself to get out of the car and slap cuffs on him, but my body was done listening to me. My eyes blinked a couple of times, disobeying my orders to stay open.

Finally, they shut.

CHAPTER 35

When I woke up, everything hurt.

My face, my chest.

More than anything, though, my right side stung like hell. I glanced down to find fresh stitches in my skin—a four-inch line, just below my ribs. A medic hovering over me explained that I'd lost a fair amount of blood from the wound left by the drone bullet. I was lucky, he said— an inch or two closer to my midsection, and I would have died on the Ferris wheel.

The medic was wearing a helmet. I vaguely noticed an electronic sound to his voice—that's when I realized he was speaking over an intercom. We were in another helicopter.

"Where—"

Before I could finish the question, he said, "Quantico. And we've got two hours left, so go back to sleep."

Who was I to argue with a highly trained medical professional?

I woke again as the helicopter was touching down. Thankfully, they'd left my earpiece in; I noticed a voice chattering its way through a biography of Thomas Edison that I vaguely remembered downloading. Some of my strength had returned—enough that I forced myself upright and shook the medic's hand.

An agent waiting at the helicopter door helped me inside an adjacent building, down a twist of hallways to a passage where the doors were paired. We stopped at a room marked "Interview 1A."

Inside was a monitoring station—like other similar rooms I'd seen, the dimly lit space existed solely to watch and record interviews occurring in the companion room next door. A large one-way mirror consumed most of one wall, while computers and monitors dominated the table in the center of the room.

Cooke and Devers sat next to each other at the table, hunched over a screen that displayed four different views of the seating arrangements on the other side of the glass. A technician sat at a desk in the corner, presumably running the audio and video.

As soon as we crossed the threshold, Cooke and Devers stood.

"Don't be all formal on my account," I said as the agent helped lower me into a chair. Cooke's expression as she looked me over said I looked bad, but there were more important things to worry about. "Where's Hughes?"

"Got flown in a few minutes before you," Devers said.

"You ready to work your magic?" I asked Cooke, nodding at the one-way glass.

Her freckles seemed to connect in a blush as she smiled sheepishly. "We'll see."

An hour later, Cooke's smile was nowhere to be found.

As bad as I felt, I took some solace in the fact that Hughes looked worse—his face was black and blue, and they'd put a brace around his neck and taped his nose. But the injuries hadn't softened him: after forty-five minutes facing Cooke's best interrogation, the only answers he'd given were his name, rank, air force ID number, and date of birth.

Now back in the monitoring room with Devers and me, she guzzled from a plastic water bottle fast enough that the sides collapsed inward with a loud crinkling sound. "I cannot believe this guy," she said, after a quick breath. "We've got him dead to rights. I'm offering him a way out, and he just won't take it. I mean, I've had plenty of subjects lawyer up to avoid talking, but I've never seen anything like this."

"How about I take a shot at him?" asked Devers.

Cooke's eyebrows rose. "I don't know, Mitchell . . ."

"What have we got to lose?"

"It's just that . . . I know how emotionally involved in this case you are—more than anyone, really—and interrogation is one of those things where emotion can get the best of you—"

Devers leaned forward, pressing his palms flat on the table. "Trust me. I *get* this guy. I can talk to him."

Cooke glanced over at me, presumably for support.

"He's not going to crack," I said. "That's pretty obvious. The only way we're gonna get anywhere is to get underneath his exterior somehow. Maybe Devers can do it."

Her expression changed, although I wasn't sure it was for the better. Finally, she shrugged. "Okay, take a shot. But if you find yourself getting angry, or upset—"

Devers raised his hands. "I'll pull myself out, I swear."

As he left the office and the door closed, Cooke mumbled through gritted teeth. "This better work."

Huddled around the monitor, we watched Devers enter the interrogation room. Cooke tapped the volume button, turning up the sound in our earphones.

Devers made for the chair across from Hughes, whose eyes were pointed at the floor. Once he'd gotten seated, arms folded in front of him, he said, "I came in to talk to you, soldier to soldier."

Hughes's eyes flicked up, and he started reciting his name again.

Devers shook his head. "I know all that," he said, his accent slightly thicker than usual. "Save your breath and just listen for a minute."

Hughes stopped talking.

"You and me," Devers said, "we're the same, you know."

Across the table, Hughes's eyes dropped again.

"Don't get me wrong, you look more like *them*." Devers nodded toward the door. "But when it comes down to it, it's really you and me. We're both from tiny dots on the map no one's ever heard of. Neither of us grew up with two nickels to rub together. We both went off, trying to prove we were actually worth a damn. Sound familiar?"

Hughes didn't answer. But his eyes slowly rose once more.

"That's right," Devers said. "You know I'm telling the truth now. You might have been a flyboy and me a ground pounder, but end of the day, we got a lot more in common than folks who haven't seen the shit a soldier sees, you know?"

While Hughes still didn't respond, he maintained eye contact.

"We've both been out in it. Following orders. Trying not to die, but also trying to show we're not the dirt-poor dumbfucks everybody thinks we are. And, for a while, when you're on a mission, you actually get to believe it.

"Then we come back from whatever godforsaken desert they sent us off to, figuring we made it. That we proved ourselves. And guess what? Not a damn thing changed. You might have gotten some education or picked up some skills, but that don't really matter. When you and I go apply for a job, try to do something else, all the person on the other side of the desk sees is a grunt from nowhere who was lucky enough not to die. Am I right?"

Hughes still didn't look away. He swallowed noticeably, his Adam's apple bobbing.

"Yeah, I think you feel me." He leaned back in his chair. "Guys like us, we never got to pick the missions, either. For me, it was, 'Patrol over here, shake down this village, find this bad guy.' For you, I'm guessing it was more like, 'Fly over there, shadow this guy, shoot a missile at that guy.' Am I close?"

Hughes remained silent but seemed to blink his agreement.

"That's what I thought." Devers nodded slowly. "And you're still doing it, right? Still taking orders?"

Despite the neck brace, Hughes's head seemed to cock the slightest bit.

"C'mon, man. I respect you. You got country skills, and you're a crackerjack pilot. But I know you didn't whip up that meta-whatever-the-fuck-material on that drone. That stuff costs major coin—whoever gave it to you, they gave you the mission, too. They called the target, right?"

Hughes's eyes returned to the floor.

"Don't sulk, flyboy. I know you *think* you picked it—they let you believe that. But deep down, you know they were pulling the strings. You didn't mind much, though, 'cause their enemy was your enemy."

Hughes puckered his lips. Underneath them, he wiped his tongue across his teeth.

"I'll tell you," Devers said, "they ain't worth protecting now, who-ever they are. Don't get me wrong, I'm sure they're pleased as punch that you're honorable enough to carry the water for them. But they sure as shit wouldn't return the favor. I've never seen anybody rich and powerful take a bullet for someone like us." Devers gave him a weary smile and waited for an answer.

When none came, he glanced off to the side for a moment. Then he took a deep breath. "There's one more thing we got in common, man. Heather."

Hughes glanced up immediately.

"That's right. Different time, different place, but you and I, we both cared about her. She was a special woman."

Hughes shifted in his chair.

"Don't worry," Devers said, giving a dismissive hand wave. "I never got with her. I didn't get the chance—I was too slow. There was always something else going on, like hunting your ass." He leaned forward over the tabletop, his tone darkening. "And then she took one in the face from your booby trap at the barn."

Next to me, I could feel Cooke's muscles tense. She half rose from her seat, and I wondered what she might do to stop Devers, if it came to that.

But it didn't. Just as suddenly, Devers slumped back in his chair again. "She protected you, you know? Right up to the end."

Hughes swallowed deeply once more.

"Uh-huh. Even as we were headed to the house, she was saying she was sure you weren't involved. That you'd never do something like that."

Hughes broke eye contact now, but Devers continued staring right at him.

"The folks who put you up to this? They don't care about you or me. And they don't care about Heather, either. She's trash to them, just like us. We're all just 'collateral damage.' But she meant a lot more to me than that. And I'm guessing she did to you, too."

Devers took a deep breath and paused a beat. "How about you do something for her now, instead of for them? One little thing. After all she did for you. She's the one who deserved it, you know?"

Silence lingered over the table for several seconds. Devers kept the pressure on with his eyes. While a range of emotions passed over Hughes's face, his mouth remained shut.

Finally, Devers stood, the chair scraping the floor loudly. "Okay, I tried. If you won't do something for Heather, man . . . if you're gonna protect Mr. Metamaterial instead of her, then maybe you really are the worthless-ass, dumbfuck holler boy everybody thinks you are."

He started toward the door, his hurt leg still dragging. It took him several seconds to cross the space with the limp, and he was reaching for the knob when Hughes spoke.

"All right," he said. "I'll tell you something."

Cooke and I turned to each other, as if to confirm what we'd just heard.

"Make sure the sound's clear," she told the technician. "I don't want to find out in an hour that this got garbled somehow."

We both looked back to the screen and leaned forward, as if that might make Hughes confess faster. A telephone rang somewhere in the room, but neither Cooke nor the technician moved to get it, so I guessed it didn't matter.

Devers was already on to his next question.

"How long you been working on this whole thing?"

"A few months," Hughes said. "Since right after my mom died."

"I heard that hit you pretty hard. You and she pretty tight?"

"Yeah."

"I know how that goes," Devers said. "You think it was the fracking?"

"'Course it was," Hughes said. "My family's lived in that house, drinking from that well, since they invented the steam engine. Nobody ever had a problem. Until now. They did their drilling, she drank that water, and . . ." His hand curled into a fist on the table.

"I gotta ask you about that plane crash. Appalachian 303. That was you, I'm guessing."

Hughes nodded. "I needed to see if air traffic control would spot the drone on radar, or if there was some other defect I didn't know about."

"So you flew it up near aircraft?"

"Seemed like the best way to test it. Approach a plane, see if anyone spotted me. Maneuver around them, see if different positioning caused any issue."

"How many tests did you run?"

Hughes shrugged. "Half dozen, maybe."

"What went wrong?" Devers asked.

"Comms got interrupted for a second, and that let the drone drift off course. It made contact with the wing, and that was all she wrote. Rest of the test was successful, though."

Devers did a small double take. "How can you say that?"

"No one saw it." Hughes shifted his weight in his chair. "I mean, I couldn't be completely sure. But I read all the news reports afterward— no mention of a UFO or contact with a drone. When they called it a 'bird strike,' I figured the cloak had worked, and they were still looking for an explanation. Worst case, they'd blame it on Chu's bunch, like you all did."

"The folks on the plane, that didn't bother you?"

He shrugged. "Like you said, collateral damage."

Devers's eyebrows rose. "Our ROE said to minimize civilian casualties."

For the first time, Hughes's expression changed. His mouth spread into a smile that made me slightly uncomfortable. "You always follow the rules of engagement?"

"I sure tried."

Hughes grunted. "Never been a war without civilian casualties."

"I thought you drone pilots did everything you could to minimize them. Followed guys around day and night till they're alone . . ."

Giving a glance off to the side, Hughes snorted. "Oh yeah, we'd follow them around. And we'd wait until things were the quietest. You know when that is? Nighttime, when they're asleep. Along with every-one else in the house. You shoot a Hellfire missile in there"—Hughes chuckled—"the whole place goes boom."

"So the women . . . and the children?"

"You report 'em as pets. Or you divide by two to trim the numbers. Whatever it takes to make it look justifiable. If you're taking out important-enough people, nobody's gonna ask questions or dig too deep."

In our control room, the telephone started ringing again, but Cooke continued to ignore it. Her eyes were glued on the screen. "Zero empathy," she said.

Back in the interview room, Devers said, "If the folks on that plane were collateral damage, I'm guessing you didn't lose any sleep over those drug dealers."

Hughes laughed.

"I'm not crying for them, either," Devers said. "But I don't get it—why attack them that day we were there? They weren't fracking."

"First off, they're drug dealers. You ought to thank me for assisting the war on drugs."

"Okay," Devers said.

"But that was a test, too."

"A test of what?" Devers asked.

"The quad's close-quarters combat capabilities. And you."

"Excuse me?"

"I watched you and the other guy hike in with Heather. He'd asked me all those tech questions, he'd shot down the fixed-wing. When I saw he'd built that gizmo, I knew it might be something I needed to worry about. So I wanted to see. After he tried jamming my control signal, I beefed up that side of the system. He got me, though, switching to jamming the video. That was sneaky."

"You almost killed us in that trailer."

Hughes shook his head. "You escaped through the tunnels."

"You knew about those?"

"Of course I did. I'd been watching that camp awhile—I knew the cookers' whole setup. And I watched you three the whole way. I was half hoping it might get you to give up."

"But we didn't."

"Nope. You came back to the house, and that was . . ." Hughes's nose crinkled. "Unfortunate."

Next to me, Cooke grabbed a nearby microphone and spoke into Devers' earpiece. "Nice going, Mitchell. We've got him for just about everything—get back to who he was working with."

The phone rang for a third time in the background. When the tech rose to answer it, Cooke whipped around and said, "Don't! I need you on this."

Back in the interrogation room, Devers crossed his arms across his chest. "Okay, time for the biggie. Who gave you the drone supplies?"

"The metamaterial?"

"That, the parts, the guns, ammo, everything. I been in your house, man—you're not sitting on a secret pile of cash."

"There's about fifty thousand dollars at my house."

"Fifty thousand?" Devers chuckled. "C'mon."

"I'm serious," Hughes said.

"Where'd you get that kind of coin?"

"Dead drug cookers don't need money."

"You took it from the camp?"

Hughes stared at Devers. "You think they were my first?"

"You're sitting on a pile of money like that, and you're eating squirrels and rabbits?"

"I don't need much. My family's lived off the land forever. And I'll tell you what, if everyone did that, we wouldn't have all these problems. It's the gluttony of this age that's got us betraying God, killing the earth."

"Gluttony?"

Hughes nodded. "People get told they need all these material things. Things made of plastic that use energy, then we go rape the earth to get the gas to make the plastic and the energy."

"So why target the frackers in all that? Why not go after the people buying the stuff?"

"Gotta start somewhere," Hughes said.

"Okay, but still," Devers said, "you can't tell me you *bought* all that stuff for the drones."

"No."

"Somebody helped you—"

"Yep."

"Who's that?"

"CarbonPro."

Devers's eyes widened, showing the white around the irises. "CarbonPro . . . the coal company?"

Hughes nodded.

Devers shook his head like he'd just taken a hard punch. "Why the hell would a company like that . . ."

"You said it yourself," Hughes said.

"Huh?"

"Enemy of my enemy. Natural gas is gonna be the end of coal. Coal can't compete as it is, the price is too low. Nobody wants to end fracking more than Big Coal."

At that moment, the door to the control room opened. A suited man I'd never seen before strode in, followed by several others, including a woman whose face I recognized immediately.

Cooke burst out of her chair and addressed the suited man. "Director McGrath?"

"We've been calling down here for about ten minutes now." With a cleft chin and silver hair at his temples, McGrath already looked like a serious customer. When he crossed his arms and shifted his weight from one foot to the other, it was enough to make me nervous, and I didn't report to him.

Cooke's face blanched. "I—I'm sorry, sir. We're in the middle of an interrogation and—"

"That's exactly what we've been calling about. Congresswoman Rapp here came to my office, concerned that we're violating this man's Miranda rights."

"He hasn't invoked the right to counsel, sir."

"That's not my understanding." Representative Rapp stepped out from behind the director now, her smile on full beam. "Mr. Hughes's attorney came to my office, indicating he was being denied permission to see his client. Not wanting this investigation to be compromised, I brought that concern to the director."

"But—"

"Melissa," McGrath said, "obviously there's been some kind of . . . *misunderstanding.*" The emphasis he put on the word was as unmistakable as the pressing look he gave her. "The prudent thing to do here is to pause the questioning of Mr. Hughes until we can sort out what's going on with his representation."

Knowing Cooke, I half expected her to unload on the director, to pound her fist on the table and tell him everything was procedurally proper. But after a silent moment, she said, "Of course, sir."

If it was possible for Rapp's smile to broaden even further, it did.

Cooke spun on her heel and, dodging my eyes, went back to the monitor. She picked up the microphone again and said, "Mitchell, take a break."

On the monitor, Devers turned to the camera, wearing a confused expression.

"You heard me," she said. "Get out of there."

CHAPTER 36

The following Tuesday morning, I was back in LA, but not at the firing range turning my target papers around. Instead, I sat in one of the guest chairs in Lavorgna's office.

"How are you healing?" he asked.

"Slowly," I said. Although my face still looked like I'd gone three rounds with the latest MMA champ, the extra days of rest had left my broken ribs feeling better—breathing wasn't as painful. The stitches in my back were really starting to itch, which the doctors said was a good sign. The bullet wound on my other side still stung, though, a lot. And the order that I couldn't surf until it healed completely was the worst part of all.

"What did the judge rule about continuing Hughes's interrogation?" I asked.

The court hearing on Hughes's lawyer's sudden appearance had been set for late yesterday morning, during my cross-country flight home. I hadn't found any press accounts last night or this morning, and Cooke hadn't been answering my texts. Of course, if we'd won, she might be busy questioning Hughes right now.

"You haven't heard?"

"Heard what?"

"The interrogation won't be continuing."

"What?" I said, bouncing to my feet. "What the hell—"

Lavorgna waved me back down into my seat. "I understand you being upset. I think you should get the details of what happened from Special Agent Cooke."

Although Lavorgna wore that damn poker face of his, the one I can never read, for some reason I sensed there was more to it.

"Sir, all due respect, you seem like you know something . . ."

Lavorgna pressed his lips together. The way he looked at me for a moment before he spoke again reminded me of the way McGrath's eyes had bored into Cooke in the interrogation room. "I know Hughes was a troubled man," he said. "I know this case is over. And I know there'll be other cases, on other days."

I stared at him for a moment, hoping he'd say more, but I knew he'd never budge if he didn't want to. Thinking of Loretta, I asked, "Can you at least tell me whether the Service is in good shape now?"

"Yes," he said, his face relaxing into a soft smile. "I've been assured our budget's going to be approved, which will give us two years until we have to worry about it again."

I allowed myself a deep breath, and some of the tension came out of my shoulders as I exhaled.

"I'd say you've earned a few days of vacation, young man. Any ideas what you might do with it?"

I'd had a feeling Lavorgna might tell me to take a break, so I'd thought about this. If I'd been healthy, a week of surfing and tinkering in my workshop would have sounded like heaven. But since surfing was out, I'd need to make other plans. "I think I'll go to Texas and visit my godkids," I said. "The older one, Michael, actually gave me an idea that helped in the case, so I should thank him in person."

"That," Lavorgna said, "sounds like a wonderful idea. Have fun."

I nodded. "Thank you, sir. With your permission, though, I have one other little request."

Lavorgna furrowed his brow, not understanding what I meant.

As soon as I left Lavorgna's, I headed down the hall to the small office that was supposed to be mine. It sat as barren and dark as I'd left it before the trip—a desk, a chair, and an empty bookshelf—but I paid no attention to that. I pulled the door shut, stepped to the window, and called Cooke on my cell.

After three rings, I assumed I'd be stuck leaving her a voice mail—she never took more than two to answer. But just when I expected the computerized message to kick in, I heard Cooke's whispered voice. "Give me a second."

I could hear background noise, like she was outside, then a heavy clunk.

"Okay, I can talk," she said, her voice still hushed.

"Where are you?" I asked.

"Parking lot," she said. "I was walking out to give you a call."

"First Lavorgna's all fishy, now you. What the hell is going on?"

"You didn't hear?"

"I haven't heard *anything*. Last I knew, I was getting on a cross-country flight, and you and the lawyers were going to court."

She sighed on the other end.

"That doesn't sound good."

"The court granted our motion," Cooke said.

"Wait, what?"

"The judge ruled Hughes had waived his right to counsel, and our interrogation was perfectly permissible. That meant we were entitled to ask him questions unless and until he decided he wanted a lawyer."

"Well, that's great," I said. "That's exactly what we wanted."

"It is, except Hughes—likely being told what to do by his new attorney—invoked the right to counsel. So we were shut down again before we could ask him another question."

"You said 'were' shut down. Like something's changed."

"I did," Cooke said. "And it has."

"What's that?"

"Things got worse."

At that point, I buried my face in my hand.

"At the end of the hearing, Hughes's attorney asked that Hughes be transferred back to a jail closer to home for arraignment and bail. The judge granted that motion, too."

"So?"

"So, yesterday afternoon, after Hughes clammed up, they put him into a van and drove him back to a holding facility in Morgantown. I drove out here last night to support the arraignment this morning. Devers was with me. But when we got to court . . ."

"When you got to court, what?"

"Hughes is dead, Seth. He hanged himself overnight."

Despite how much my ribs had healed, my breath suddenly felt short again.

"Are you still there?" Cooke asked.

"Yeah. But that's . . . You don't really—"

"I don't think it's on the level, no. Not a chance. I think the transfer was orchestrated to get Hughes back somewhere that CarbonPro could shut him up." She sighed again, even louder than before. "But, as the director has reminded me several times now, what I think is not what we can prove."

"Without Hughes, can we go after CarbonPro?"

"There's nothing linking them to this at all, other than Hughes's word."

"But . . . how can they get away with this, Melissa? How can—"

"You saw exactly how they're going to get away with it," she said.

"You mean Rapp?"

Cooke grunted. "Who do you think's her biggest campaign donor?"

I put a hand to my forehead. "I can't believe this. CarbonPro could be passing metamaterials to some other disgruntled guy like Hughes right now, and there's nothing we can do—"

"I didn't say *that*."

"What do you mean?"

"There's something we can do," she said. "And we're doing it."

"What's that?"

"What the FBI always does. We're going to go out and build a case. We've got the metamaterial—we can run that down. And we can get all up in CarbonPro's business without them knowing. The director and I talked—if CarbonPro was brazen enough to try this, it's likely not the only illegal thing they've done."

Suddenly I understood what Lavorgna had been getting at. "Other cases, huh?"

Although I obviously couldn't see her, I pictured Cooke nodding. "Other cases."

"Will you . . ."

"No, no," she said. "I've got plenty of work to do, and that kind of stuff isn't really my bag. I think Director McGrath found exactly the right person to put in charge, though."

"Oh yeah? Who's that?"

"Who do you think, dummy? Mitchell."

"Devers isn't exactly the guy I'd pick to investigate Big Coal."

"Don't underestimate him," she said. "I think his eyes have been opened."

"You mean by Simon."

"Yeah, that." A long pause followed. "So I'm back to my usual work at Quantico. What's next for you?"

"Lavorgna told me to take a vacation."

"That's good, you should. And, hey, maybe we'll get to do this again soon. Or, if nothing else, you can come back and take me to that Chinese restaurant again."

I smiled at that. "Only if you promise to practice with your chopsticks."

◆ ◆ ◆

In the end, I almost had to carry her onto the airplane over my shoulder. She didn't weigh all that much, but it still probably would have hurt, given my condition.

After we'd landed at DFW and gotten the rental car, her litany of questions continued. "Where are you taking me? You didn't go to any trouble, did you?"

"Relax," I said. "It's all taken care of."

When we reached the edge of the park, I pulled in next to Shirley's minivan. No surprise that she and the kids had beaten us—their little house sat just a half mile away. Getting here through the Metroplex had taken more time than I'd expected.

Looking out across the green field, a multicolored play structure sat on the opposite side. I could see Shirley, her back to us, and the kids climbing around. "This is it," I said. "We're here."

"I don't know if I should do this. Bob—"

"Bob's at home," I said. "He's in good hands, remember?" When I'd explained that I wanted to give Loretta a few days off, the facility where Bob took his treatments had volunteered to host him for a couple of nights. "You need a break, and this'll be fun. We've got a nice steak dinner tonight and tickets to *Hamilton*."

Whenever Loretta sent me off on a trip, she seemed to think I got to stay in four-star resorts, have fancy dinners, and go out at night. I decided it'd be nice to actually do it, and to let her tag along.

She didn't seem to be paying attention to any of that, though. "I haven't played with little children in . . . decades."

"It's not hard," I said. "They're good kids. Besides, you're gonna be too busy helping them with this to have any other worries."

When I pressed the bag into her gnarled hands, she gave me a confused look over her spectacles.

"Just open it," I said.

She peeled back the opaque gray plastic, revealing the black-and-neon-yellow box inside. "What on earth . . . ?"

I waited a moment to let it sink in. Finally, I said, "It's a radio-controlled drone. I thought we'd fly it around with them."

ACKNOWLEDGMENTS

I owe the state of West Virginia a lot.

For starters, I went to kindergarten there; my very first school memories involve climbing onto a bus bound for Alban Elementary School. When we ended up moving away, my classmates gave me a book called *Sharks!*, not realizing the little paperback would set me on a twenty-year journey toward marine biology. Later, to avoid starting high school as the "new kid," I asked to go to boarding school, where the guy who ended up being my classmate, teammate, and best friend hailed from West Virginia. Visiting him each summer, I got to spend countless sunny days cheering on horses at the Charles Town Racetrack and checking out girls at the pool in Jefferson Memorial Park. Since then, I've developed even more friends in the state, including law-school classmates who've become some of its most accomplished trial lawyers.

All of that's why, when I considered where to set Seth Walker's next adventure, West Virginia jumped to mind. It's a staggeringly beautiful place filled with proud, complex people who've contributed to our national narrative in critical ways. Yet, as rural and remote as it can be, it's also ground zero for some of the most important issues confronting our country. While I very deliberately tried to avoid sugarcoating any of these challenges in *False Horizon*, I do hope my sincere affection for the state and its people comes through on the page.

To help ensure I portrayed West Virginia as accurately as possible, I enlisted longtime residents Captain Heath Marcus (USN) and Chris Regan as early readers, both of whom provided invaluable insights that found their way into the manuscript. Kas DeCarvalho gave additional feedback, particularly on character issues, while Tom Millikan remains my go-to source for electrical-engineering questions. As always, I consulted a number of pilots about ideas for the manuscript, and Barry Shelton provided me with what became the title. I'm grateful to all of them for their help, as well as to Professor Steven Franconeri of Northwestern University for our discussions about neural function and complex processing. Any mistakes you see on the page are mine and mine alone. All the technology presented in the book—even the most futuristic—is real-world stuff. If you're interested in learning more about any of it, details and resources will be posted on my website, http://josephreidbooks.com/.

In terms of this book reaching your hands, I need to extend a huge and heartfelt thanks to Gracie Doyle, Sarah Shaw, and everyone else at Thomas & Mercer for their tireless work and assistance. I'm particularly indebted to my editor, Liz Pearsons, for her steadfast support of me, this book, and the Seth Walker series. My agent, Cynthia Manson, remains my tireless champion. Ed Stackler is, as always, the Sherpa without whom I'd still be wandering about on the mountain.

Finally, thanks go to my wife and daughters. More than any other ingredient, writing a book requires time, and all three have been particularly patient about the hours I spent away from them, hunched over a keyboard, trying to live out this real-life dream of being a writer.

ABOUT THE AUTHOR

Photo © 2017 Makela Reid

The son of a navy helicopter pilot, Joseph Reid chased great white sharks as a marine biologist before becoming a patent lawyer who litigates multimillion-dollar cases for high-tech companies. He has flown millions of miles on commercial aircraft and has spent countless hours in airports around the world. Published in both of his academic disciplines, he is also the author of *Takeoff* and *False Horizon* in the Amazon Charts bestselling Seth Walker series. A graduate of Duke University and the University of Notre Dame, he lives in San Diego with his wife and children. For more information, visit www.josephreidbooks.com.